Dark Little Dreams

An Anthology of Dark Fiction

Edited By
Brett Reistroffer

BAD DREAM ENTERTAINMENT

WWW.BADDREAMENTERTAINMENT.COM

Anthology Copyright 2016

Copyrights to the individual works contained in this collection belong to the credited authors:

Intellectual Porperty ©2014(English) Santiago Eximeno ; *The Love of a Good Entity* ©2014 Christopher Nadeau; *Buried in Work* ©2015 MP Johnson; *BuzzWord* ©2015 Brian Culp; *Dr. Aljimati: Professor of the Forlorn Sky* ©2014 Mark Patrick Lynch; *The Fox God and the Fox* ©2014 Louis Rakovich; *Midnight and Jefe Bowman* ©2014 Eric J. Guignard; *The Bone Washer* ©2014 Travis Burnham; *The Wilds* ©2015 Tim Jeffreys; *Mousetrap* ©2013 Robert G. Ferrell; *Witchy Man, Woman Skin* ©2014 Anna Yeats; *Where Sheep Have Fangs When You Count Them* ©2014 Gerri Leen; *Nevermore* ©2014 Jay Seate; *Love the One You're With* ©2013 Birney Reed; *My Little Babies* @2008 Brett Reistroffer

Edited by Brett Reistroffer

Printed in the United States of America
First Edition: 2016
eBook ISBN 978-0-9960381-5-7
Hardcover ISBN 978-0-9960381-6-4
Softcover ISBN 978-0-9960381-7-1

Published By:
Bad Dream Entertainment®
www.BadDreamEntertainment.com

Cover Design by Brett Reistroffer

The 'EyeBrain' logo is a registered trademark of Bad Dream Entertainment, Seattle, WA.
Original trademark design by Darcray - www.Darcray.com

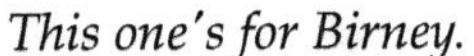

This one's for Birney.

Table of Contents

Introduction

By Anthology Editor Brett Reistroffer

Something strange and unsettling happens when you take the darker side of fiction and bring it closer to home. Sure, the endless possibilities afforded to storytellers by far-flung fantasy hold no bounds to astound, astonish, mesmerize, and horrify readers; but when you strip it all away and cut closer to the world we all live, breath, and walk in, stories tend to take on a different meaning. After all, what point is there to fantasy and science fiction other than to escape from the probability of one world for the possibility of another? Even when used as analogy or metaphor to our own lives, high-concept fiction is still told through the lens of altered perception, the eyes and mind of characters we can never quite know and a world we don't quite recognize. The result is rich imagery and absorbing stories that readers can safely lose themselves in and explore to near endless depths. They key word there is 'safe'. But what happens when those characters just might be people we know, and the world one that we actually do recognize? Things aren't so safe anymore.

This is how we come to 'contemporary dark fiction'; tales

told from the guise of almost real characters in the almost real world, stories that couldn't possibly be true but, maybe, could be. Is the person you meet at the bar taking home more than just your conversation? What is your average workday really doing to those bits of your brain you've become so very adept at turning off? Just how lost can we become in our modern technology? Not all the tales told in *Dark Little Dreams* are coming straight from the haunts of your own neighborhood, some fall far from it, in fact. But what they all do share is one foot planted firmly in familiar territory, where we as readers are most vulnerable. There isn't much room to escape when the story you're reading contains more grains of truth than you're willing to count.

Brett Reistroffer

May 2015

Intellectual Property

Santiago Eximeno

Translated to English by Alicia L. Alonso

"So what do you think?" asked Lidia, smiling and holding an unlit cigarette between her left-hand fingers.

She'd told me her name just a few minutes earlier, as if by doing it she created an indestructible bond between us, an intimate link that would allow her to fearlessly open up her heart to me, setting trivial talk aside. For over an hour I had listened to her monologue in complete silence, paying attention to her words and gestures, not feeling the least desire to know her name. For her, the excitement of talking to a stranger had intensified to the point of becoming unbearable, and she had been dragged into confessing her secret as if giving away a priceless treasure. For a few instants I wondered whether it was her real name or she was offering me an invention. I could find no logical reason for her to deceive me. She wanted to share with me something more than simple words, and confessing her name was a necessary preamble.

"I guess there's not much I can say," I answered.

We were sitting next to the stage, at a battered, dark wooden low table. A young waitress had placed us together with arbitrary criterion, ignorant of our relationship. Prosaic reality told me that the only reason we met was because we had both bought our tickets too late. Lidia was pretty, or at least there was a shine in her eyes, and she had one of those smiles that make you believe you had made more than a few mistakes in life. She spoke endlessly, and that was exactly what I was after: some banal conversation to start with, certain confidences later on, and the sharing of intimate thoughts at the end. We would not get much further. When we got up from the table we would both go our separate ways and our lives would never cross again. And, even if they did, it was quite probable that she wouldn't remember me.

I, however, could never forget her.

"I know," said Lidia, lighting her cigarette with an elephant-shaped lighter, a curio a workmate had given her as a gift. "It happened a long time ago. I have almost forgotten it. I certainly hope the guy is already dead. In fact, for weeks I prayed that he would have a horrible accident."

I smiled and signaled the waitress over.

"We'll have the same, please," I said, pointing to our empty glasses.

Since I was a kid, people would use me as their confessor. My classmates would share with me their most intimate secrets; teachers would reveal to me details of their everyday lives that I had no wish to know. For many years I thought about it, trying to understand why strangers approached me just so they could load their intimate details into my ears. Perhaps it was because of my shyness, my silences, my attentive expression. I didn't know. Somehow my aspect, my presence, led them to trust me and open up their heart to me, just as Lidia had.

On the stage, the band members were giving the final tests to their instruments and sound equipment. They chatted among themselves, took swigs of their beer, pointed at the spotlights while protecting their eyes with the palms of their hands. I had been going to the Thursday show for over three months. The venue was now a second home to me. This was the first time I shared my table with a stranger. Normally I lingered at the bar, slowly drinking my black pint of beer while enjoying the show. Now, the decision to sit at a table had provided me with this unexpected pleasure.

The waitress served our drinks just as the lights were being dimmed.

"What do you think I should have done?" asked Lidia, sipping her vodka and orange.

"What you did was the right thing, Lidia," I said, pronouncing her name, relishing the feeling reflected on her face when she heard it from my lips.

She smiled and lowered her eyes. After the drummer had presented the band members one by one, the musicians started playing their improvised jazz. We listened to the first song in silence for a few minutes, enjoying the music. Lidia soon felt the need to retake the conversation.

"So, what did you say you did? Journalism?" she asked.

"No," I answered. "I'm a writer."

The band dove into an especially lively song, and I couldn't help tapping my foot to the beat. They played well. The syncopated movements of the bassist blew the audience away. A row of sincere applause followed, interrupted by the first notes of a new song.

"A writer? How interesting," said Lidia.

But I could read a certain disappointment in her eyes. She would have preferred a journalist, or else a North American spy stranded in this country, involved in an obscure case of political corruption and waiting for a group of brave Marines to rescue him. I regretted not having impressed her. Somehow, even though I knew it was not what I wanted from her, I felt attracted by how she moved and by the way she lowered her eyes. She wasn't really that pretty after all, but her body exhaled an ineffable something that made her an attractive woman. It was probably her story, the anecdote she narrated like a mantra. People always attracted me after I'd listened to their story. Upon arriving at the venue, I'd dropped my wedding ring into my pocket. Perhaps I was trying to make up for lost time, trying to feel again what my wife no longer made me feel.

"Yes," I said. "Writer. Short stories, especially. Novels don't attract me. They require too much attention."

"You've never written a novel?"

I took a sip from my drink and applauded the end of a song.

"One," I answered. "Afterwards, I lost interest. It was too autobiographical. I prefer to keep things short and sweet."

She smiled. Many people react like that to clichés used at the right moments. I had the impression that she didn't understand anything I was telling her, but that didn't bother me at all. I'd already listened to her story, and the rest had no importance.

"Did it sell well?" she asked.

The musicians were saying goodbye in the midst of applause. The evening was coming to an end. I started clapping and Lidia did the same. We looked at each other, smiling. We'd both got what we wanted. I stood up and gestured to her to remain sitting.

"I have to go. You'd better stay," I said. "I have your number. I'll call you tomorrow."

Her eyes said *yes*, almost imploringly.

"Oh, and… about the novel… I only wrote it. I never said I published it."

She made a noise similar to a guffaw and bid me farewell with a ridiculous shake of her hand.

"By the way," she shouted as I was leaving the place. "What the hell were we talking about before?"

~

It was a sweltering night outside. The street lights had just been turned on, luring moths out of their hiding places. The clammy atmosphere turned the city into an oil painting about to melt. I walked a few meters towards the nearest bus stop. A couple passed me in a flash. I asked myself what their story was. I wondered if they wished to tell it to me. A group of teen boys smoked and joked around under the bus stop marquee. I kept to the side, trying not to listen to their conversations. I already had my story. I didn't need another one.

I thought about Lidia. Would she ever read her tale, her little vital anecdote, as one of my stories? Perhaps she'd never bought a book in her life, nor felt any interest in doing so. I hadn't told her my name, so she would not be prowling her neighborhood bookstores or the nearest department store searching for my books. No, her little story would end up being part of some forgotten anthology on the shelves of an old bookstore, and she would never hear about it. Other readers, eager for some small amusement to fill the empty shell of their everyday life, would buy the book and plunge into its small world of deceptions, sharing the true pain inside it, making it theirs for a few minutes. They would turn Lidia's loss into something new, unique, personal and indivisible, and different for each reader.

The bus came, a blurry crimson stain shredded by the lights from other vehicles. It didn't stop. The teens booed and screamed as the driver, with a well-rehearsed gesture, shrugged his shoulders. As the bus took a turn at the roundabout ahead we discovered that it was out of service. As we waited, two people joined the group: an old woman who stared at the ground while compulsively twisting her fingers, and a serious looking man reading a book that was bound in newspaper. Was he ashamed of what he was reading? Did he, perhaps, prefer not to share it with anyone? As a writer, both options offended me. I heard the faraway rumor of an ambulance siren. It was a hot night, perfect for drinking in excess.

A few minutes passed, as slow as the pages of a particularly boring novel. Then, in the midst of the teens' racket, a girl pointed at the street. Another bus was approaching. I told myself it would have been more intelligent to take a taxi. The idea of a new story wandered around my head and had comfortably settled into my memory, but it would not be completely mine until I had transcribed it. The feeling of sharing a private story, a secret, with a woman whose name I could hardly remember anymore, made me feel uncomfortable. I needed it to be mine, only mine, so that I could transmit it in all truthfulness to my readers. That's what intellectual property was all about.

The bus stopped and opened its doors, and we all climbed inside. I took a seat behind the old woman, who was calmer now. The teen boys took the back seats, trying to chat up two pale-faced girls dressed in black who ignored them. I looked at the face on my wrist watch. It was past eleven-thirty p.m.

The air conditioning inside the bus helped me to relax, and I mentally reviewed the information stored in my head. I still had a few stops ahead of me, and nothing better to do. Lidia had married very young because of an unexpected pregnancy. As a preamble it was too common, too cliché. But then she'd told me about her infidelity. It wasn't surprising, seeing what her life had been like, but at least she'd cheated on her husband with his own sister. That would be enticing enough for most readers. Lesbian adultery, her husband abusing her when she decided to abandon him, the final fight involving a knife. There was no question about it: I could sell the story to any of the magazines I worked for. It was a story you could read in one sitting and then forget a few hours later, just as Lidia would no doubt forget her own story that same night. As in previous occasions, I felt the first signs of guilt in the form of a stabbing pain in the back of my neck. But it was gone in an instant. I had already accepted my punishment for the gift I had been given, and there was no point in regretting it before I began a new story.

I got home sometime after midnight. It had started to rain, which increased the stifling atmosphere that the first days of summer had brought along. I crossed the entrance and, before calling the elevator, fumbled for my wedding ring inside my shirt pocket and placed it on my finger. My wife wouldn't be able to tell the difference, but I would feel more comfortable wearing the ring at home. I climbed into the elevator and got off one floor below mine, as usual. Walking up the last flight of stairs to my flat was part of my therapy, of my need to hold on to the reality that slipped through my fingers whenever I sat in front of my typewriter.

I remembered a conversation with another writer, a man who'd published a couple of novels in a reduced literary sector, but still enjoyed a certain acknowledgment from a particular audience. He'd read some of my short stories and felt they were full of commonplace images that transmitted life. We shared a coffee and happily chatted about it. I paid polite attention to his praise and criticism, and answered his cliché questions with monosyllables and an occasional wisecrack. Where did I get my inspiration? From life itself, and from the people that surrounded me. A typical answer, yes, but it was an honest one. However, he was surprised to know that, in this computer age, I still used my old Olivetti Lexicon 80, the typewriter my father had given me as a gift when I was seven.

"Nostalgia or need?" he asked me, with a knowing smile.

I smiled back, leaving an intentioned pause for dramatic effect and sipped my coffee. We were actors in a play, an improvised comedy, and for some precious seconds I was the absolute protagonist.

"Is there a difference?" I answered, and he gave me a smiling look of complicity, as if he really understood what we were talking about and we really did share the secret of literary creation.

I placed the key in the keyhole and paid attention to the distinctive crack of the door as it opened. The woman's story vibrated inside my mind, begging to be put down on paper. I walked inside and softly shut the door. I'd left the ceiling fan on, and a fresh breeze glided through the hallway like a myriad of flying insects fluttering through the night.

"I'm home!" I said out loud.

The kitchen lights were on. I considered preparing some dinner after I had transcribed the story. Right now, it was the story that I had to give all my time to, before it lost its strength. I went into the bedroom, turned on the light and sat across from the typewriter. Before I had left, I was convinced I would come back with enough material for another short story, so I'd removed the protective cover and placed a blank sheet of paper in it.

I started to type.

At first I hesitated, as I always did when facing a blank sheet, but soon the words became sentences, the sentences paragraphs, and the anecdote of the woman I'd met at the bar materialized like a painting slowly spreading over a canvass. The fragmented images dwelling inside my mind became black on white at the mechanic rhythm whispered by the typewriter keys. I knew that later on, as usual, I'd have to correct some typos and polish some sentences here and there, but the first draft would be practically the definitive version that would be published.

When I finished, after having changed the paper six times, I was exhausted but satisfied. Now the story was totally mine. It was my property. I could do whatever I wanted with it.

I grabbed the paper sheets, stood up and went to the kitchen. I found a bottle of orange juice and two apples inside of the refrigerator. I poured myself a glass of juice, sat at one of the stools I'd bought the previous week at a neighborhood shop, and ate the apples while revising the story on the kitchen top. I found the errors I expected. Mere trifles, the result of hurried typing. Nothing serious. Now that the story was no longer inside my mind—nor in the mind of the woman who'd told it to me—I was euphoric. I thought of celebrating it with a drink, but my more responsible side refused. I remembered the problems that alcohol had brought to me in the past, the memory lapses that caused stories to be lost and pages to remain blank. Truth be told, it had also helped me to discover my potential as a writer, my gift for transmitting ideas to millions of readers. But the price I'd had to pay was high, too high.

I went back to the bedroom and sat at the foot of the bed.

I placed the papers aside and looked at the woman lying on the bed sheet. I'd tied her wrists and ankles with flexible cords, attaching them to metal loops I'd previously nailed to the carpeted floor. Every morning, I tended to the wounds she inflicted on herself while trying to break free, shaking from side to side like a caged-up animal. Using an alcohol-soaked gauze I would softly clean her skin, avoiding her fingernails, avoiding her stare. Sometimes, I attempted to initiate a conversation. Sometimes.

The woman lifted her head and looked at me. There was no trace of sanity left in her wild eyes, in the impossible sneer of her mouth, in the thick veins that protruded under the white skin of her neck. She grunted something incomprehensible while a fine line of drool slid down her mouth. She flailed her arms and legs in a final attempt to grab me. She couldn't. After a few seconds she calmed down and lay still again, waiting. A nauseating smell filled the room, a smell that I hadn't noticed while I was typing away, but which now claimed its own space inside my mind.

"You soiled yourself again, didn't you?" I whispered, and she shook her head spasmodically.

I would have to wash the bed sheets and hang them out to dry again, exposing them to the curious attention of the neighbors who kept asking me about my wife. All the stories I'd made up to justify her sudden disappearance had proven useless. It was funny; no one believed my fictions, but my short stories—real, complete stories—were usually taken for the inventions of a writer.

The woman lying on the bed grunted again and tried to sit up. Avoiding her contact, I leaned over, turned on the night lamp and read the cover on a pile of papers bound in wire comb that lay on the night table.

"Marta," I muttered, remembering my wife's name.

The woman turned her face towards me. In the configuration of her face bones, so sharp they looked like they were going to pierce the skin any moment, I could still see lost traces of what she had once meant to me. I could still remember her sweet voice against my ear, telling me her little secrets, sharing her life with me. I held the book between my hands and looked at her. Everything she had ever been was there in my hands, in a hundred yellowish paper sheets badly held together.

"Marta," I repeated, but she could not understand my words.

I had forgotten so many things… the perfume of her skin, the joy in her eyes. Stale clichés to hold on to a reality that disintegrated in front of my own eyes, in the stench of her own feces. I never understood why she didn't stop, why she continued to tell me everything even though she knew what she was losing. I think that, in the end, she understood it was not senile dementia, nor Alzheimer's disease. In the end she understood that, for some unexplainable reason, all her memories were erased instants after she'd told them to me, after my endless hours at the typewriter. Even when she read them she was unable to associate them as her own. I suppose that, as every good writer, I had a muse. And as happens with every muse, her source of ideas was not eternal and she had finally emptied herself out.

Marta turned her head and vomited on the pillow. What did she eat today? I couldn't remember. I tried to keep her on a correct diet, for her.

For the baby.

Nervous, I caressed her bulging belly. She shook, trying to avoid the contact, and stared at me with her lost eyes. In that perturbed gesture I perceived that, if she could break free of her bindings, she would kill me with her own hands. That's what she had been reduced to; that's what she had become. An animal with primary instincts, with no recollection, no memories beyond basic needs. I had destroyed her as a person, and her destruction had birthed my masterpiece. My only novel.

Oh, how I yearned to publish it.

But, as I caressed her belly and felt my child move inside her, I knew I had to wait. I'd bought half a hundred books on pregnancy, and I was already an expert. I could deliver this child by C-section if necessary, it would present no difficulty. I doubted Marta would survive the operation, but she had already contributed significantly to my success. When I published the novel, I would definitely reach the fame that the short stories refused to give me. The novel would feed my ego, it would replenish me. I would never have to write again.

At least, no more short stories.

I was planning a Part Two, a sequel of my masterpiece. At a time when all consecrated authors revisited their old scenarios over and over again, it was almost compulsory to write a sequel. I was not thinking of a six-book saga, no. Just Part Two. My child would contribute to it by giving me the epilogue of the first part.

Oh, God, how I wanted to listen to its first cry.

And, then, transcribe it.

The Love of a Good Entity

Christopher Nadeau

Sheila couldn't remember the last time she'd smiled. There was a picture on her bedroom end table. It had been taken at a wedding—not hers, of course. No one had asked her, and the photographer caught Sheila in a rare moment of mirth with her brother Simon. Some days, she stared at that picture and tried to remember what Simon had said that was so funny.

She never could.

Sadly, Simon was no longer capable of reminding her; he'd been in a coma for nearly five years.

They had always been close. Some would've said a little *too* close. The siblings had often been seen holding hands and sitting next to each other. The wedding in the picture wasn't the first one they'd attended together. It was the last one, however.

Nobody had all of the facts, but it was apparent that someone had attacked her brother with a baseball bat in his own apartment. The attacker was never found and, considering Simon had tested positive for pot and coke, the crime was a low priority; just another over-privileged junkie leading a no-doubt kinky lifestyle.

As much as she loved her brother, she couldn't excuse his excesses. She also couldn't forgive him for leaving her alone. She'd never had any real friendships and had spent much of her time conjuring.

She realized early on that science and magic were often indistinguishable at the higher levels. One fanatic's demon was an analytical person's alien life form. Once it became clear that neither of these individuals was wrong, one could presumably summon with impunity.

At first, she'd assumed she was dreaming that Simon had once again let himself into her apartment, her tone filled with equal parts scolding and affection as she asked him who he was hiding from this time.

"Married woman or bookie?" she said.

The Simon look-a-like said nothing. He merely stared at her, and that was when Sheila noticed the difference. The serenity in the eyes did not belong to her brother.

"Who are you?"

The look-a-like smiled with its mouth closed. "You tell me."

Sheila felt her heart stop for a moment; this was too much power. She wanted more and hated herself for it. "I would prefer it if you told me." She didn't sound convincing to her own ears.

"I am little Ronnie Silver, who influenced the other second graders to start calling you Fatty-Fatty Four Thighs."

Sheila could only blink at the intimate knowledge this creature possessed. It wasn't just peering inside of her, it was *dwelling* there.

"Is that all?" she managed.

The creature shook its (Simon's) head. "I'm also the song you wrote when you were thirteen, the one Mrs. Frist made you read in front of the whole class."

Sheila felt a shudder of self-revulsion, something she'd not experienced in decades. It was the feeling of a constantly ridiculed fat girl with glasses and no friends. It was a pain felt by children deemed unworthy of respect in an era when parents believed every word that teachers told them.

The creature smiled. "I am the screaming, bleeding girl crying and begging for release from the trunk of a Ford Taurus belonging to—"

"Stop!" Sheila tried to jump to her feet and wound up getting tangled in her sheets, falling onto the floor instead. "*What* are you?" she said, voice muffled.

"That is a very different question."

The creature walked over and offered Sheila its hand. Cautiously, she reached up and took it, immediately lifted off the floor and to her feet. Simon wasn't that strong at the height of his health-kick phase.

"You brought me here," it said casually. "You must define what I am."

"Why do you look like my brother?"

The creature smiled. "Who should I look like?"

Sheila thought about that for a moment and confessed she had no idea.

"Then that's why," the creature said, as if this answered anything.

Sheila shook her head; wasn't it just her luck to conjure such an annoyance? Instead of something terrifying or, God forbid, handsome and willing to please, she got to deal with a Simon clone with a fondness for first-semester of college philosophical rhetoric.

Also, it was obvious that it had no intentions of going anywhere else for the foreseeable future.

~

As the days and nights passed, Sheila reached the conclusion that the creature she'd summoned, who she refused to give a name, knew her better than anyone ever had or would. She was terrified by this, but also comforted. She wondered if the creature was a projection of her id and decided that was too simple an explanation. Maybe it didn't hurt matters that it looked like Simon, but that only brought up a whole host of irresolvable internal conflicts she refused to admit to herself.

Still, there was a definite level of comfort with its presence. It was almost like having—*No,* she chided herself. *Never complete that thought.*

"You seem troubled," it said one day out of the blue.

Sheila paused in her housecleaning and frowned without looking at the creature. "What makes you say that?"

"Interesting," the creature said.

"What is?"

"You didn't deny it."

She responded with an annoyed glance. No further words passed between them for the rest of the day. She felt soothed by the silences, as if they filled a vacuum, the creature's presence preventing her from descending back into her customary self-loathing loneliness.

"Are you ever going to leave?" she asked one day.

The creature furrowed its smooth brow. "Am I?"

Sheila giggled. "I asked first."

"But only you can answer."

She wanted to say the answer was most likely no, but she chose to look away instead, trying to convince herself she wasn't falling in love with this summoned entity who looked like Simon.

~

"Why can't you ever go outside the house?" Sheila asked.

The creature shrugged, smiling. "The world of people is out there."

She found the twinkle in his eye charming, but she refused to give in this time. "So what? The world's full of people."

"But I only belong to one of them."

She hated herself for blushing, but had no control over it. When the creature spoke, she often saw Simon as he should have been: handsome without the blotchy skin, his teeth straight and white, his sandy blond hair well-kempt. Not to mention attentive, caring and devoted only to—

Jesus, she thought. *What's wrong with me?*

"What would happen if you went outside?" she asked.

The creature shuddered and looked away; she'd never seen it do that before. "You would lose me. I would lose you."

Tears filled Sheila's eyes. "I don't understand."

"You do," the creature said.

It was true, she did. She had summoned him and her mind kept him here, exactly as he was. If he walked outside, the wills of others would come into play and he would be torn apart. Why did that scenario sound so familiar?

"The Bradbury story," he said.

Sheila nodded. Right, the Bradbury story about the disembodied Martian that couldn't maintain its disguise as the son of a grieving couple once it accompanied them to the local marketplace. It was one of the most emotional and tragic things she'd ever read.

"I won't let that happen to you," she said, voice shaking.

The creature gazed at her with a warmth unlike any she'd ever seen. "I will always be yours."

Sheila rushed into the kitchen, glanced over her shoulder to make sure she wasn't followed, and started swooning. She'd never felt so alive. The world was filled with magic and wonder and she was at the center of it all!

It was only later that night, in bed, that Sheila realized she'd started thinking of the creature as 'he' instead of 'it'.

~

Sheila wasn't sure when she started allowing him to share her bed, but soon it was as if he'd always been next to her. She still resisted naming him, however. Somehow, she felt more in control if she held that one thing back. Besides, he didn't require a name in order to pleasure her, did he?

Sheila, who'd not been with more than a few lovers, found herself in the odd role of sexual mentor, and she reveled in it. It made her feel vital and needed. And the entity (she could no longer view him as a creature) was an eager apprentice.

It was during the quiet moments that she questioned her sanity. The entity, perceptive as always, asked her why she was so far away tonight.

Sheila forced a chuckle. "I don't trust happiness."

"Do you think it plots to cause you pain?"

She ran her hand along his (Simon's) cheek. "I think it's an illusion, a sweet one. I think one day I'll lose you, no matter what you say to the contrary."

"I am yours, without you, there is no me."

"That sounds like every crappy pop song on the radio."

He studied her for a moment, the corners of his mouth turning down. "You resist what makes you happy."

She shrugged into her pillow. "What makes me happy has never been right."

They fell silent, her wondering when the bubble would burst, while he no doubt puzzled over her baffling concepts of human morality. That was the night the dreams started.

~

The dreams were vivid and always the same. She walked into Simon's hospital room, something she'd not done in months in real life, and paused in the doorway. He was still in a coma, still connected to machines, still far away from her. Slowly, she entered the room and approached his bedside. "I'll never leave you."

"You already have."

She stared into his unmoving face. "No…"

"Yes, you have."

Sheila turned around and gasped. A shadow stood in the doorway, its size increasing and decreasing with each beat of her heart.

"You've replaced me, Sheila." It was Simon's voice, but it seemed to come from everywhere. "After all we meant to each other."

"No, it's not like that." Her protests rang hollow in her own ears. "I can't just devote my life to… watching you *die*."

"I'll only die when you've abandoned me completely."

The shadow grew until it covered the entire doorway. Sheila shrank away, the room growing darker, darker, darker…

~

The entity had a difficult time handling the tension developing between them. He could be so child-like at times. His incessant questioning threatened to cause in her a nervous breakdown. Like most males, he focused almost exclusively on problem-solving. "How can I help?" and "But why do you feel this way?" became his mantras. Try as she might, she couldn't get him to understand that she just wanted to talk about the dreams.

She knew that no matter what choice she made, it would be the wrong one. It was the Story of Sheila. She'd always believed that people like her existed so that the worthier, happier people wouldn't have as much to worry about in life.

"Don't you love me anymore?" the entity asked. "Don't I please you anymore?"

Sheila rolled her eyes. What a ridiculous thing to ask her. Her entire life had been a holding pattern until the entity arrived. She wanted to fall into his arms and disappear forever from a world that had rejected her for a long as she could remember. But Simon didn't want that, and Simon always got what he wanted.

~

There was only one way for her to bring the entity with her. She covered him from head to toe, dressing him in sweats and a hoodie that obscured his face. Naturally, people stared. She didn't care. All that mattered was what everybody *saw*: a hidden individual walking with a plain Jane.

They entered the coma ward with no resistance. It was rare to be stopped on wards like this one and ICU. One never knew when someone was coming to visit a loved one for the last time.

"You all right?" she called over her shoulder.

"I don't… not sure." The entity's breathing had grown raspy, his voice hoarse.

She didn't dare turn around for fear of giving into sympathy. She'd come too far, ignored too much to let that happen now.

"Just a few more feet, okay?" she said, shakily.

"Okay."

Her heart sank. Like a loyal dog, he trusted her implicitly. She had time for one last bout of regrets and they hit her in the chest like a blow from a heavyweight boxer. What the hell was she doing? Simon was a vegetable. The being she'd conjured was alive, or at least alive enough to be her companion.

But it wasn't a companion she wanted, was it? Why else had she made it in the image of her brother?

"We're here now," she said. "It'll be all right now."

"Thank… you." He sounded weak, diminished.

She entered first on wobbly legs, pausing in the doorway as déjà vu took hold and made the room spin. The *beep-beep-beep* of her brother's life support served as her anchor to reality.

"Hi, Simon. It's me. I came."

No response, nor was one expected. She knew there was little remaining of her brother except a shadow, but that remaining part of him still held sway over her.

"Are you… are you there, Sheila?"

She turned slowly to face the lover she'd created, his shuffling gait causing him to struggle into the room. He looked thinner, the sweats she'd dressed him in hanging off his body as if on a hanger. What she could see of his face appeared ashen.

"I don't feel like… here," he managed.

"It'll be okay." What was one more lie?

"I-I love you," he said.

Lower lip quivering, Sheila turned away, back to her brother, her true love. Perversion, mutation, it didn't matter anymore.

"Can you even hear me?" she said. "I came. Message received. Now what?"

Somewhere far off, she heard the entity ask if he was still here. She wondered what she expected to happen. Simon wasn't going to suddenly sit up and proclaim himself better. Nor was he going to project his essence into his look-a-like like something out of a paranormal-themed TV melodrama.

"I'm so stupid," she said.

A raspy voice called her name. She ignored it. Her insides were hollow.

"Please?" the voice said.

She frowned, glanced over at the collapsed heap on the floor. It was as if someone else turned her head.

"P-please?" he said again. "Losing… me."

Sheila wiped the tears from her eyes. "I know you are."

"Help… me?"

"I can't." The words came out choked-sounding.

His moaning was difficult enough to endure, but his sobbing nearly drove her over the edge.

Her companion, the entity, fell over on his side, his hands now turning to ashes. She took one hesitant step forward and stopped, realizing it was already too late. She gazed down at the dry, cracking flesh from which a low moan came, non-stop and filled with agony. She thought she heard her name but couldn't be sure. She heard one last, single moan and realized it came from inside her.

Through a teary-eyed mist, she turned away from the rapidly vanishing remnants of her only ever chance at true love and focused instead on Simon. She let the beeping of his life support calm her before speaking.

"Are you happy?" she said. "Is this what you wanted?"

She felt foolish. He probably couldn't even understand what she was saying. Still, she could have sworn his mouth moved. She blinked and leaned forward. No, it *was* moving. Both corners tugged upward into what looked like the beginning of a smile. She had just enough time to gasp before Simon flat-lined.

"No," she said in a hoarse whisper. "Don't go. Please don't—"

She heard the door fly open behind her, followed by echoing footfalls as the medical staff hurried past her and to her brother's side. Even as they set about trying to revive him, she knew they would fail.

Simon always got what he wanted.

Buried in Work

MP Johnson

Troy couldn't remember how many days had passed since he climbed headfirst into the tunnel, or how many men had gone in with him, but he was certain that everyone else on the crew was now dead. He couldn't confirm this visually because no light penetrated the tunnel. His eyes had adjusted to the darkness only enough so he could almost tell when his eyes were opened and when they were closed. Almost. But still he knew everyone was dead. He could tell by the sandwiches.

There were other clues, of course. He hadn't moved any further down the tunnel in a long time, and he hadn't heard any noise from the rest of the crew for almost as long. But he could find other explanations for these facts. Nobody in the crew was particularly talkative, which was why he liked working with them: all business and no bullshit. And the lack of movement could easily have been attributed to a holdup somewhere further down the line. Try as he might though, he couldn't explain away the increasing number of uneaten sandwiches that slid past him at mealtime.

The tunnel went down into the earth at an angle of maybe forty degrees. It wasn't steep enough for the crew to slide down on the dirt, nor was it wide enough for them to crawl through. It was barely wide enough to squeeze into. Lying on his back, Troy could touch the top of the tunnel with his knees. He tried to avoid doing that though, because when he did, dirt poured down and the whole thing threatened to cave in.

With sliding and crawling out of the question, he and the crew had propelled themselves downward via a chain that ran the length of the tunnel, rooted somewhere below, the bottom perhaps. If there was a bottom. Lying on their backs, they went hand over hand, headfirst, climbing down the chain, grunting all the while. Two ropes ran alongside the chain. Troy guessed it was more likely one long rope looped around, attached to pulleys at the top and the bottom. The meal ropes.

Now, as it had so many times before, the chain rattled and the ropes moved. He reached out, just far enough into the darkness so that the downward-moving rope ran between his thumb and his forefinger. He held his hand there until a paper bag slapped his palm. With a snap, he tugged the bag free of the clothespin that held it onto the rope.

Holding it close to his chest, he ripped the bag open to get to the sandwich inside, devouring it almost immediately. Some sort of meat spread today. It was hard to tell because of the dirt that had accumulated in his mouth, clogging his taste buds. Sometimes it was cold cuts. Sometimes it was peanut butter. Once, it was egg salad, but it had gone bad and he puked almost immediately after finishing it. The puke was still on his face, crusted somewhere between layers of sweat and grime.

At first, the sandwiches had only gone down. Lately, he had noticed more and more coming back up on the upward-moving rope. Sure, some of them could have been missed because someone on the crew fell asleep, but with the chain rattling within inches of your face and the ropes sliding by, it was hard to keep dozing.

"Unless you're dead," he mumbled.

He wormed his arm out in front of him, so his bicep pressed against his ear and slapped the steel-toed work boot of the man who had entered the tunnel ahead of him.

"You dead, O'Reilly?" he asked.

Or was O'Reilly behind him? Once in a while, in the darkness, Troy got confused. Was he aiming downward, or had he turned around to head back toward the surface? He doubted he would have been able to execute such a maneuver in the cramped tunnel. Sometimes though, he woke up on his belly instead of his back, and even that seemed like acrobatics in such confined quarters.

Reorienting himself was as easy as spitting. Whichever way the saliva went was down. "When you get caught in an avalanche, the first thing you want to do is start digging, but you got to make sure you don't just dig yourself in deeper," someone—Troy couldn't remember who—had once told him. Troy had marveled at the wording: "When you get caught in an avalanche..." This person had said 'when' rather than 'if', like he could see the future, like he knew Troy was going to need that info one day.

On those mornings when he woke up on his belly, spitting wasn't necessary. When he released his morning piss and it streamed past his lips, past his nose, threatening to erode the crust of dirt on his face, it told him everything he needed to know.

Now he just wanted to know if anyone else was alive. When O'Reilly didn't answer, Troy pulled the man's boot off, stripped the sock off and tickled cold, exposed flesh. It felt dead, but Troy had to be sure. He twisted the foot hard to the side until he heard a bone snap and the foot went floppy. No screams. No gasps.

"O'Reilly is dead!" he yelled, to nobody in particular.

Nobody responded.

"What am I doing in this tunnel?" he asked, and the question terrified him.

Troy did not question orders. He had never questioned orders. Not because he didn't want to know, but because he didn't need to know. It was about trust. He trusted his boss, Mr. Sweeley. He hadn't questioned Mr. Sweeley's orders when he climbed headfirst into the tunnel, and he certainly wasn't going to question them now.

"Mr. Sweeley pays me to do what I'm told. Mr. Sweeley is paid to think about it," he said, but he found himself disbelieving the words as they came out of his mouth. He shook the disbelief off because it didn't make sense. If Mr. Sweeley had made a mistake, he would have pulled everyone out. There are laws preventing him from endangering his crew.

That is how society runs. Mr. Sweeley would not ignore those laws.

Troy had done a lot of work like this for Mr. Sweeley. Teardowns and buildups. Muscle work. Sweat work. He and the crew had once spent a day in a field smashing cinder blocks into powder with sledgehammers as the sun seared their bare skin. Troy hadn't questioned that job. In fact, he had enjoyed it quite a bit.

But this tunnel job hadn't brought him any joy.

"Mr. Sweeley!" he yelled.

He felt fur brush past his cheek. A rat. One of many. Once in a while, he would wake with one pawing curiously at his lips. This one wanted at his nose. He could feel its whiskers as it jabbed its snout into his nostril, trying to find a part of him that hadn't dried up and crusted over. He swatted it away.

When the rodent squealed and scurried off, Troy held his hand in front of his face. He tried to squint through the darkness to see it, but he couldn't. How, if he couldn't see it, could he be sure it was okay? With rats scurrying and nibbling, how could he be certain that they hadn't taken one of his fingers?

He tried to count his digits by tapping each one on his nose and counting each tap.

"One."

"Two."

"Three."

The thought of other missing limbs interrupted his count.

Fingers were one thing, but what about his legs? They had fallen asleep early on. Maybe they weren't there anymore. Maybe all he had down there were a couple of gnawed-on sets of bones, encrusted with dirt, little bits of flesh dangling red and limp like ignored surrender flags.

The chain rattled and he stuck his hand by the rope to catch his lunch. As he tore open the bag, he realized that he wasn't terribly hungry. Hadn't he just eaten? No, he must have fallen asleep at some point because he was on his belly now. He must have turned over in his sleep again. Or had the tunnel caved in? No, the sandwich rope still flowed freely. Troy could still breath. There had been no collapse.

Something had changed though. There was no sandwich inside the bag. There was something else, something flat and stiff and triangular. He rubbed the object between his fingers, trying to understand it. One side was relatively smooth while the other was lined with fur. An ear, he decided. A dog's ear, like the ear of a German Shepherd. Or was it the ear of a rat? He tried to hold it in such a way that he could measure how many fingers wide it was at its widest point, but his fingers were suddenly tingly. To gauge its size, he pressed the narrowest part of the ear into his nostril. The ear didn't go in very far. When he let go of the thing, it fell out of his nose. A dog's ear. A rat's ear would have been small enough to stick into his nostril and stay put, even amidst the clots of dirt.

"Do I have a dog?"

A ghost of a sensation ran through his tingling fingertips:

the feeling of scratching a furry skull at the base of an ear like the one that now lay next to his face somewhere in the grime. That felt good. He wanted to feel that again. But in order to do so, he needed to finish this job and earn his paycheck. Then he could go home and pet Brute. That was his dog's name: Brute. He just needed a reminder about his duties.

"What is my job again, Boss?"

When he got no answer, he twisted his body and moved his arms, reaching out for O'Reilly's feet. Instead of touching a bare foot, as he had expected, his fingers sunk into a mess of hair. He drew his arms back in shock. He had turned around. He must have fallen asleep and turned around, and now he was touching the hair of Big Ed, who had entered the tunnel behind him. But he couldn't understand how that was possible. There was no room to make such a maneuver in this tunnel. Worse yet, he knew he would have to turn back to finish the job, and he had to finish the job.

"Big Ed, are you alive?"

Big Ed didn't answer. Troy reached out again. This time, when he touched the hair, it scattered. It ran away from his grasp, and his fingers sunk into cold, wet mush. It felt like the meat spread on his last sandwich. At first, he thought it was Big Ed's brains. As he dug deeper, he felt toe bones amidst the muck and realized he hadn't touched hair at all, but fur. The fur of the rats that had been dining on O'Reilly's dead flesh.

He heard the familiar jangling of the chain and automatically put his hand by the rope. A few seconds passed before he had a paper bag in his hand.

"Didn't I just eat?"

He realized he hadn't, because his last meal hadn't contained a sandwich. Still, he wasn't hungry yet. More out of instinct than desire to dine, he ripped open the paper bag. Again, what he found inside didn't feel like a sandwich. He ran his fingers over the object. It was soft and bony. It had wisps of hair on its back and a smooth underbelly. Some kind of animal, with five uneven tails and a sliced edge where it's head might have been. Was he supposed to eat this bony, multi-tailed dead thing? Was that the job?

He continued to poke at the object. Then he realized those weren't tails, those were fingers, much like his own. That sliced edge was where it would have connected to an arm. He threw the hand into the darkness, probably next to O'Reilly's dead face.

His next move was not calculated at all. He simply reached out and grabbed the rope. At first, it tore out of his grip and he felt his skin burn off his palm. He withdrew his hand with a yelp. Blood trickled into the crooks of his fingers. Then he did it again, but this time he squeezed the rope tighter, with both hands, stiffening his spine and tucking his chin against his chest to brace himself for the collision with O'Reilly's rotten feet.

But he slipped right by O'Reilly, perhaps because the man had been suitably devoured to allow for more space, or perhaps because the tunnel got wider there. If that was the case, it was only around O'Reilly because it got tighter when the rope dragged him passed others. Steel-toed boots crashed into his head. Cold fingers with dirt-encrusted nails raked down his work shirt. He scraped the tunnel walls and dirt rained around him, filling up his ears, clinging to his nose hair. He kept spitting it out of his mouth, but it just turned into mud and dangled in bands from his lips.

The rope quickly escorted him past one coworker after another. Most didn't move. Most were cold. But one reached out for him, feebly seizing his shirt. The man hissed dryly, "Please, I need a break, Boss."

Troy slapped his coworker away.

Then Troy panicked. Had he grabbed the right side of the rope? Was he going down or up? He was moving headfirst, so he must have been aiming downward, to finish the job. The right direction. Unless he had fallen asleep and turned around again. No, he had never turned around, he reminded himself. He had just gotten confused because of O'Reilly's rat-covered feet. Besides, he figured that leading with his head was better than leading with his legs, since he couldn't feel them. They'd just flop around worthlessly, slowing him down. If they weren't busted already, they would be for sure.

After easily careening past so many others that he lost count, his head hit someone's feet hard. He felt a flash of pain in his skull that ran down into his neck. He thought he might black out. Maybe he did. Amidst the blackness, he couldn't really tell. Either way, the rope slipped out of his grip for a moment, burning his flesh deeper. He wondered if he'd have any meat left on his palms after this. Or maybe he would be left with melted nubs of skin at his wrists.

He could only think of one way to protect the flesh he had left. He maneuvered his hands under his shirt and tried to tear it off, or at least rip off a piece of it. At that moment, he understood how much his time in the tunnel had weakened him. He had to strain to tear his shirt off – his old, worn-out work shirt that already had holes in both armpits. To make matters worse, his shoulders began to throb, protesting against the way he had treated them, the way the rope had threatened to tear them out of their sockets. But he couldn't stop now. He wrapped his shirt around his fists and got a good, slightly less painful grip on the rope, taking off again.

The man whose feet Troy had crashed into didn't want to get out of the way. Troy kept his grip, but suddenly it felt as though the rope was slowing down.

"Please don't stop!" Troy shouted.

He didn't want to wait until the next meal, when the rope would start running again, to finish his journey. Thankfully, it didn't stop, but he didn't make it past the hard-booted man either. Instead, the man hitched a ride. The rope had dragged Troy so that his head was in the man's crotch, and both of the man's legs were draped over Troy's shoulders. It was as if he had been giving the man a piggyback ride and they had both fallen flat on their backs, locked in that position, and now they were both going headfirst through the tunnel. It was far from comfortable, but the man clung tight and Troy refused to let go of the rope in order to shake the parasite loose.

They passed about ten more bodies before Troy finally shrugged free of the man and crunched past him. Soon, he saw something he hadn't seen for a long time: Light. It was right in front of him. For a moment, he was so excited he almost didn't notice that he could now see every rat-excavated eyeball cavity, every maggot-stuffed mouth. Trying to ignore the dripping meat of the men that lined the tunnel, he looked back and rejoiced at the sight of his legs. They were still there! Or at least his pants were, and they looked full. It would take a closer inspection to determine the state of everything underneath them.

The light grew closer and his heart beat faster and soon he was at the end of the tunnel. He let go of the rope and squirmed the few remaining feet, belly down in the dirt like a snake. But when he reached the mouth of the tunnel, he panicked. The exit was blocked. Gripped in the dead, calloused hands of Jack Spanning, the crew's foreman and the man who had volunteered to go first, was a thin wire grating.

Troy peered through it. On the other side of the roadblock was a well-lit room. It looked like a kitchen. There were no cupboards though, no stoves. The kitchen-esque part of it was the linoleum floor, a brown and orange diamond pattern.

In the middle of the room, Mr. Sweeley stood with his hands on his hips, holding up his substantial side belly, staring at corpses piled on top of each other on the floor. Pieces had been removed from the halfway undressed bodies – hands, ears. Mr. Sweeley just shook his head from side to side, clearly disappointed.

"All out of bread," he mumbled. "Can't even feed my guys proper."

"Not many guys left to feed, Boss," Troy said.

Mr. Sweeley looked up, seemingly unsurprised. "I figured as much. Good to see you're still going, son."

Troy nodded. "Can you help me out of here?"

"Sure." Mr. Sweeley stepped to the edge of the tunnel and yanked off the grating. He gripped Troy's bloody hand and pulled him through, easing his fall.

"I've just got to lay here a bit, try to get my legs to wake up," Troy said.

"You do that," Mr. Sweeley replied, going back to the stack of corpses.

Troy rubbed his hands over his thighs as blood pierced his veins again.

Mr. Sweeley kicked at the dead bodies, shaking his head again and grunting, making his disappointment at the situation exceedingly clear.

As Troy tentatively brought himself to his feet, Mr. Sweeley smiled at him. "You've always been a trooper, son. Let's go upstairs. I'll write out your paycheck."

Troy looked down at his bloody hands, his dirt-caked boots. He thought about what he had been through for this job, thought about the men he had left behind in the tunnel. What was that welling up in his gut? Disbelief? Anger? It spread quickly, and he noticed his hands shaking, even as they dripped red puddles on the linoleum. Could he just accept a paycheck, after all he had been through? It didn't seem right.

And the pile of corpses on the kitchen floor? He noticed now that they were not all human. One had fur. One was a German Shepherd. And it was missing an ear.

"Brute?" he said.

The dead dog reached out with a paw stripped almost to the bone. It tried to edge its way out of the pile, but under the strain its belly ripped open and human hands poured out, glistening and half-digested with stomach acid. This was too much. Troy realized he could not just accept this. There was no way.

"Boss," he said.

Mr. Sweeley's smile vanished. "Yes, son?"

"I think I need a raise."

BuzzWord

Brian Culp

So, there's this woman you figure is exactly half your age, and she holds the fate of your son in her hands, and about four questions into the interview, she's asking why you left your last job. She does this without looking up from your résumé, her finger hovering over what's called a *gap*. So you direct your answer at her forehead. You tell her with a face long accustomed to hiding things that you were looking for a bigger *challenge*. For a way to partner with *like-minded people* who shared your undying *passion* for taking application design to the *next level*; something on the *cutting edge,* no wait—you mean the absolute *bleeding edge* of technology. You pause; it's good theater. More than that, you then say, gearing up for a punchline memorized in front of a mirror the evening before, you were looking for an opportunity with a company that's out to '*disrupt the status quo*'.

This is a lie.

The first of many you will tell this day.

In fact, it's the first of many you'll tell this woman, this consumer of young adult vampire fiction, fresh out of college, who knows nothing whatsoever about what it's like to be a functioning adult with things like a mortgage and alimony and bills from your child's doctor—a doctor who treats your son every few weeks with Botox injections, not because the child is vain, but because he had a birth defect. The Botox, when injected into the tendons around his knees, helps him stand and walk and participate like the other kids in his class, and that's all you want so desperately for your child: just to be normal. And maybe this desperation has seeped into the very fiber of who you are, and all you really want out of this interview is not to come off as pleadingly, frantically, pathetically, desperate.

You want to interrupt the girl, this HR teenager, and tell her to do something other than spend what remains of her youth in this tiny, claustrophobic, cubbyhole of an office. You want to explain that life is about to get much harder over the next fifteen years than it's been over the previous fifteen. More than anything, you want to take off your mask and speak as one human being to another. I'm only here, handing you these lines, you want to say, because I need fuel to pay for my kid's next trip to the doctor.

But she's transitioned to her next question before you get your chance, and you answer it by listing *workaholic* and *perfectionist* among your shortcomings, because that's what you put on your LinkedIn profile, and the lolita from HR seems to eat it up as though you were reading from a script.

For the most part, you are.

Point of fact: the narrative you're presenting for this interview is one of *outlaw*, even though you've never fired a gun, worn a ski mask, jumped from an airplane, or slashed some asshole's tires after they filched the parking spot—a spot you'd clearly been signaling for, only to have some fucker in an Escalade barrel into it before the guy you were waiting on could finish backing out; the Escalade fucker not considering for one second that you might be pressed for time because you had an important interview to get to. Unfuckingbelievable.

The plot hole in your narrative, as Escalade guy confirmed, is that you're not an outlaw. Not when the mask comes off. What you are instead is the kind of person who pays library fines. Who offers to pay for dinner, even when you're the one invited. Who apologizes first, even though your ex was the one who started three-quarters of the arguments and four-quarters of the affairs.

In any event, the *outlaw* version of yourself *takes risks* and *breaks rules* and *sticks to his guns* and *fights for the cause* when necessary. He's someone with *core beliefs* and *guiding principals*. You finally tell the HR child whom your son might date someday that you consider yourself a *thought leader*, zealous about *enhancing UX* as if UX is even a real thing.

She nods. She seems to think it is.

Exiting the interview, you shake her hand again. And on the way out to your car, you take a paperclip you palmed from the reception desk and pop it between your teeth. You bite down, angry at yourself and your performance, not knowing what explanation you'll give to your son. The paperclip tastes of hand lotion and sweat and electricity.

To your great surprise, you're offered the position the next day.

~

Two weeks later, you report to work 15 minutes before the prescribed time, check in with the HR woman and are handed a thick stack of papers and manuals to peruse at your leisure. You settle into your new cubicle, boot up your computer, and wait for someone to come speak to you. No one does. So after 15 minutes of this, you get up and search for the company's supply closet. You find it without too much trouble. Four shelves deep. Fully stocked. Unmanned; it's yours to plunder.

So you seize two large handfuls of ballpoints, highlighters, three Steno notebooks, some binders, folders, and dividing tabs. A Sharpie for good measure. Above all else, you grab a new pack of Post-Its. And by pack, you mean a bundle. A big stack of five different colors. The Post-Its are shiny, boundless, breathing things, each pad ready to be set free from its glistening cellophane prison. These instruments you've carefully chosen—pen, paper, and your imagination—seem alive; they vibrate and pulse with potential. They are bright pinks and greens and oranges and nutritious purples. They seem adrift in this sea of brown walls and olive cubicle partitions.

For a brief moment, you feel a genuine thrill.

Except then you arrive back at your desk, and you see your first email. Over the course of the next six hours you'll attend no less than four meetings, each one further dulling the edge of your enthusiasm. What baffles you is that seemingly intelligent human beings keep using words like *key metrics*, *iterative processes*, and *variant groups*; each of these words uttered without a trace of irony.

Sometime during meeting number three, you stifle either a yawn or a laugh, you can't decide which. But that's when you remember your new collection of prizes. You retrieve a pad of Post-It's from your coat pocket, click the top of a pen that's the color of optimism, and start to write down a few of the phrases.

Then, when you're sure no one is looking, you carefully fold the square, pastel notes in half, and then fold them in half one more time.

And tuck the notes into your mouth.

The morning meetings wrap up around lunchtime. During the next hour, you'd really like to just sit quietly by yourself and read something by Vonnegut that you're about halfway through. But you know how this game is played; you don't want people to think you're weird. "Who sits by themselves during lunch and reads?" they will ask. "Who reads Vonnegut, anyway? Isn't he dead?" And you don't want to face questions like that. You desperately want to be a *good fit*. You desperately want to stand and walk and eat just like everyone else.

So you accept the invitation and head to the company lunchroom with some of your coworkers. One of them calls you Bro. Another mentions an app and you pretend to have heard about it. Another brags about a great little place they found on AirBnB while they were in Ibiza this summer. Or maybe it was

HotelTonight. Or Uber. You have no idea what Uber does, but it sounds important.

You consider asking why they didn't just use the phone, but that would be weird, so you swallow your question where it goes for a swim in your bowels with the Post-It notes you ate during meeting number three.

That's about when your manager just happens to pass by. He says Hey, and sits down to start *chewing the fat*, and of course you're nobody's fool: this whole thing has been orchestrated. Your coworkers aren't interested in lunch. They're here to size you up. They're here to see whether or not you'll be a *good fit*.

You swallow down that observation as well.

About this boss: he's only a few years younger than you, thankfully, but desperately needs a wife who will choose his wardrobe. His jeans have wide bottoms that went out of style at least five years ago. And his beard is less a beard than it is a statement: *See, fellas, I'm so focused on my job 14 hours a day that I don't even have time to shave. Well, that and I'm kinda hip. You know—one part boss, three parts Bro.*

He cracks a joke that's not funny, then laughs aggressively. You think that this vigorous laughter might be his best job skill. When he's done laughing and checking to see that everyone gathered has laughed appropriately along with him, he folds his hands and arches his brow just so. This is his let's-get-serious-for-just-a-moment-because-while-I-am-mostly-fun-and-games-I-do-keep-an-eye-on-the-bottom-line look. He asks those at the table what it is, *exactly*, the company does. "What it quote unquote *really* does," he says, using verbal italics at every opportunity.

You want to answer, but you're seasoned enough to know that outlaws play better in the interview room than in the lunchroom.

So you say nothing.

Instead, you retrieve that wonderful turquoise pen that can do just about anything—the one capable of jotting down an idea that will change the world. You snatch the pen from your shirt pocket and give it a click, ready to transcribe *exactly* what the manager says next.

The manager looks at each of his charges, pausing dramatically before delivering the punchline. "We're a company that *disrupts the status quo*," he says.

Your pen spasms across the lines of the Post-It, and you're thankful you haven't just taken a swig of your iced tea that's the color of bile, and thus have no ammunition to shoot from your nose and onto the chest of your boss who is also three parts Bro.

The spasm becomes more animated as you draw something else on the Post-It. You scrape pen across paper a few more times. Under the words both you and your boss/Bro have filched from some Internet listicle on Mashable or Quora or Buzzfeed or God knows where, you've drawn a crude stick figure, beard and all, that looks like something you've seen in a truck stop bathroom.

You carefully fold the Post-It in half, and then fold it half once more. This time, the Post-It goes into your jeans pocket. Because you can't let anyone see what you've drawn. You can't let anyone see that under the words, attached to the stick figure, is a giant, ejaculating penis.

Late that same afternoon, you start to feel queasy. A mild fever, perhaps. A film of sweat covers your face. The back of your neck feels like the flesh of the fetal pigs you used to dissect in biology class. You reach into your jeans pocket.

The Post-It is gone.

Shit.

Someone is going to find your stick figure drawing you hoped would resemble your boss, but instead looks like a giant, spurting phallus, and turn it over to the HR co-ed. Naturally, she'll launch an inquiry, one of your Bro coworkers will remember thinking it a bit weird how you took lunchtime notes using a new pad of lime-green Post-Its. Two and two will be put together, and that, as the saying goes, will be that. As sure as night follows day, you'll be escorted out, and then have to drive home to face your child. You'll have to explain that he'll be foregoing this month's Botox treatment because, well, mostly because you're weird.

You're weird, and just couldn't keep that fact to yourself.

So you head to the bathroom, and once you're sure no one else is in there, you lock yourself in a stall. You pull your pants down to your ankles. Maybe your jeans pockets have holes. Maybe the note has slipped through one of said holes, you hope against hope, and the thing has become wedged underneath one of your socks.

It's not.

But something else is there instead. Something weird. Something that looks like a large purple welt.

The purple welt is on your thigh, about halfway between groin and knee. At about the place, you suppose, where the bottom of your jeans pocket rests against your leg. You touch the welt and wince in pain, feeling the edge of something sharp and square underneath. You give the welt a gentle squeeze. Under your flesh, something feels trapped. Something that feels like a piece of paper that's been folded in half, and then folded in half once again.

A wave of nausea washes over you and you exit the stall, pants still around your ankles, and waddle over to the sink.

You lift your shirt and stare at the mirror.

Your brow knits in horror.

Pressing against your distended belly are what appears to be several hundred corners of folded paper. Worse, they're moving, roiling, churning, and you think they look ready to burst through your abdomen at any moment. Perhaps, you conclude, the note you wrote at lunch has become pistil to the stamen of all the other notes and words you swallowed throughout the day. Or, perhaps it even started with the paper clip on the day you interviewed. Your words and your boss's words and your co-workers words have copulated, leaving you impregnated with a thousand million hundred items of jargon and banality and buzzword.

I just needed fuel, you think.

And now I have all *this* growing inside of me.

You look around the featureless white walls of the bathroom in a crazed panic.

You need these things out. Now.

So you find the letter opener you've tucked into your coat pocket—wait, you brought a letter opener in here?—and stare at yourself again, mustering the courage for what comes next.

You drive the point of the letter opener deep into your gut.

You gasp in pain, but refuse to cry out as you work the dull blade left to right. You're a Samurai committing hari-kiri, and will handle this grim task as such. You're an outlaw, holed up in a bunker, shot and snake-bitten, ready to open the wound and suck out the poison, ready to stitch yourself up and reemerge, guns blazing.

Tears and blood and bile the color of iced tea splash off of the white linoleum below.

Now that the incision has been made, you shuffle back over to the stall, reach into the gash wrist-deep, and despite the blinding pain, scoop out note after note after lime green folded Post-It note, one giant, gruesome handful after another, and drop each of the offending words into the toilet.

You flush once, then a second time. But as you're tucking your entrails back into your abdomen and listening to the roar from the flush, someone's voice sounds from outside the bathroom door. Someone with aggressive laughter.

You desperately grab for the stapler you stashed in your other coat pocket and do the best you can, frantically stapling closed the makeshift incision. You scurry out and wipe up blood and viscera from the sink and floor with a fistful of paper towels just as you hear the laughter die down.

The door swings open.

Your boss's eyebrows arch in recognition and he asks, "Safe to come in?" He seems to expect a witty retort, and so you flash a big grin and tell him that you'd advise against a second bowl of chili at lunch.

A chuckle bursts out of him as he claps you on the shoulder and says he enjoyed the lunch conversation, and you nod, hoping that he won't notice the sweat on your forehead. Or anything else.

As the door closes, you mention that you're really excited to start *rolling up your sleeves* and *align your skillset* with the company's vision.

You wince as the door swings shut, because this, too, is a lie.

You swear it will be the last one you tell this day.

Back at your desk, another wave of nausea passes over you again, this one not as strong as the last, and you run your fingers along your stomach, hoping that blood isn't seeping through your new white shirt. You figure there must be some WebMD article, or blog page, or at the very least a TEDtalk that will help make sense of what's transpired. Your stomach feels warm and angry while you enter the words "fear" and "dreams" and "debilitating, panicking, anxiety" into search boxes.

And sure enough, you find it: a TEDtalk that will surely make you feel better.

Except the speaker on the dark stage reminds you of your boss: a shade under 40, and fish-belly white, and dark-haired, and beholden to facial hair that's about a week short of a full beard. This, you decide, is what frat guys look like when, mid-race, they sneak a glance over their shoulder and see the 40s gaining on them. What the man says next floors you. He mentions there's—get this—a fucking app to 'track your happiness'.

While your eyes squint in disbelief, one of the guys you had lunch with today—the one who called you Bro—materializes like a cartoon villain. He slaps you on the back and asks you what you're watching, and then gives you a curious look. He asks if you're OK.

You tell him you're fantastic. Resolution broken.

He says you look a little pasty.

You answer by coughing into your fist. The cough is wet and loose.

You point at your monitor, and the guy rolls his chair away.

You then notice your fist.

Blackish blood, which point in fact may be the ballpoint pen ink you drained into your 2nd and 3rd coffees of the day, has splattered all over your hand, and has turned the monitor into a work from Jackson Pollock. You reach for a Kleenex and wipe your mouth and hand and monitor, hoping that the guy who called you Bro won't notice.

You hope he won't notice you're disintegrating.

Except that deep down you want him to notice. You want desperately for someone to notice you, and ask what the hell is wrong. Ask you about the reasons you're so weird all the time.

So you begin screaming.

You scream maniacally at your monitor. You scream to anyone who will bother listening that you shouldn't be here; that you should be outside this building whose exterior reminds you of your high school, which in turn reminds you of a prison, which in turn reminds you of a psych ward, which in turn reminds you of a building in an office park full of other buildings meant to house people for years on end in tiny cubicles of space. You should be outside these walls, with a pen or a paintbrush or just your voice, forcing words and colors out, rather than swallowing them down.

You scream until your teeth crack, and yet no one responds. You scream the word *patient* over and over, which some tiny shred of memory keeps telling you the HR woman was saying over and over during that initial interview.

And through it all, the TEDtalk guy prattles on reassuringly about the power of lucid, waking dreams and their ability to help people and companies *disrupt the status quo*. And as he relays the message in all his bearded earnestness, your mind splits in two while the scream simmers down to a hysterical giggle. Then you void your bowels, filling your jeans with toner ink and thumbtacks and dry-erase marker felts, and everything else you've eaten from the supply closet throughout the day.

You come apart at the seams in full view of every single one of your new co-workers in this modern, open-air floor plan. And your only salvation in that moment is that you've already decided what to tell your son; what to say when you get home with a box of office supplies tucked under your arm.

What you'll do is set that box of Post-Its and pens and highlighters on the kitchen table. You'll call your son into the kitchen. The two of you will speak, one human being to another, and you'll advise him against making the same choices you have. When he asks you what the hell that means, you'll explain that TEDtalk guy has it all wrong. What you should be aiming for, son, is not simply filling your days with waking dreams, but filling them with ones worth dreaming in the first place.

Dr Aljimati: Professor of the Forlorn Sky

Mark Patrick Lynch

I'm near the barrier before *La Vite* comes in. I'm here early. The crowds will arrive later. They will gasp and sigh at the lines of the rail network's answer to supersonic passenger flights.

Beside me is a dusky-coloured man in a tired suit that doesn't quite fit. It's worn to a shine at the elbows and knees, mottled across the shoulders with what I imagine is chalk-dust rather than an excess of dandruff. Through professional necessity I've become something of a people watcher, and I take this gentleman's measure from the edge of my eye, fielding more direct glances as I pretend to look around the station concourse. If he notices me watching him, he doesn't appear to care.

He's in research and education, I think, though I doubt he has many students. But those few pupils will be sincere and dedicated; they're there to be taught by him specifically, rather than having landed in front of his desk through a whim of sorting processes.

It strikes me that he has held university tenure for many years, maybe most of his working life. He's published the results of his lengthy and often solitary deliberations, and though his name is referenced in academia it is only for those intricate think-papers on matters no one else would really take the time to investigate that he is known. He is not, in any sense, a grand gestures man. He's footnote material, and I can't see that he's ever risen above that. But there's some hope, even there.

He wears circular, gold-rimmed eyeglasses, has greying hair and a salt and pepper beard. His scent is that of spices and an old man living alone with too many books, a combination I find at once enticing and slightly unsavoury.

I place him in his early sixties though he looks older because the lines on his face are deeply carved, his eyebrows wide and bristly. His ancestry is, somewhere in the mix, Middle Eastern. He probably arrived as an immigrant, from a scholarly background, and is a nationalised Anglo now, though a part of him will always feel that he does not quite belong. His dreams of childhood skies will differ from mine.

He does not fidget, though nor does he stand perfectly still. He moves carefully to accommodate his burden. I sense unrest in him, a churning below waters that on the surface seem no more unsettled than a calm, placid lake before the morning mist has lifted.

Born under lower stars, he's short, and in fact only comes up to my chin. (And let me tell you this much about myself: I'm not the tallest woman standing in the station today, not by a long way.) For some reason, I'm surprised the doctor isn't wearing a hat. I would expect one of those old-fashioned affairs with a band above the brim. A hat and an off-tan raincoat would be right, because he's something of an anachronism. He'd make a good character actor, chasing Indiana Jones with bureaucratic intent through museum halls before Indy goes off on one of his archaeological jaunts.

Since he arrived, clutching to his chest an accordion-layer satchel bulging with much-handled papers that every so often ping paper clips like stray artillery shells, he has not said a word. All he's done is stare from behind his eyeglasses into some existential distance where the tracks snake from the platform and lose themselves in an intricate criss-crossing of spaghetti metal.

He's not a passenger. The best reason I can think for him to be waiting for *La Vite* is that he's meeting someone travelling aboard it: a colleague probably, someone to show his findings to. Whoever it is, it wouldn't be a lover; his passion doesn't extend into the physical that way. It's been subjugated by the same desire that powers religious dedication. He has his books and his sublimely seductive studies, and in such a situation I believe he'd find it hard to make time for the needs of a woman – or a man if he swung that way, though I don't think he does.

But I'm tired of standing here at the barrier and intuiting him. I've seen all I need to know. He's a professor, a professor of the sky by his expression. And with the weather's natural state in a flux that can best be described as freaky, I think he probably hugs his briefcase because it contains papers relating to some minor discovery he's made, one which might signify something larger to the Deep Considerers who are brave enough to study whatever's going on above our heads.

I christen him Dr Aljimati, professor of the forlorn sky.

Forlorn sky, did I say? *Forlorn and forgotten sky*, it probably stands better as.

Here's a reason.

No one likes to look up, not these days. Don't talk atmospherics. Concentrate on dealing with what happens beneath… which has, thankfully, somehow remained normal. The whole country acts like that, the whole world. The only time we see the sky is by mistake. We glance in a puddle and it's there, impossibly reflected, or else it catches your eye and, forgetting, you glance up to see what's wrong.

Because you *do* forget, being so used to the blue and the grey and the sunset shades of years before. Then it hits you again, descending like an illustrated boot in a *Monty Python* animation, and you have to remind yourself you're not crazy and that everyone, and I mean *everyone*, is coping with the same thing.

Concerned with what's beneath the sky right now, dealing with what's right here along the station concourse, my legs are telling me I shouldn't have worn a skirt today. It's cold. There was snow first thing this morning, though of course no one saw it falling; it just appeared, spreading like tiny stains on the ground. I need some warmth.

Because I don't want to wheel my suitcase into the reservation of tables around the drink and food outlets with the dreary newsagents flashing fiction apps, I ask the professor if he'll look after my luggage while I search out a coffee dispenser. Something that takes credits and spits heated liquid in plastic cups; a cup thin enough that I can warm my hands around and then put its contents to work on heating up my insides.

I'll be five minutes, I promise.

Perhaps surprised at himself, Dr Aljimati agrees to stand guard.

I say, "Would you like me to buy you one? It's the least I can do. That's if I can find a machine that's working; I don't want to get caught in the queue at the café."

"That would be very generous," he says. He blinks slowly, as if I have thawed him from an enchantress's spell. He lowers his satchel halfway down his tie, and when he turns to me and speaks I see his lips for the first time, between the blades of frosted grass his moustache and beard form. They move with exaggerated care, shaping words. "A coffee, yes. A coffee, please, that would be nice."

"Milk? Sugar?"

"Black," he says. "Only black."

I leave my luggage with the professor, feeling oddly as though I'm abandoning more. I didn't expect him to say yes to the coffee. Most people wouldn't. Perhaps those years cloistered in study have left him in a state similar to the one experienced by Asperger's sufferers, reckless with honesty and not looking for subtlety in the dance of social encounters.

After hunting around, I find a coffee and hot chocolate machine next to a potted plant with long green stems that stretch outwards like a rubber sculpture. It's not native to the Isles, the plant. An invader, like the sky. There are Styrofoam cups on a shelf beside the machine, and brand-name options and prices still in euros and pounds on the dispenser. I fumble a credit card into the hesitant slot and press a few touch-screen options. I hear internal gurgling, and then a stream of liquid sloshes into the first cup I put on the overspill grid.

It's supposed to be mild-blend coffee, but it looks like the kind of mud-water in which are found infectious plagues spelling the end of mankind. That one's the professor's. I spare the extra money for myself and get a hot chocolate.

I think about Dr Aljimati as I shuffle with short steps, careful not to spill the loaded drinks I'm transporting, back to where I left him and his duty of care.

What if he has learned something that will make a difference? Something that will perhaps guide the high gods of science to work out the medicines needed to return the skies to how they used to be? If he's a professor of clouds and rainbows, of high atmospheric musings, then why *can't* he come up with a solution? There seems to be no reason why he should not. It's people like him who made things so bad in the first place. They've got to know how to fix it.

"Coffee," I say to him when I reach the barrier.

"Thank you."

He seems more relaxed now, and his satchel briefcase hangs loosely from one hand. I hadn't noticed before, but his fingernails are as wide as shovel blades. When he takes the cup, I feel strength in his hands, a man's strength.

I want to talk to him, even though it may not be for the best.

"I heard of someone who was struck by lightning," I say. "He didn't know it was coming. Well, how could he? There was nothing on the forecast. He was struck before the thunder, the very first hit. Chances are already a million to one in a storm, right? How impossible can it be to get struck first time?"

"Ah," says the professor, and raises his Ebola virus mud-water to his lips. His gaze is beyond the barrier, seeing something an infinite distance away. "Yes."

But I persist. "I don't understand how they work the forecasts. Weathermen, you'd think they'd be out of a job, wouldn't you?"

Dr Aljimati nods, but the action is like a cat's nod before it drifts off to sleep. "Hm," he says to my chatter. "Hm" and "Yes" and "Quite so". But he does not say, "Excuse me," and push away. He does not say, "I am sorry but I cannot talk to you, I must leave now." He is settled here, awaiting whatever Fate brings him on the train.

We drink the remainder of our machined potions in silence. What he thinks of my airy comments and me, I don't know. But he is avoiding my eye now. I should use this, take the hint.

The station is filling and I'd have to speak louder for the professor to hear me now. In five minutes *La Vite* will be here. People want to catch a glimpse and are already pushing forward. I know I can't stay, even if I could think of something new to say, or find a way to draw out of the professor the possible healing remedies he might have to cure the sky. The crowds, the coming train, they mean I've to get busy myself.

"Well, thanks for looking after my luggage," I say, and then, as if I can't help myself because of who he is, because of that laboured answer he might hold in his straining satchel, I surprise him by giving him a quick hug.

Then I'm gone, bumping my artful way through the crowd, dodging and hustling, pulling my suitcase, wonky wheels squeaking as I go.

In the ladies' I open the wallets and purses I've lifted from the crowd, including the one from inside the professor's jacket pocket. There's money, real notes and coins, as I suspected there would be. Older men still carry real money with them and not just cards. Though it's not ready cash in the hand, and it takes time and work, I'd be able to sell the plastic for profit. The name repeated on the professor's identity papers is Imran Karhboul. There's a dental appointment reminder in the same name too. A business card describes Mr. Karhboul as a teacher of music. Yeah, whatever. I drop the empty wallet in the trash bin, along with the scoured purses and other raided trophies, exiting the ladies' as the cacophonous rush of the arriving *La Vite* fills the platforms. I leave the station.

Above me, the sky deepens through that colour it takes on at this time of day, the colour we don't have a name for yet. Mile high stone columns float around statue clouds of frozen birds and screaming houses. What might be an analogue to the sun pulses and laughs. I think maybe I see a tree up there, about an office block tall, with spreading branches and faces in its bole and the filigrees of its bark, long tendrils of roots trailing underneath. Or perhaps they are fairies or hippopotamuses. But then I blink and look again and it is something else entirely.

Aware of the hard-money and credit cards I've taken, all of which are weighted like ballasts in my pockets, I haul my decoy suitcase full of rags and turn my head back down to the ground. I don't consider hope or cures for the sky. I walk on into the snow that isn't falling but somehow still is.

The Fox God and the Fox

Louis Rakovich

Deep in the savanna, a long time ago, there used to be a place called the Valley of Long Grass. The air in the valley was hot, the soil hard, and the animals lean and tenacious, and ever hungry. In the day, the sky was a gold cloth, in the night, a floating pool of blood. Gold and blood, those were the lives of the predators who lived among the stems–they would work, trade, and hunt the small creatures that roamed there, and they would kill each other, often and with brutality.

Their god they called the Spirit of the Valley. She was a pitiless and vengeful god, and had no kindness for the weak beasts of the earth. She rewarded force and bloodshed alone; an animal who wore his kin's toes around his neck wore also her smile on his shoulders.

But she wasn't a god of flesh and blood, and in her wrath she couldn't strike an animal down. She was a god of strange and violent thoughts, of slippery stones, of whispers coming from wide cracks in the ground. She worked slow, and she worked small–but unless an animal redeemed himself in her eyes before her work was done, he would die.

~

In the valley, long ago, there lived a fox. He hunted, he traded, and he built a deep, sturdy den for his family to live in, but he killed rarely, and with a weak heart.

Fortune had smiled on him when he was born and blessed him with good ears. He would be working in the sun, constructing hunting tools with his lustrous black paws, and when he heard the sound of unfriendly feet he'd rush into the den and bar the door. With his ears he kept his wife and child safe.

He had one friend, a small and cunning civet. The civet kept his wives and his gold locked deep in his nest, and around the nest he had placed many inventive and cruel traps. Often, unwelcome visitors would fall into deep holes, or lose their limbs or their heads on his ground. The civet made himself coats out of their skin and chains out of their teeth and toes, and cut their meat into cubes which he dried and sold.

~

One day, a warthog and his crew decided to outsmart the civet and sneak onto his grounds through the fox's land. That day, the fox's ears failed him. He didn't hear the footsteps of the intruders until it was too late, and as he sprung to his feet a hoofed hand cast a rope around his throat and pulled. The fox felt his heart beat in his eyes and his tongue swell up in his mouth. He fell into a hot and nauseating darkness.

When he awoke, hours later, the grass was quiet. No moving feet, no voices. On shaky legs he limped to his den to find the corpses of his family lying bloody by the door. The fox sat down on the ground, his ears drooping, and stared into the reddening sky. Then his head fell. He lay on his side, curled up into a half ball, and went to sleep.

The civet's voice guided him out of a frenzied dream. The little beast put his paw on the fox's shoulder and told him of the warthog's failed attempt to steal his gold:

As the warthog's crew arrived at the civet's grounds, they had begun to chant and shout, "Your friend the fox and his family are dead, and you're next!" They stepped forward, calm and confident, for they believed that no traps had been hidden between the civet's territory and his neighbor's. They didn't know that the fox never visited the civet in his nest. One by one, they fell to the ground, their feet bitten by sharp wooden teeth, their throats pierced with thick spikes. The warthog saw what had become of his crew and retreated.

When the civet's tale was over, the fox spoke. His voice was hoarse and quiet, his tone unchanging. "Damn the warthog," he said, "and damn the Spirit of the Valley for allowing this."

"The Spirit of the Valley has no mercy," said the civet. "She favors the strong over the weak. Paint your face with the blood of those you've killed and you'll prosper. Wear their face as a mask and you'll be showered in riches. You know this."

~

The fox spent the night by the corpses of his family, his yellow eyes open and bloodshot. Then morning came, and with a sigh he got up and set to dig a hole. The civet, looking at him from the windows of his nest, thought he was digging a grave.

But the fox dug wide, not deep, and collected the dirt in a tall pile. Then he stopped and disappeared into his den. The civet saw him come out a few minutes later, carrying sharp tools and a jug of water.

The fox spread the bodies of his wife and child on the ground, and with his tools he made deep cuts all along their stomachs and chests. He reached inside his wife, and one by one, extracted all her organs and laid them by her side. He did the same with the child. The civet watched as the fox worked, an expression of stark madness on his pointy face.

When the bodies were empty, the fox poured the water onto the pile of dirt and began to knead the wet lumps with his bloody paws. To preserve their dead flesh, he smeared the black mud over the bodies and filled them with grass he had torn out of the ground in violent motions. He stitched the bodies up, and stitched the child onto the mother so that it appeared to be hanging on to her neck with its arms. He disappeared into the den again. This time he emerged with a long wooden pole on his shoulder.

He stuck the pole into the ground, fastening it in its place with the remainder of the viscous mud. Then, he lifted the stitched bodies and tied them to the pole, so that they stood upright. He then knelt and cried, and from the civet's window, it looked as though the fox was praying to a god handmade in his image.

~

The next day, the fox got up at dawn and went to sit by his

family. The mud had dried in the heat, and its color had changed from black to a dark reddish-brown. He asked for his wife's forgiveness, and prayed to the Spirit of the Valley to give him strength so that he may go and kill the warthog. But the strength didn't appear, and the fox remained seated on the ground, his fur dirty and his ears drooping.

His eyes were fixed on the muddy figure before him. When the civet came to check on him in the early afternoon, he hardly noticed his presence. In that moment, the civet thought that his friend wouldn't have minded his footsteps even had they been unfriendly. The fox had nothing left to keep safe.

Each morning over the following days, the fox would go to sit by his family. They had become nearly unrecognizable–a fox-like statue of muddy crust–but he would talk, and cry, and beg for forgiveness. Then one day, through his own frantic muttering, he heard a stranger's voice. He looked down. A small mongoose was kneeling by his side, his hands put together and his head lifted toward the muddy figure. He was deep in prayer.

"What are you doing here?" asked the fox.

"I saw you praying," the mongoose said, "and so I thought that I would join and pray to this, this fox god." He rattled the snake skeleton which he wore around his neck, and added, "One can never be too safe."

"Go away," said the fox.

The mongoose smiled. "I'll go now, but I'll be back tomorrow. You can't keep this new god all to yourself."

And indeed, the next morning the fox found the mongoose waiting for him by the muddy figure. He prayed for gold, for plenty slithering creatures to eat, and for the strength to kill and not be killed when the time comes. The fox couldn't bring himself to tell him that the figure was not a god, but his own creation, made in a moment of sorrow and insanity. He listened to the mongoose pray, and the sight of the deluded little beast amused him so, that for a moment he forgot his grief.

~

For three mornings the mongoose prayed and the fox sat by his side. Then, on the fourth morning, the fox came out of his den to see the ground around the muddy figure covered with golden fur. The mongoose had told the meerkats of the new god, and they came–all three dozen of them–to pay their respects.

"When did it appear?" they asked the fox as he approached. "What does it ask for? What should we call it?"

"It's the Fox God," said the mongoose, sure of the truth in his words. The fox didn't argue.

Once the mongoose and the meerkats had left, the civet made his way from his nest to his neighbor's den. "What's going on here?" he asked. And the fox told him everything, starting from his preservation of his family with mud and grass, and ending with the arrival of the meerkats.

"This could be dangerous," the civet said.

"Don't worry," said the fox. "They're small animals, and harmless. If this puts their minds at ease, then so be it."

But the next morning the mongoose and the meerkats brought the hyena with them, and the civet locked himself in his nest to keep clear from trouble. The fox greeted the hyena. "Have you come to pray to the Fox God?" he asked.

The hyena nodded. "What does it want, your god? The Spirit of the Valley asks for the hearts of all those I kill. I burn them, and The Spirit of the Valley keeps me safe. What does the Fox God want?"

In that moment a curious idea came to the fox's mind. "It wants..." he said, and grew silent in thought. He realized there was a way to avenge the death of his family, even with a weak heart such as his. He swallowed, and looked into the hyena's eyes.

"It wants sacrifice. Yes, it's told me it wants sacrifice. The Fox God wants the soil around its statue soaked with swine's blood. It wants you to bring it the warthog."

~

That night the fox slept badly, haunted with wild anticipation. At dawn, he went outside and sat to sharpen his knife. Soon he heard the sounds of commotion in the grass. The hyena had brought the serval, the caracal and the crocodile with her, and together the four were dragging the badly bruised warthog in the direction of the Fox God's statue. The mongoose and the meerkats followed.

The hyena pushed the warthog to the ground. "We brought him," she said to the fox.

"Good." The fox looked down into the warthog's black eyes

and smiled.

An expression of anger and fear appeared on the warthog's face. "I've killed you," he said. "How can you stand here? I've killed you."

"The Fox God brought me back to life," said the fox, and the meerkats cheered. For one brief moment he almost believed his own lie. He turned to the hyena. "Take him to the statue."

The large animals dragged the warthog along, and the meerkats ran around them in golden circles. The mongoose stuck his chest out and walked proudly and slowly. He had dressed up for the sacrifice, in a coat of snakeskin and large, rattling bracelets made of bird skulls painted with blood and gold. He considered the fox the prophet and himself the discoverer of the new religion, and as such he had reason to be proud.

The hyena let go of the warthog. The fox took him by the short hair on his head and pulled him to his knees.

"The Fox God wished for this swine's death. Everyone who helped bring him here today will be rewarded," he said. Then, holding the sharpened knife, he bent down and whispered in the warthog's ear, "I'll cut your throat."

The warthog's blood sprayed over the fox's face. He smiled, and it poured into the spaces between his teeth. The taste of metal made him dizzy.

~

The animals cheered, and prayed, and left. When they were gone the civet came to talk to his friend.

"This isn't right," he said. "Maybe the Spirit of the Valley would have ignored prayer, but not sacrifice. And look at you," he gestured toward the fox's bloody face, "you have pig's blood in your eyes. Before, you were weak, but at least you weren't a liar. Now you're presenting your weakness as strength. You're protecting it, building it a crib of wild and blasphemous lies. You've gone mad."

"I have," said the fox, "but I'm not mad anymore. You use traps and weapons to kill. I discovered I can use animals just the same. Am I weaker than you?"

The civet thought a moment. "You are," he said. "There is one way to win favor in this place, and it's the way of the Spirit of the Valley. In other places, there are other gods, and maybe they value deceit and illusion as strength. But here you kill, or you are killed. Knowing this, you failed to win favor with our god, and your family paid for your weakness. And now, still knowing it, you spin lies and cause others to lose favor with the Spirit, and when they're punished for their blasphemy, their blood will be on your hands also."

The civet returned to his nest. He locked the door, covered his wives with blankets and lay by their side. He knew the Spirit of the Valley to be a jealous god, and after the fox's deed he was afraid of what the night may bring.

~

Hours later, the fox awoke in the dark. Although he knew it to be empty, he felt a presence in the room. The ground began to shake, as if scores of invisible and heavy feet were running around the den. It was the Spirit of the Valley—a vast bodiless thing, moving about in the night like the cold breath of a giant creature. There was no mouth to say the words, but in his large bat-ears, the fox could hear the spirit calling him outside.

He went. The muddy figure of the Fox God was a shadow against the red sky. The Spirit of the Valley spoke. Her voice beat through the fox's body, rocking his heart, pumping in his ears. "You want a god of mud and dead flesh? I'll give you what you want."

And the Spirit of the Valley breathed life into the Fox God. A sharp smell of blood washed over the valley; the figure twitched; a soft cracking sound was heard. The Fox God lifted its arm, took hold of the pole tied to its back, and pulled. The pole snapped out of the ground and slid through the ropes. The Fox God was left standing on its feet without support, holding the wooden pole in its hand. In the dark, it looked like an animal ready for battle.

The fox ran back to his den and barred the door. But the Fox God didn't go after him. It disappeared into the red darkness.

That night it walked around the valley, leaving death wherever it went. A god of body and mass, it could touch an animal–it could strike an animal down. Its work was simple and quick. It killed the hyena, the serval, the caracal and the crocodile; it killed the mongoose and the three dozen meerkats.

At dawn, the Fox God returned to the place of its creation. It tore down the fox's door and remained standing in the doorway. Through its eyes and mouth, the Spirit of the Valley spoke for the second time.

"If it was revenge you were after, you should have killed the warthog yourself. Instead, you had your god of flesh bribe my followers to do your killing, and you forgot that when blood spills in this land, it spills for me. You wanted a god of flesh, so here you have one. You brought your punishment on yourself—don't weave lies if you don't wish to see them come true."

The fox saw the muddy figure leap toward him, the wooden pole held high in its hand. Sudden, sharp pain spread from his head to his toes like a bolt of lightning. He fell to the ground.

The Fox God stood a moment, and then collapsed onto the body of the dead fox, an empty shell of flesh and mud.

Midnight and Jefe Bowman

Eric J. Guignard

In the days of the blue and grey, there lived a sprig of a lad named Leonard Jephet Bowman, though most folks just called him Jefe.

He was a rambunctious child, taken to slipping toads down the backs of girls' dresses and pulling their hair when they squealed. He squashed every insect he saw and tied bottles to cats' tails with yarn stolen from his Ma's knitting box. More than once, Jefe set a rock in a fire pit until it turned scalding hot and then, carrying it in a cloth, threw the hot rock at someone he didn't like. Not only would the victim get a rock bangin' on their dome, but when that person picked up the rock to throw it back, they'd burn the skin off their fingers.

Well, the Devil took kindly to young Jefe Bowman because, as everyone knows, ol' Scratch just loves naughty children. Whenever Jefe was in the throes of a moral conundrum, Satan rushed up and whispered a few sweet words into his ear so the boy wouldn't ever accidentally fall onto the path of the righteous. If the Devil was a school house teacher, Jefe became his star pupil. He kept an eye on the boy, watching over the years with considerable pride the ruckus Jefe caused.

But we'll get back to Lucifer later.

The story of Jefe Bowman takes place within the fringes of the Great Smoky Mountains, where he and his family lived, a half day's ride south of Gatlinburg, Tennessee. They were hard-workin' people in those parts, carving out a bit of civilization from the stubborn wilderness, and days on the Bowman farm, in particular, were ones filled with great labor. Each day, Jefe was up before the sun touched the sky and he toiled long into the afternoon.

"A boy's idle hands are meant to hold a shovel," Pa liked to say.

"Up at dawn to grow a lawn," Ma would add.

"Hard work develops a straight back," Pa would then counter.

And if that weren't bad enough, Ma would throw in for good measure, "If the Lord wanted you to revel, he'd grow our barley high and level."

Being a boy, Jefe didn't care to work and instead just wanted to play and play and play. But when ordered by his folks to complete chores, he just nodded his head and said, "Yes, sir. Yes, ma'am."

Then, once the fields were plowed and cows milked, wood chopped, water drawn, and crops harvested, Jefe could do as he pleased. Pa paid no mind to what trouble he got into, so long as all the day's toils were completed.

Fortunately, Jefe had two older brothers, Elmer and Odie, to share in the chores and to play with afterwards. They were good brothers for roughhousing but, like the Devil, they were instrumental in Jefe's raucous behavior. They taught him every mean trick they knew and even invented some new ones on top of those. They hid fire ants in folks' knickers and cut holes in the bottoms of drinking cups. Hurling pig dung at neighbors walking to church was a particular favorite of the Bowman boys.

Elmer and Odie knew those tricks well by practicing them on each other. They were always at each others' throats, fightin' over anything that came to mind, like if a fart in the wind smelled of one lilac or two. If there was mud on the banks of the Tennessee River, one brother would say rain was comin' and the other would counter that a drought was settin' in. That's just how they were, always taking adversarial sides of a dispute.

When the great 'War Between the States' spread through those parts in 1861, Jefe's brothers left the farm to join the army. As they had all their lives, each took an opposite side of the conflict in order to get the better of the other. Elmer rode with the 9th Cavalry, a Rebel Regiment under General Breckinridge's Expedition. Odie became a rifleman with the 10th Infantry, a Union Regiment under General Gillem.

Jefe was mad at them both. He was mad because they left him alone on the farm with Ma and Pa to do the work that was once divided by three brothers. He was mad at them for taking different sides on an argument that shouldn't have concerned either of them. Most of all, he was mad because there wasn't anyone left to play with. He felt loneliness at their absence and knew there wasn't going to be a family reunion anytime soon. Jefe wanted to play, but all he knew were the mean tricks Elmer and Odie had taught him. The sad fact of the matter was, the more of those tricks he played on other folks, the less likely anyone wanted him around, so he became an outcast.

One afternoon, Jefe's woes got the best of him, and he sat on the dirt road outside his family's farm with his head between his knees, sobbing pitifully.

The Devil heard Jefe crying, and he wanted to know what distressed him. Y'all may not know this, but Satan actually has a tender spot for crying children, especially those he favors. It's a sad affair, even for Scratch, to see tears fall from the face of rosy-cheeked youth. He put on his coveralls and straw hat and moseyed up the road to meet Jefe, red tail trailing in the dust behind like the rut left in a field after a plow's passed over.

"Mind sharin' what vexes you, son?" Satan asked.

"I ain't got no one to play with. Ma and Pa are busy workin' all day, and my brothers left to go fight in the war. The other kids say I'm too mean, and the neighbors call me a bad apple," Jefe replied.

"Well, I know a thing or two about apples," Lucifer replied with a grin, "and there ain't nothing wrong with you. You just make *different* decisions than other folks. That makes you pretty special in my opinion."

"Thanks, mister. You want to play with me?"

The Devil leaned back his head and roared in laughter. "Boy, there ain't a thing that would please me more than to tear up this old land with you. But I've got a pile of other obligations to keep me busy."

"I understand. You're just like the other grown-ups. You got *important* things to do."

Satan winced at that; he didn't ever want to be considered *just a grown-up*. He empathized with the impish boy and felt a tremble in the black hunk of coal that sat where a normal fellow's heart might beat. Though Scratch is the Lord of the underworld, with all manner of sorcery and abominations at his disposal, he'd much rather be playing than working. Collecting souls and punishing the wicked is a thankless job, after all, and Satan didn't have much in the way of friends either.

The Devil contemplated the matter and said, "What you need is a dog."

"We've already got three," Jefe said with a sniffle.

"Are you talking about those mangy coon hounds that sleep under the porch all day? Naw, those are your Pa's dogs. A boy needs his own dog, and that's as true as an outhouse needs stink."

"I guess," Jefe said. He shrugged his shoulders and traced a finger through the dirt.

"What say you, should a new whelp come scamperin' by this very moment?"

"I'd be pleased to meet him, I suppose."

At that, a black mongrel of a pup bounded up the road, as if following the rut left by Scratch's tail.

"Well, look at that. Here he comes now," Satan said.

Jefe saw the dog and grinned large as a Yankee tart. The mutt was shaggy with big ears that flopped at each step and a bushy tail that wagged back and forth like a bent compass needle searching for north. It was about the size of a one-year-old calf, with plenty more room to grow. A big pink tongue lolled from its mouth, and black eyes twinkled in the summer sunshine. There was something wild about those eyes, like a nefarious joy, as if they were searching, not for a rabbit to chase down, but maybe a pack of uppity Baptists from the revival tent.

The dog was pure black, dark as winter shadows under a starless sky. Jefe knew right away its name was to be *Midnight*.

"I reckon the two of you are going to have a heap of good times, from here on out," Satan said.

Jefe didn't reply, but tousled Midnight behind his floppy ears. The two looked into each others' eyes and felt right away the warm affection of friendship, that companionship sought in a kindred spirit.

Satan didn't say another word but just ambled back down the road with a whistle on his lips.

If Jefe got into trouble before, it was plumb multiplied now. Scratch don't give away anything for free and, though he didn't ask for anything as insidious as a little boy's soul, what he did gain was a priceless fount of personal pleasure by watching the rapacious antics of a rascal youth and his hell-borne dog. O!

Did Satan grin and chuckle at the mishaps caused by Midnight and Jefe Bowman.

Those two tore up the countryside like a gale wind blowing through a nest made of sparrow feathers. They urinated in wells and shepherded snakes into peoples' beds, laughing all the while. One time, Jefe pretended to be an Indian and rode Midnight like a horse through the mountains, shooting poisoned arrows at livestock. Another time he wanted to be a pirate, so he flooded the Cherokee Valley and sailed over it on a log raft, sparing no prisoners. Once, Jefe wanted to fly, so he and Midnight leapt across the face of a full moon. Those people that saw, fell to their knees in fright.

He wasn't asked to do chores now, and Jefe hardly ever went home. When he did, his folks shuttered the windows and bolted the doors.

"That dog is the devil's imp," Pa told him.

"Yes sir, I can't argue with that," Jefe replied.

Years trekked by and, so too, did The Great War. It went back and forth, so as sometimes the southern states were winning, while sometimes the northern states were winning. There sounded great wailing everywhere Jefe went, and he got mighty tired of hearing about the conflict. It seemed the war was *never* going to end, and people aren't keen on playing while their families are shooting at each other. He thought of his brothers often, and felt bad they had been away such a long time.

That afternoon, Breckinridge's Expedition fought off

Gillem's Division at a small conflict known as *The Battle of Bull's Gap*. Both of Jefe's brothers were gravely wounded during the battle and each lay in medical tents on opposite sides of the county. He decided to visit them and resolve matters once and for all.

He visited Odie first.

"Howdy, brother," Jefe said.

"Howdy," Odie replied. "I've heard some wild tales of your doings."

"Midnight and I are just havin' some fun. Ain't much harm in it, I reckon."

"It's nothing I wouldn't do, given the opportunity," Odie said. He had a musket ball lodged in his chest and didn't look too good.

"I came here to settle this matter of the *States' Rebellion.* What will it take for you to go home? Ma and Pa are mournin' the absence of their sons, and I feel a mite bad, even if they won't talk to me. There ain't no one left to help with their chores."

"I'll never quit fighting," Odie said. "I'd rather die than lose to the likes of Elmer Bowman. I ain't gonna let him beat me in *anything!*"

Jefe thought about that, and then he and Midnight crossed over to the Confederate side to pay Elmer a visit.

"Howdy, brother," Jefe said.

"Howdy," Elmer replied. "Been a long time since last I saw you."

"I just visited Odie and asked how'd he like to end this war."

"What'd he say?" Elmer asked. He had a musket ball lodged in his chest like his brother and looked like he was two feet away from being six under.

"Odie said he'd rather die than lose this conflict to you."

"He did? Well then, I'd rather do whatever he ain't. I'd live just to spite him, even if I lost."

Jefe thought about that, too. As always, each brother wanted the opposite of the other.

The next day Odie died, and Elmer recovered.

Jefe and Midnight crossed the state line and headed south to Atlanta. From there, they tore a path of rambunctious antics and destruction all the way to the ocean port at Savannah, the likes of which the South had never known. It was said that wherever they traveled, the earth was scorched in their path.

Jefe knocked over telegraph poles just to watch them topple against each other like a line of dominoes. He set fire to cotton gins and storage bins because the flames were pretty to look at. When they came across farms, he was reminded of the hard labors he once toiled at, so he laid salt across the fields until the crops died. Wouldn't no children have to harvest while Jefe Bowman was around. To celebrate each child's emancipation from chores, he found a bridge to collapse or road to bury, the same way men might smoke a cigar after dinner. The broken and twisted railroads were his doing, too; he loved to watch the trains crash. The steel rails that folks found wrapped around tree stumps came to be known as "Jefe's neckties".

Those who knew better fled when they learned Jefe and Midnight were coming their way—there wasn't nothing safe! Those two caused so much destruction in Georgia, most people refused to believe it could be the sole work of a boy and his dog. The newspaper men and politicians blamed it all instead on the nearest Union forces under General William Tecumseh Sherman.

Truth be told, General Sherman was lazy and drunk in his camp up in Chattanooga, and contemplating retreat. When word came he had brought about the collapse of the South, and was the harbinger of Union victory, he was as surprised as anyone else. That didn't stop him though from nodding his head and accepting every laurel and accolade that fell his way.

And so it went, the cause of the South was defeated, so that Elmer could live knowing he'd lost, while Odie died victorious. Jefe thought it better that way; one brother gone home was better than none at all.

Jefe never aged another day after that. He didn't die either; he just stayed the same sweet age when logic don't apply, and the concerns of good and evil are so much wisps of smoke blowing away over the mountaintops.

Maybe it's because the Devil doesn't have children of his own that he felt such a kinship with Jefe. He saw himself in that boy, mischievous and misunderstood, marked as a *ne'er-do-well* the moment he was born. Ol' Scratch looked upon Jefe as one looks upon a setting sun, awestruck at the wild, flashing colors in the sky, but knowing they are fleeting; soon they will fade and only the inky darkness of night will remain. Sometimes, when one looks at a sunset, they wish that moment could last forever.

The Devil wished it too, in Jefe Bowman.

To this day, Jefe and Midnight wander the South, gettin' into scrapes and wreaking havoc. Sometimes they chase each other in circles, 'til a twister rises from their path. Other times, they might spit in the wind 'til the resulting storm sinks ships.

Of course, sometimes they also decide to stretch their legs a bit and see what the rest of the country looks like.

One time, Jefe thought it funny to poke a cow with a broomstick until, tired of being tormented, that cow lashed out and kicked over a lantern in its barn. The resulting fire burned down Chicago.

In the mid-1930s, they were caught red-handed pulling up all the grazing grass in Oklahoma. A mob of enraged homesteaders came after them, and Jefe ran out of there so fast, the dust he kicked up in the air covered five states and lingered three years.

The last they were seen was during a hurricane in New Orleans, just before the Mississippi River rolled in to submerge half the city. Most folks don't believe the flood was on account of a boy and his dog skipping stones against the levees until they broke, but you and I know better.

Some say Jefe Bowman is the Devil himself, but it ain't true. He's just a child, the likes of which we all were at one time or another.

He's just a little boy playing with his best friend.

The Bone Washer

Travis Burnham

On my very first day, I'd been forced into the Preparation Chamber, in amongst the beetles, and the stench and the flesh, and the bones. I bore the trial because the Prepared was Ainsley's great uncle—beloved Ainsley, who had convinced her father to find me a position in the Bone Washer's guild.

Outside the chamber, Bordo, the Chief Arranger leaned in so close I could see the perspiration beading on his nose and brow. Bordo loathed that he had to depend on someone so young for such a crucial part of the Preparation. With the execution of the previous apprentice for seditious words and the death of the elder Bone Washer, the task of preparing bones had fallen to me. Though inexperienced, I was the most qualified.

"Listen well, Caleb," he said in a hissed whisper. "I hated this man, but if you hurt so much as one sacred beetle, or misplace so much as a knucklebone and disgrace our guild?" He scowled, painfully twisting my ear. "I'll beat you so badly that you'll never walk again."

Bordo, pale and bald, but thick in body and arm, had the strength to carry out his threat. Proof abounded in my circle of peers. Another apprentice a few years older still walked with a limp—when he'd mislaid a left intermediate cuneiform bone, Bordo hammered the bottom of his feet with a lead pipe so that he would always remember where the cuneiform bone could be found.

Weighed down with my accouterments, I took a deep breath and opened the oaken door that lead to the body. The room was dark and warm from the vented air that circulated the smell of decay. The stick of incense that I held did little to keep the fetor at bay. Though there were other sounds, they faded to nothing when pitted against the dry-quiet skitcheting sound of beetles on bone and stone floor. That, and the quiet larval munching of flesh being consumed. The beetles were merely the parents, whereas the larvae did all the eating of the vessels and skin and muscle that anchored them to this world and barred entrance to the afterlife. It was only the dead's bones that were eternal.

As I entered, the beetles retreated from my dim light, glossy brown and tan flecks flashing across their shells as they scattered. Theirs was a dark world, and my jar of glow algae was a quiet but distinct interruption. I walked as if barefoot on broken bottles, aware that any misstep might be my last if there were an insect beneath.

The light fell upon Old Vanslyke who, in life, had been a minor noble full of political ideas that made him unpopular with the guilds.

Though the larvae writhed upon his skeleton, I felt as though they crawled upon mine, worming their way through my flesh. I did not want to be ungrateful for my position, but still I suppressed a shiver and muttered the invocation of apology, waving the incense above the corpse, hovering low where the larvae seemed slow moving. Their bewhiskered bodies, with alternating bands of brown and black, moved as one, slinking off the Prepared and into safer shadowy places. As the incense ashes were spent I, with a shaking hand, carefully collected them in my pocket.

As instructed, I set down the glow jar into its designated place and unrolled the canvas stretcher alongside the bones, which freed my hands to remove the brush from the other pocket of my robe.

Before touching the body, I spoke the requisite words, "*Viscus senium os tolero.*" Flesh decays, bone endures.

I don't know what disturbed me more, the mass of moving beetles and larvae, or the thought of touching something that had been a someone a scant week ago. Though Vanslyke had been found in his bed, some had suspected foul play in his passing. They were but a few however, and no more than the usual cast of elderly characters who suspected foul play at every passing.

The Flesher had been asked to do an examination beforehand, but found nothing amiss. It hardly seemed surprising, for though Vanslyke had been lively, he'd also been well into his sixties. He'd probably had enemies, due to his belief that guild members and the lower classes must remain in their place, but apparently none of these enemies considered murder.

I took a deep breath and reached forward. I made to brush away those stubborn beetles who'd not abandoned their meal... but there were none. I'd been told there would be dozens or more tucked away in the skull sutures and between various joints, the dark spaces between.

Despite the warm humid air, a thin cold layer of sweat slicked my skin as I grasped Vanslyke's tibia, fibula, and tarsal, and began laying him out on the stretcher—feet west, head east.

"*Proficiscor vestri pes super semita.*" I set your feet upon the path.

Most of his joints were still articulated; cartilage being a food of last resort for the larvae. I meticulously worked my way up—patella, femur, pelvis, vertebrae, ribs, sternum, mandible, skull—at each step carefully checking to make sure I'd not left a bone behind. I used the hundreds of fine ribbons that were threaded through the stretcher to tie the bones down along their outline. From the stretcher, Bordo, as Master Arranger, would take them. My muscles ached. The concentration and tension on my eyesight brought on a headache that would define all headaches from that point forward.

As I placed the final bone and tied the complex knot to keep it in place, a square of thin watery light flickered against the opposing wall. Someone watched from the viewport, probably Felix the Thermic, who was responsible for the overall wellbeing of the beetles, as well as caring for the wood furnace and vents that kept the temperature and humidity at a level the insects found comfortable. I felt secure knowing he kept an eye on me.

Finished laying out the Prepared, I set up the straps that fastened to my shoulders and would allow me to carry the stretcher by myself. I stood and walked carefully, working the pins and needles from my stiff limbs.

I made the sign to the insects and uttered my departure prayer.

"*Gratias ago scarabaeus.*" Thank the beetles.

At the exit, and then past, I felt the displaced air as the door shut behind me. A tangible relief washed through me, loosening my knees and releasing the fist clenched around my stomach.

I turned and Bordo was there.

With a lead pipe.

"Welcome back, Caleb." He ran a practiced eye over the Prepared, assessing. "I trust you had a nice visit with the beetles."

I held my breath, legs wobbly, back throbbing with the weight of the Prepared.

Finding nothing amiss with his cursory examination of the skeleton, he thrust out his chest and gave a snarl of disappointment. "He'd best be the color of moonlight when I see him next. Not even a hint of greasy yellow or over bleaching. Break or lose a bone and I'll do the same to you."

"Yes, Master Bordo."

He grunted and dismissed me, thrusting his chin towards

the Vat Room.

I was merely a link in the chain, the Bone Washer. Before me, the Flesher—trimming muscle and tissue, removing the brain, then drying—and after me, Bordo, the Chief Arranger, whose job it is to lay out the Prepared and, more importantly, set him apart from other skeletons so that loved ones can identify the deceased from hundreds of others in the ossuary. Whatever else can be said about Bordo, he's very good at his job.

The reek of strong chemicals filled the Vat Room, as well as barrels and tubs, alembics and beakers, jars and clay vessels. I knew but a fraction the functions of the items and substances in this room. Threadbare rugs lay upon the floor, while shelves covered every bit of rough stone wall. Off to the side were my quarters, a small room with a bookshelf and a single bed that had once belonged to Master Osvaldo.

When I had first joined the guild, Osvaldo had me commit the Washer Code to memory. Despite my young age, I knew more of the Washer's art than anyone else in the castle or surrounding area. I spent all my nights poring over texts and journals, trying to glean the processes that he'd been slow to show me while still alive—my attempt to be worthy of my position, and of Ainsley's effort on my behalf. Some eight years ago, she'd pleaded and pleaded with her father. He'd surrendered and placed me before the guildmasters—if not for her, I'd have been just another bloated corpse in some dark alley.

I often wished that Ainsley's father had found me a different profession, or another guildmaster had chosen me. Why not an apprenticeship with the Kite Maker's Guild, or the Lamplighters? Or even the Mercenary Guild? I pictured myself filling out a uniform with muscles gained from long days of hard riding and hard fighting. Ainsley would love such a man.

But Master Osvaldo had chosen me. Instead of starving, I was a washer of bones. As powerful as my disgust for the larvae and beetles was, it was just another obstacle for me to overcome.

I thought of the previous journeyman Bone Washer, Joshua, who'd made the mistake of saying the wrong things to the wrong people. Just two weeks ago, I'd watched him twitch at the end of a rope for speaking out against our corrupt nobility.

I set aside my busy thoughts and stoked the fire, easing the Prepared into the hot water and ammonia bath. As I opened the Code, I nodded off before I'd even finished the first paragraph.

~

I awoke sprawled across one of the numerous stained and threadbare journals, the candle guttering low. I jolted and ran to the ammonia bath—would all of my work and study be for naught? A small amount of fat from the marrow cavities floated on the surface. I relaxed, thankfully having woken just in time. I skimmed it and then with tongs checked for the early warning signs of pits or discoloration – a clear signal that the Prepared was ready to move to the next step.

A soft knock.

The door opened quietly, but no one was there, the hallway black as pitch beyond.

"Hello?" I asked.

"Good evening, young Caleb," said the darkness. Felix the Thermic stepped from the shadows. "How was your first experience with the beetles?" Gnarled and ancient, and a hand shorter than me, the Thermic was built in the spindly manner of a dead tree, all mottled bark and skeletal branches. He was something of a father figure to the young ones in the guilds. Friendly, and no friend of Bordo's, he was probably checking on me to ensure there were no mishaps with my Washing.

I breathed a sigh of relief. "I near enough died of fright, Felix. As for my first experience? It's as if I can still feel them crawling on my skin."

Felix chuckled, his voice deep and resonant, contradicting his age. "I think you'll grow to love them. They certainly seem quite accustomed to you."

"Accustomed?"

"Never in my time have I seen the beetles act in such a way," he replied. He groomed his unruly eyebrows with a gnarled hand. "Usually the larvae are quite reluctant to leave the Prepared. They linger in the joints and crevices. It often doubles the Washers' time just coaxing the larvae to leave their meal and shelter."

I turned the spigot on the vat that drained the water from the Prepared, who had been in the bath long enough I gauged.

Felix looked at the bones. "Vanslyke. Bordo really hated that man."

"Bordo hates everyone."

"Though it's hard to say in these matters, Vanslyke was probably Bordo's father. Regardless, when the Master Arranger confronted Vanslyke, the noble simply ignored him, wiped Bordo away as if he were something unpleasant that the Lord had stepped in."

I hadn't heard this particular rumor before, but even with this information it was difficult for me to dredge up any sympathy for the Master Arranger.

"The nobles," Felix continued, "have little regard for those of us in the lower classes."

I tried to remain focused on my task. "This is true, but if it hadn't been for Lady Ainsley—"

Felix pushed his point. "The suppression of last week's grain riot only illuminates the king's poor mental health. There were children, babies even, among the dead. There's a storm coming, Caleb, and there are no buildings in the middle ground to offer shelter."

Fear began crowding my thoughts. What did Felix want me to say? I thought again of Joshua, spasming in the noose, and the nine farmers who'd been hung this morning for misrecording their barley yields. I chose my words carefully. "You, of course know, Thermic, that my allegiance lies with the guilds, but does this seem like a wise conversation after what happened to Joshua?"

Felix gave a thin smile. "Of course, young Caleb, of course.

Let's avoid such talk." He patted my hand. "You're a good lad." Doubling back to the previous conversation, he continued. "Quite unique, the reaction of the insects towards you today."

"I didn't stray from what I've been taught," I replied, still worried about the previous conversation, but also concerned that perhaps I'd done something wrong with the Preparation.

"No, you didn't. At least not from what I saw," mused Felix, tapping a finger against his lips. "Not from what I saw," he repeated, speaking to no one but himself, as if I'd become a ghost. He waved a hand in casual farewell as he walked out of the chamber.

Trying hard not to be distracted by my worldly concerns, I turned back to my work on the Prepared—alcoholbath to dry him, brush to remove debris, and finally the sweet smelling stream of colorless Trichle, the substance best served for stripping away the stubborn greases and oils.

~

In stark contrast to the rest of the dilapidated castle and ragged hovels beyond, the Presentation Room was in pristine condition. Finely upholstered chairs ran from wall to wall in rows, while enormous murals depicting glorious scenes of the afterlife stretched into the darkness beyond the rafters. Falling past long windows, heavy curtains the color of blood glowed as they resisted the sunlight behind them. The Prepared was in front while the living milled about the rest of the room.

It was only the nobles that were worthy of these ceremonies. I, of common blood, would more likely spend my eternity in an unmarked grave, but for me this seemed preferable to having my flesh consumed by the larvae in the Preparation Chamber.

For most nobles this was merely an opportunity to strut and preen, gossip and machinate, but even with the jaded personalities represented here, I heard murmurs of appreciation. Despite the fact that it had been my first time going through the process, the attendees were talking about my Preparation: the cleanliness, the lack of abrasions, the smoothness of the bone, the impeccable color. Could it be that all my hard studies were worth it? I felt torn between two feelings. Unwarranted as the compliments felt, the room buzzed, and many a conversation and gaze fell upon me. Would Ainsley see me in a different light?

Vanslyke's presentation ceremony was little different than any other, but for at least one it was clearly different. In a landscape of dry eyes, Ainsley tried to stifle her unseemly sorrow.

My thoughts fell back to a time when I would discretely watch her. One of the library windows overlooked the courtyard and the west side of the castle, and from there I could watch her spar with the sword master, or practice horsemanship. It's a curious thing about beauty, that even from a distance it's still evident. For Ainsley, I thought it was maybe the set of her shoulders and her long purposeful strides, or the way her laugh echoed off the stone walls.

Here in the Presentation room, at this distance, I could more closely examine her. Though Ainsley looked uncomfortable in a gown of midnight blue and tears aplenty, the most incongruous addition to her attire was the sling around her broken right arm. Hers was not a traditional beauty, but a pleasing combination of cropped, disheveled hair, a nose a little too big and a mouth a little too small. Well past the age at which she should be playing at war—fourteen or so—she'd broken her arm while defending a wooden fort suspended in the boughs of the large oak tree in the center of the apple orchard. At some point Master Osvaldo had told me she wanted to be a soldier.

Ainsley's father, the son of Lord Vanslyke the Elder, had views in stark contrast to that of his father. He held the opinion that the lower classes, even women, should have rights, and Ainsley was a product of his upbringing, recognizing neither class nor gender when judging others.

Across the Chamber, Ainsley caught me looking at her and, before I could look away, gave me a weak smile through her pain and mouthed thank you. She could only be thanking me for the Preparation. Maybe, truly, all of those nights of little sleep had been worth it. Could she love a Bone Washer?

When I attempted to snatch another glance at Ainsley, I noticed Bordo scowling at her.

Then his eyes locked with mine.

He'd also seen Ainsley's and the other nobles' appreciation. Though I didn't want it, I drew the attention of the nobles, attention that perhaps Bordo himself craved.

Moving efficiently toward me through the throng, he speared forward, his face a tightly controlled mask of jealousy and rage.

~

Phalanges to metacarpals to carpals, the days blurred together.

I'd spent much of my energy the previous week avoiding Bordo. Like the beetles and larvae that disgusted me, I took to finding crannies and dark niches, out of the way places in the castle where I could sit with a candle and book undisturbed. Perhaps by seeking out these quiet places, I would find some degree of empathy for the insects. Learn to love them as Master Osvaldo had.

One evening, as the sun's light bled out, I sat beneath a smoky torch I'd lit along a rarely used corridor, poring over one of Osvaldo's books contrasting ammonia and lye solutions for the first boiling in Preparation. It was eloquent how he juxtaposed the compounds by their properties and cleansing abilities.

When I heard footsteps approaching, my heart hit a double beat until I realized almost immediately that the step was far too light and quick for the Chief Arranger. When I identified the owner of the tread, I made my book the center of my universe, my shyness making me wish I were invisible.

When a pair of soft, high boots stopped in front of me, I had no choice but to look up.

The blunt end of a wooden sparring sword nearly touched my nose, Ainsley eying me across the hilt and down the blade. She held the weapon awkwardly in her left hand, the sling still supporting her right.

"What knave have we here? Speak, knave, lest I need to run you through as a trespasser."

My words dried up. I hadn't seen her this closely since we'd played as children. The torchlight flickered against her smooth skin, lit her green eyes, and cast pulses of red through her chestnut hair. With her confidence and swagger she was everything I wasn't.

She was beautiful.

Gripped with the urge to kiss her, my face grew warm and I looked down, desperately hoping that she wouldn't see the flush.

In one smooth motion she sheathed her sword and reached down to snatch the book from my lap. "What language is this?" she said, flipping through the pages. "It looks like the meanderings of a worm drunk on ink."

I was a poor conversationalist, used to the company of books and bones. "It's… it is… The Code."

"The Code?" She raised an eyebrow and dropped her voice to a conspiratorial tone. "A secret code?"

"I suppose."

She threw herself down beside me and continued flipping through the book. Even through the heavy fabric of our clothes, I could feel her warmth where our arms lay against each other.

"You must teach the Code to me at once."

"I… can't."

"I suppose because then it would no longer be a secret." She heaved an exasperated sigh. "You learned folk are all cut from the same cloth. Dreary and tedious." She tossed the book into my lap.

She carried herself with a naïve grace that allowed her to not look down on me and, because of this, I wanted desperately to prove to her that I wasn't dreary, that I was worthy of her friendship.

"I graciously forgive your lack of facility in the social graces." She fixed me with an imperious eye before continuing, "Because of what you did for my grandfather." At the mention of her grandfather, she seemed to deflate, like an actor who had lost her character.

"*Viscus senium os tolero*," I said in sympathy without thought. Though his flesh would rot, he and his bones would persist in the afterlife.

Annoyance flickered across her face at the standard condolence, but disappeared just as quickly. She said, "He was vigorous, you know, despite his years. It wasn't his time."

The same quiet that had stolen my words crept upon her, our silence only interrupted by the spluttering of the torch and the sough of the curtains, weak guardians against the wintry night air outside.

"My father and my grandfather had their disagreements. Father believes that people should be treated well, despite their station, whereas my grandfather felt that people shouldn't rise above their proper position, should know their place. Of what mind are you?"

"I haven't the time to think of things other than Washing. I only know that I don't hunger, or fear for my safety." I took a deep breath, and pushed out the words. "I have you to thank for that."

She seemed to not hear my thanks, brushed it away like cobwebs. "You and Granda might have gotten along." She looked down. "I know he could be insufferable," she whispered. Then steel poured into her voice, and she said, "But he was still my Granda and I'll find his killer. I'm a persistent hound."

How could I respond? I didn't believe her grandfather had been murdered. Grief caused people to grope for answers, to search shadows for villains. Osvaldo had even alluded to these misconceptions in one of his journal's entries.

She suddenly offered her hand. "We have yet to be properly reacquainted. I'm Ainsley, if you've forgotten."

"Caleb," I added, crushed that she hadn't remembered.

"Caleb," she said, as if tasting a new food. She turned to look at me and again I blushed, this time at her attention. "I like you, Caleb Bone Washer. You have an honest face." She stood and dropped her sorrow like a dirty garment. Pulling her sword from its sheath, she was once again the knight-errant. She tapped my shoulders with the flat of the blade and grinned. "I dub thee *Lord Converser*, because of your facility with the spoken tongue. Our paths will cross again soon, my Lord, I'm certain."

And then, racing around the corner, she was gone, leaving a

tight, hollow feeling below my sternum.

~

Days passed. Grand Dame Sabin, the great aunt of Lord Pickering, was the next Prepared. I went in the early morning to collect her.

Bordo was there, of course, fulfilling his role as Master Arranger.

"Good evening, Master Bone Washer." He spit 'master' out as if it was a gobbet of snot that had been rattling in his throat.

I think Bordo would have beat me down on the spot, but despite only having performed one Washing, it seemed that many considered that one Washing so superlative that I had gained a tincture of fame that now afforded me a small amount of protection from him. I was also the sole Bone Washer, though they were searching for suitable understudies. Even with these factors I could feel his barely restrained anger seething below the surface.

I said nothing, afraid that anything might be a catalyst for violence. I went to move around the Chief Arranger, but he grabbed my arm so hard I felt tingles down to my hand. As if reading my thoughts, he growled, "This kind of fame is short lived, Washer, and I'll be waiting on the other side."

I pushed past Bordo and plunged into the chamber. The hot air washed over me. Though warmer than the chilly hallway, it afforded no relief because again I felt the crawling sensation, as if the beetles were burrowing into my muscles and bones, crawling inside of me and worming their way through my organs.

The beetles retreated from my light as before, moving as one, seeming to obey some unspoken command.

I went through Sabin's Preparation, mechanically speaking the words that would help guide her into the next life. I left the chamber, but there was no respite from my fears. Beetles and larvae in the chamber, Bordo everywhere else.

Back in my room, Sabin simmered in her Preparation bath. As I reached for a book, I froze. There, on my outstretched arm, crawling from my sleeve, was a beetle. Chills like cold razors slid down my spine.

It was illegal to remove beetles from the Preparation Chamber. The Master Arranger decided and presided over punishment. I could picture Bordo's gleeful expression if he were to hear the news that I'd been caught with a beetle.

My mind came to the forbidden idea of simply crushing the beetle and burning the remains, but killing a beetle by accident implied strict punishment, by intent meant long imprisonment, or worse.

The beetle sat there, looking at me, as if trying to communicate in some insectile language. It vibrated its wing casings and exuded a smell that was not altogether unpleasant. I looked for its beauty, and found some in its brushed patterns of black and tan and white. He was simply an innocent cog in a massive machine, not unlike myself. The thought of violence suddenly seemed abhorrent.

I reached for a pair of tongs—an impromptu beetle

manipulation tool—but the beetle simply shivered its wing casings and ambled back into the cuff of my robe.

Not wanting to miss the happy coincidence, I dampened the fire and made my way to the Preparation Chamber, sticking to the shadows as best I could.

~

There were only a select few that were allowed access to the Preparation Chamber. I stopped in the alcove that held the jars of glow algae and chose the smallest one. Though there'd been no registrations to my knowledge, I double checked the log that the nobility required us to keep, in order to be sure there were no bodies scheduled. I wasn't interested in any unwelcome visitors.

I hid the light beneath my cloak.

The door swung open in front of me, and immediately something felt wrong.

The Chamber felt… occupied.

I moved forward and knelt to restore the errant cuff beetle to its home. It obediently flew deeper into the chamber and landed on—

I expected to see an Expedient, a deer or a cow that would get the beetles from one Prepared to the next. Instead, limned in the algae glow light, lay a Prepared, a quite obvious human form, though I'd checked that none were scheduled. How did they get the body in here without my knowledge?

Frustration swelled in me. I should have been informed. What if the larvae were left too long upon the skeleton? They would have begun upon the sinew and the bones would have been disarticulated. It was a stroke of luck then, that I'd stumbled upon this Prepared, though I'm sure someone would have told me sooner or later. Who could have put it in here? At first I thought of Bordo, but as the Master Arranger he stood to be discredited as well if a body spent too long in the Chamber.

My clumsy thoughts then stumbled upon the possibility.

Perhaps this body was not meant to be Arranged, but disposed.

Murder?

My mind raced through possibilities. Who had keys to the Preparation Chamber besides me? The Flesher? He was a large, simple, jovial man. Felix? He was old and practically a father to me. Though they certainly had the opportunity, I would sooner suspect myself. Who else had easy access to this room?

Bordo. Of course.

As the Master Arranger, he lived next to the beetles. Could it have been him? With his violent nature and mood swings could it be anyone else?

I drew closer to the beetles and their unplanned meal, fear dogging every footstep that Bordo might walk in on me, but still hoping that there simply been a mistake and I hadn't been informed.

Larvae obscured the Prepared, but I could still see some details. Not large, about my size. Probably female judging from the width of the hips. My eyes snapped to the detail that I didn't want to see: a broken radius, a broken arm.

Vomit crawled up my throat as I fled.

~

I barely waited for the door to open before entering. Felix's room was hot and humid, and the roar of the furnace played backdrop.

Weak, I groped for speech. What I had to say just spilled from me in shaking words. "I found Ainsley in the Preparation Chamber. Bordo must have killed her." Saying it aloud made it real. It took all my strength to not break down into sobs. "Maybe he even killed Vanslyke somehow!"

"Bordo? Kill Lord Vanslyke and his granddaughter?" Felix frowned. "That's a serious accusation."

Felix motioned towards a seat. "Sit and warm yourself by the fire. Perhaps we can get some sense out of you. I've some hot water ready and I can make you some tea."

Despite my sorrow, suspicion rose in me. Why did Felix seem so calm? Did he not believe me about the body?

Felix asked, "Why do you suspect Bordo?" as he busied himself with the preparation of our drinks.

I hesitated, but replied. "You yourself said Bordo hated the man and what better way to further his hatred than kill Ainsley —Lady Ainsley. Or maybe she found something out." My words were tumbling and clustering, making little sense as I groped for reasons. "And with his sadistic nature—"

"It's true the man has a violent temperament," Felix said, smoothly interjecting and handing me the tea, settling down across from me with his own drink in hand. "Have you told anyone else?"

"No." I held the tea in my hands, felt its warmth, but I didn't bring it to my lips.

Felix seemed to come to some kind of internal decision, and all of a sudden his tone and demeanor changed. "We'd best alert Lord Cabal, he'll get to the bottom of this." He looked down at my untouched tea and stood. "Is the tea bitter? Let me sweeten that with some honey, and then we'll be on our way."

He rummaged in the cabinet behind me.

Suddenly, I felt a pain at the nape of my neck as if stung by a bee. I clapped my hand to the aggrieved spot and spun to face Felix.

Felix frowned. "If you'd simply had the tea, this would have been so much more pleasant. You would have just fallen asleep." He wouldn't look me in the eyes. "I'm afraid this is quicker, but not as kind."

I ran my hands over a raised welt surrounding a small puncture wound. "You… you poisoned me?"

Heat spread down through my extremities and swept up over my skull—fire in my veins. I tried to stand, but my limbs spasmed and my back arched painfully. My tongue felt thick, my throat dry.

Felix's brow furrowed in sadness. "I'm sorry that you stumbled across Lady Ainsley, Caleb. Her passing is a tragedy. She was so young. But small people can fit into small places and overhear things they shouldn't overhear. The other guild masters and I will fix this broken city and Vanslyke is just a casualty for the greater good.

"As was Ainsley." He rung his hands, guilt etching his face. "And you. I can't have them finding Ainsley and tracing her back to me. I'm so sorry, Caleb. So sorry."

Numbness raced through my limbs and the teacup fell from senseless fingers. I fell to the floor as a pain gripped my midsection and drove a throbbing up through my brain. My vision pulsed white static.

"It's Vanslyke's fault," Felix continued. "If he hadn't been such a steadfast bigot, if he'd embraced the guilds and not stood in the way of our elevation to nobility, then perhaps we wouldn't have removed him."

He frowned. "If only I could have trusted you to side with the guild, but you seemed so steadfastly noncommittal. How could I trust you?" He patted my hand, then brushed away the hair I'd felt fall across my eyes. "Don't worry, the pain has passed. It will be over soon."

I felt my heart slow, and then stop.

"No." My lips twitched, but no words escaped my lips.

I didn't want to die.

~

Dim light woke me, my vision splintered into a thousand fragments, as if I looked at one scene from many perspectives. I sensed I was in the Preparation Chamber. My worst fear realized. I tried to move, but felt at odds with myself; not all in the right place and drawn in different directions.

Sounds came to me, but I felt them, more than heard them,

vibrations that set my frame to shudder. It was a voice, muted, mumbling, talking to itself. With difficulty, I focused, intent on understanding.

"I'll miss you, poor, foolish, interfering Caleb. You were one of my favorites," said Felix. "And you were so skilled. Your work on Vanslyke was nothing short of art." I sensed the regret in his voice. "And to think it was your first Preparation."

I lost focus on his words. There was no pain, but I felt the beetles among me. In me.

What happened? I struggled and stumbled through my memories. I remembered dropping the teacup, which tumbled and then shattered. Convulsing and then darkness.

Was I dead? Was Ainsley somehow here with me?

He grunted and the world shifted beneath me. "It's a sad day when the old must dispose of the young. But when the guilds are in power, there will be so much more equality. No starvation, no injustice."

I tried to move my hand, but it felt like I willed all of my fingers, all of my toes at once, none of them wishing to comply. I concentrated, pitting willpower against the maelstrom of my confusion.

Materializing from a mosaic of shadow and light that was cast from many different directions, Felix's face swam into a blurry impression, unfocused but obviously him. I could more smell him than anything else. And when he moved, I felt more than saw it, sensed the vibrations in the air between us.

I tried to form words, but there was nothing there with

which to form them. Instead, I tried to move my hands, and I moved.

"What's this?" Felix said, curiosity with an edge of worry. "Get back to work you foolish insects."

I looked away from Felix, and the horror of what I saw unfolded before me. It was my body, gutted and fleshed, an empty husk beneath a wriggling carpet of beetles and larvae. I struggled to care, but it seemed the emotion was beyond me. My old body was gone.

Now I was more.

I was one. I was one thousand. One-hundred thousand.

I was the beetles and the larvae, and they were me.

Millions of beetle and larvae feet moved as one at my command.

"Why have you stopped eating? Get away from me!"

A million pairs of beetle wings beat the air and flew.

I crept and flew towards the voice, Felix's voice.

His words turned to pleading, pleading to screams, finally to shrieks and then silence.

He was mine and I was among him.

"Gratias ago scarabaeus."

The Wilds

by Tim Jeffreys

The day was overcast and still, the sea calm. It was exactly the kind of day Connor knew would make Pa uneasy. They had their boat out on the water early, without struggle. They cast their nets with no fuss, then sat and waited. Connor ate the sandwiches his mother had prepared, glancing now and then towards shore. He could just see the outline of the bay. The silent, steel-coloured sea and blank grey sky made him feel like he was drifting in a void. He looked at Pa, who sat turning his head to and fro as if detecting sounds all about him. There were no sounds though, except the lazy lap of water against the sides of the boat and the occasional cry of a gull somewhere in the distance. His father stood and said:

"Something's wrong."

"Sit down, Pa. It's just the day."

"It's that kind of day when things go wrong, so calm and quiet. And something has gone wrong. I can sense it. Let's get the nets in."

"Pa...?"

"Something's wrong, you mark my words."

Connor shook his head, then, seeing there would be no

argument he stood and helped his father draw the nets in. There would be no catch today.

Maybe next time. Connor was addressing his thoughts to the unseen fish swimming below the surface, evading the dinner plate because Pa couldn't relax when everything was relaxed around him.

"I was looking forward to a nice bit of trout as well," he told his father after they had drawn the empty nets back onto the boat.

"There'll be other times for trout," his father said. "Let's get back."

Crouching, the man brought the engine sputtering to life and turned the boat toward shore. As they approached the bay, Connor noticed a figure on the sand. Pa saw who it was before he did.

"There's your Rae. Waiting for you."

"She's not waiting for me, Pa. And she's not *my* Rae."

"You like her, don't you?"

"We're just friends."

"You know your mother thinks of her as part of the family. She'd be heartbroken if you two didn't…"

Connor threw his father a black look, silencing him. "We're just friends."

"Well, if she's not waiting for you, what *is* she doing?"

"How should I know?"

"I think she's waiting for you."

"Pa!"

They were close enough to the shore now to see Rae clearly. She was a small figure, seeming smaller still in big black boots and an oversized jumper that reached almost to her knees. She had been walking on the beach, but now she turned and waved to them. Connor raised a hand but abruptly lowered it, feeling his father watching him. As they struggled to get the boat up onto the sand, Rae bounded over to them, pretending to help but really only getting in the way. Connor didn't mind. He had known Rae all his life. They were the same age and she was almost like a sister to him. The little house where she lived with her elderly grandfather was only a short walk across the clifftop from his own. Her parents had gone to the mainland long ago with a promise to return, but so far they hadn't. Rae often said that when her grandfather died she would have no one, and when he heard this Connor would throw an arm over her shoulder and tell her: "You'll have me."

She would smile at this, shyly, as if she didn't quite believe him. His parents thought that he and Rae would get married one day or at least spend their lives together.

"Hello, you two," she said as the boat hit the beach. "Caught anything today?"

"Only a bad case of paranoia," Connor said, but his father ignored this.

"Not today, sweetheart. You two run along. I'll finish up the mooring."

"All right, Pa. I'll take the nets."

Connor slung the rolled-up nets over his shoulder and

began walking up the beach with Rae beside him.

"What're you doing down here on the beach?" he asked.

"Oh, nothing really. You're back early."

"The day's too still. It makes Pa nervous."

"I see," Rae said with a little laugh. "I've got something for you."

"Yeah? What is it?"

From the folds of her clothes, she produced a small paper-wrapped parcel.She held it out to him.

"It's not my birthday until November."

"I know. It's just something I wanted you to have. Open it when you get home."

"You're not coming up to the house?"

"No. I've got to check on Grandpa. Tomorrow's Sunday. Come and see me?"

"Maybe."

"No maybes."

"All right. I'll come."

She smiled, walking backwards away from him. Then she turned and hurried off in the direction of her house.

When he arrived home he dumped the nets in the yard and called to his mother. She came out of the house wearing her apron, looking fretful.

"Where's your father?"

"Coming. Why? What's wrong?"

"Della's here."

"Della? And Lewis?"

"Your brother's not here." His mother looked tired and distracted. "Just Della."

"Where's Lewis then?"

"Ask her."

Connor moved past his mother and entered the house. In the family room, he saw someone seated in the wing-backed chair facing the fireplace. The chair's back was to him as he entered.

"Della?"

She sat up and turned around in the chair. The sight of her stopped him in his tracks. It had been two years since his brother married Della and moved to her family's estate on the other side of the coast. Connor had been a boy of fourteen then, with only a developing interest in the opposite sex. Now, he was struck by the sight of his sister-in-law. With a quick estimate he realised she would now be about nineteen or twenty. She wore a flowery linen dress and lounged in the chair with her knees apart, her bare legs directed towards the fire. One leg was stretched out, her foot raised on his mother's sewing box. Her eyes were big and blue and considering, her long yellow hair disheveled.

"Della?" he said again.

He rounded the chair and faced her. She smiled looking up at him, tilting her head to one side.

"My, Connor, I hardly recognised you."

"What happened to you?" he said, glancing at her outstretched leg.

"I hurt my ankle on the walk over here. Can't you see it's all swollen? Your Ma's been so kind."

Connor looked. As he did, Della turned her leg as if inviting him to admire it. Her ankle did look a little swollen.

"Where's Lewis?"

"Honey, did your mother not tell you? Lewis has gone missing."

~

"It's Sutter's Wilds," Della said.

Connor's mother had insisted that everyone sit down at the kitchen table, though none of them were in any mood to eat the stew she'd heated up and dished out. Connor had to help Della to the table. She couldn't put weight on her swollen ankle, she said, so he'd had to half-carry her. She smelt of old sweat, but he got a vague puzzling thrill from her nearness to him. Before they reached the table, Della had smiled into his face and said: "Haven't you gotten strong?" and he'd blushed.

"Sutter's?" Pa said, turning a bread roll in his hands, pinching bits off it and crumbling them between his fingers. "Lewis used to ask me about that place. I worried about him moving out that way. He hasn't been walking in Sutter's, has he?"

Della was slouched against the table, her head propped on one hand. For a moment she didn't answer Pa. She frowned and rolled her eyes towards the ceiling as if she was unsure what to say or afraid of divulging some secret.

"Lewis has been walking in Sutter's for years. Didn't you

know? He used to walk the edges. That's how we first met each other. He came strolling by my Daddy's house one day. After the wedding he started going in a little deeper. I told him not to. I told him when you're like me and born and raised right close to Sutter's you know not to go in too far. That's all anyone tells you soon as you're big enough to understand. But he wouldn't listen to me. He used to go off walking for hours and when he'd come back you could hardly talk to him and his eyes were all distant, like. Sometimes I wouldn't see him for days. He'd come home real quiet and thoughtful. I was starting to feel like I didn't know him anymore. My own husband."

"Della," Ma said, "why didn't you come and tell us this sooner?"

"I threatened to. I told Lewis I would. But he would always get angry. He'd say it was no one else's business where he went walking. It wasn't until now, with him having been gone three days already, that I decided I'd better come and tell you what's been going on."

"Three days!" said Pa.

"Yes. I've worried myself silly."

There was a silence. Connor surveyed the anxious faces around the table. "But," he said, "the things people say about Sutter's Wilds, they're just stories, aren't they? Aren't they?"

Della looked at him. "Strange things happen there, Connor. Always have, always will. You ask anyone who lives out that way. They'll tell you."

"Lewis must have gotten himself lost," Pa said, standing up.

"You're not thinking to go in and look for him?" Ma said.

"What else are we going to do?"

"It's a good few hours walk to Della's place. By the time you get there, it'll be almost dark."

"Maybe I'll find Lewis there, waiting. Maybe he's found his way home already."

"I'll come with you," Connor said.

His mother turned to him. "No, you won't. You'll stay away from that place, that's what you'll do."

"But, Ma, it's just stories."

"No, Connor. Me and your father will go. You and Della can stay here. It's obvious she can't go anywhere."

Connor looked at Della.

"It's all going to be fine," Della said.

Connor pleaded with his parents to let him go with them, even as they set out across the yard, each wearing waterproofs and carrying a backpack. For some reason, he was uncomfortable with the thought of being left alone with Della. A light rain had started to fall by then. Pa waved Connor back to the house.

"Get back in there. You've got to stay and look after Della."

"But, Pa…"

"Listen to me, Connor. You're not going out to Sutter's Wilds and that's final."

Stomping back to the house, Connor saw that Della was back in the chair by the fireplace. She had returned there without help from anyone.

"You going to take good care of me, Connor?"

"What do you mean?" he said.

"You have to look after me, sweets. Your folks said so."

"You're Lewis' wife. Not mine."

She turned in the chair to look at him. "Honey, Lewis ain't here."

He didn't answer.

~

The next day, without the sound of his parents banging about the house, Connor slept late. It was an urgent need for the toilet that finally woke him. Getting out of bed he hurried to the bathroom, blinking the sleep from his eyes. The house was silent. The bathroom door stood ajar, and pushing against it he realised too late that someone was inside. It was Della. She stood naked, drying herself from the bath.

"Oh, I… I'm sorry… I didn't…" He tried to grab for the door handle to pull the door closed again, but it swung away from him.

Della looked up, smiled at him, and went on drying herself.

"It's all right, honeybun. No harm done."

"There's a lock," he told her, apparently unable to move, or shift his eyes away. His face had grown hot. "We normally lock it."

"It's fine, hon. I'm done here. You wanna get in?" Carefully, she wrapped the towel around her slim form, tossed back her wet hair, and slid past him. "You go ahead."

By the time he got back to his bedroom, Connor's

embarrassment had turned to anger. What was Della doing leaving the bathroom door unlocked like that? Then to just stand there drying herself instead of covering herself up straight away? She was his brother's wife, and now he couldn't get the image of her naked body out of his mind.

He stamped about the room, shedding his nightclothes. Pulling on the trousers he had worn the previous day, he felt something in one of the pockets. Baffled, he took it out. It was the little wrapped gift Rae had given him the previous morning on the beach. With all the fuss over Della's arrival, he'd forgotten all about it. Standing shirtless by his bed, he tore off the wrapping. Underneath was a small box. Opening this, he found inside a pendant made from small pebbles that had been glued together to form a disk and attached to a black cord. Probably, he thought, Rae had made it herself. She had a talent for making things. Surprised and delighted, Connor strung it at once around his neck. It was then that he remembered how he'd told Rae he would visit her today. He was glad, too. Anything was better than staying at the house all day with Della.

As if to prove him right in thinking this, he heard the door creak open behind him and he spun around. Della hung in the door space, still wearing only a towel, her wet hair hanging over one side of her face.

"Did you want me, Connor?" she said.

"What?"

Della didn't seem to notice the trace of annoyance in his

voice. "Did you holler?"

"I didn't say a thing. I was getting dressed."

"Oh? I thought I heard… never mind." She began to back out of the door space, her eyes moving about his room, but then she stopped. "Oh, that's a nice bed. Looks real comfy. The one in Lewis' old room is awful. Lumpy and hard. Wanna swap with me?"

"Swap? No. This is my room."

"Oh. Well, maybe share then?"

"Share?"

"I could get in with you tonight. We could keep each other company."

He stared at her. "No," he said. "I like my own bed. Besides…"

But she interrupted him, saying casually: "Oh, well. Just a thought. What you up to today, sweetness?"

"I'm going to see Rae."

"Rae? She your girlfriend?"

"No, she's… just a friend."

"Righty. I guess I'll see you later then. I'll be right here. Let me know if you change your mind."

"Change my mind? About what?"

Della laughed. "About the bed, silly." And with this, she closed the door. He heard her footsteps cross the hall and grabbed his shirt.

Leaving the house after a rushed breakfast, he kicked the door open and stomped down the yard with his face flushed, his thoughts buzzing.

The day was sunny but a cold wind blew in from the sea. Approaching the lonely little house on the clifftop, Connor noticed Rae and Earl, her grandfather, walking up the path from the beach. He stood and waited for them, gazing out across the water. Earl was slow to get to the top of the path, Rae helping him all the way. When Rae saw Connor waiting for them, she smiled and waved a hand. She was carrying something and held it up for him to see.

"Look what I found!"

It looked like a jaw bone. It was about the length of Rae's forearm.

"What's that from, you reckon?" Connor said, taking it from her and turning it in his hands. "Maybe a whale?"

"Basking shark, most likely," Earl said. "A whale's jaw'd be a good deal bigger than that. How're you doing Connor?"

"Not so bad." Connor looked at the old man and smiled. Earl got confused a lot lately, and it was not every day that he recognised the boy. Some days he called him Lewis, after his brother; or sometimes even by his father's name, Lou. Both Connor and Rae had long given up correcting him. Today though, Earl appeared clear of eye and clear of mind.

"Been walking on the beach?" Connor said.

"Getting some air," Earl said. "And trying not to get blown sideways by that wind."

Connor and Rae exchanged a smile. Connor handed the jaw bone back to Rae. "What're you going to do with it?"

"I think it'll look good on the wall in my room." They walked on a little along the path. "So, you can keep your promises then?"

"I'm here, aren't I?" Connor followed Rae and her grandfather as they walked on toward the house. "Hey, guess who's at my house. Della."

"Della? You mean, Lewis' Della?"

"Yep. She said Lewis went walking into Sutter's Wilds three days ago and she hasn't seen him since. My folks have gone off to look for him. Della stayed. She hurt her ankle on the way over here."

"Sutter's Wilds? What did he go in there for?"

"Della said he was fascinated by it. He went walking there a lot, she said."

Earl broke in. "He should know better than to go walking in Sutter's. There are some places on this earth that just feel wrong, and that's one of them."

"But it's just stories," Connor said. "Isn't it? There's nothing really wrong in Sutter's Wilds, is there? I mean, like people say?"

"I went in once," Earl said. "When I was a young man about Lewis' age. I went in and then I got the hell out as fast as I could."

Connor stopped walking. "Why? Did you see something?"

Earl opened his mouth to speak, but then he looked into Connor's expectant face and stopped himself. His face softened. "I just got spooked, that's all. Funny place, Sutter's. Lewis'll be fine. Your folks'll find him and get him out of there."

They walked on in silence. Inside, the house was narrow and cluttered. Earl went off towards the lounge, muttering that he was going to sit in his chair and close his eyes for a few minutes. Rae, clutching her beach treasure, led Connor to her room.

"Come on, you can help me decide where to hang this."

Rae's room was even more cramped and cluttered than the rest of the house. Almost every available surface was covered with things Rae had found on the beach: different coloured pebbles, feathers, and rusty bits of metal. Connor sat down on the bed—the only place he could—with his chin propped in his hand, gazing at the floor, whilst Rae went around the room with the jaw bone, holding it up against the wall. Eventually noticing Connor's dejected pose, she said:

"You worried about Lewis?"

"No. Not really."

"What is it then?"

"Oh, just Della. She's so strange."

"Well," said Rae, after a pause. "Maybe you just need to get to know her better. Now's your chance."

"I don't want to get to know her better. She bothers me."

"Why?"

"The things she does. She makes me feel so…"

Rae crossed the room to perch beside him on the bed. "So what?"

Connor let out a sigh. "I don't know." He could feel her

looking at him.

"Did you like your present?"

"What? Oh, the pendant. Yes, I love it. You're really clever, Rae. You're going to be an artist."

He met her gaze. She was smiling in a child-like way, her eyes bright. On impulse, and to his own surprise as much as hers, he leaned toward her and kissed her on the lips. When he drew back she looked at him, blinking. A strand of dark hair had fallen across her eyes. He pushed it aside and kissed her again. After a few moments, he eased her backwards onto the bed. He was propped above her when she said:

"What… what're we doing?"

"Pa thinks we're going to get married. My mother thinks so too."

She gazed up at him. She looked bewildered.

"Do you… do you want to do this?" he said.

"Get married?"

"No, this. What we're doing now."

"I suppose I do. If you do."

He looked into her eyes for a few moments, then sat up. First, testing her reaction, he took off her boots and flung them to the floor. She remained still, watching him. Then his fingers went to the cord that was wound through the waistband of her trousers and unfastened it.

"Wait," Rae said suddenly, watching him. "I… I can't."

"You've known me all your life, Rae. Everyone thinks we're going to get married."

"I know. But this is… I don't know. I'm scared. That's the first time you've kissed me and now… " She brushed his hands away from her waist, hurriedly refastened the cord, then sat up and got off the bed.

"Rae," he said, with a trace of annoyance. "Can't you just —?"

"It's too fast, Connor." She scurried around to the other side of the room to find her boots, sat down on the floor, and pulled them back on. Watching her, Connor felt his annoyance at her dwindle.

"I'm sorry," he said. "You're right, Rae. I'm just confused."

She looked at him, showing a thin smile. "I'm not sure I want to get married."

"No, me neither. It's just Della. She's got me so flustered. The things she says."

Rae looked at him, tilting her head to the side. "What does she say?"

"Oh, nothing." He turned and picked the jaw bone up off the bed. "Anyway, weren't we deciding on a place to put this?"

He looked at Rae. She was staring at him, not smiling. He felt his face beginning to flush.

"Look," he said, "can we please forget what just happened? We're still friends, right?"

"Sure," she said, in a small voice, glancing away.

~

He walked all the way home muttering to himself and kicking at mounds of grass, stray bits of wood, or whatever else happened to be in his path. Arriving home, he discovered that Della had prepared a fish soup for dinner. He smelt it as soon as he entered the house and was reminded of how he hadn't eaten since breakfast. He went to the kitchen where he found Della and sat down at the table without speaking.

Della smiled and placed a bowl in front of him.

"Connor, sweets," she said in mock reprimand. "I thought you were supposed to be taking care of me, not the other way around."

He watched her as she went back and forth to the stove. The straps of her blue dress kept falling off her shoulder. She would glance at Connor every time she hitched one back up, the expression on her face seeming to say: what a lot of fuss clothes are.

"How's the ankle," he said.

"Oh, it's a little better."

There was a long silence. Then Connor said, "What happened between Lewis and you?"

She was standing at the stove, her back to him. "What do you mean, hon?"

"Didn't the marriage work out?"

For a long moment she froze, not saying anything. Then she turned to face him, one hand propped on a hip. "At first it did, for a few months. Then Lewis got real distracted. He didn't want me no more, I think."

Connor thought for a moment. "What do you mean he didn't want you? Do you mean in bed?"

Della laughed, throwing her head back. "You don't mince your words, now do you, Connor?" She said this in a way that suggested she approved. "Hon, just lately Lewis didn't want me anywhere. Not in the kitchen, not in the dining room, and most decidedly not in the bedroom. You get me?"

He shrugged, tore off some of the bread she'd brought to the table, and began eating the soup. Della had her back to him again. He couldn't help noticing the way her hips moved in the loose hanging dress.

"You're a funny one, Connor. I suppose you're just getting to that curious age. I know what that's like. How old are you, fifteen?"

"Sixteen."

"When I was fifteen or so I knew a boy named Leighton. I think that was his name. He was a bit older than me. He must have been about eighteen then. He looked real sweet and clean, with little round spectacles. You know the type. He used to play real sweet too, carrying my bags back from the store, or my books if he met me walking back from the schoolhouse. Anyway, one summer's day he asks me if I want to lie down for a minute in the long grass out behind the road near the stables where my daddy kept the horses back when my mother was alive. I did it as well, thinking him so sweet and everything." She laughed to herself. "And, you know what, he did all sorts of things to me. I can feel myself blushing just thinking about it. He wasn't such a sweetie as he made out, let me tell you. I told him later that if my Daddy found out what he'd done, he'd get his horse and run him down. This was a few years before I met Lewis. I think I knew really why he wanted me to lie down in that grass with him. And I was curious. Like you get at that age. It's just curiosity. As natural as breathing."

She turned and looked at Connor as if she expected a response, but Connor didn't know how to respond. He found he couldn't look at her now.

"How's the soup, hon?"

"Soup's fine."

"Anything else I can do for you?"

"Right now, I'm fine."

Della chuckled under her breath, although he had no idea why. She put her back to him again and sang to herself as she began tidying away the pots and pans.

Connor's lowered gaze followed her about the kitchen.

~

A sound woke him in the night. It was the creak of his bedroom door. The room was pitch black. He sat up in bed, and with his thoughts still muddy from sleep, said: "Pa?"

"It's me, honeybee."

"Della?" He looked for her but could see only darkness. "What do you want? Are my folks home?"

"Ain't no one in this big old house but you and me, Connor. That's the problem."

He rubbed his eyes. "Problem? What time is it?"

"I'm scared, Connor. Can't you hear the wind blowing around the house? It gives me the willies. Please, please, please let me get in with you. Please. I'm lying in the next room and my imagination's showing me all sorts of things."

Connor fell back against his pillows with a sigh. He was too sleepy to argue with her, or at least that was what he told himself. "Fine. Fine. Do what you like."

"Oh, thank you, Connor. I won't be no trouble, honest. You'll hardly know I'm there."

He heard the door close again and her footsteps padding around the bed. The blankets were lifted and then he felt her weight settle on the mattress beside him. He lay still, feeling suddenly wide awake. Della didn't move either. He could hear her breathing. He sensed she was turned towards him, her eyes watching the dark where he lay. Then she said in a low voice:

"Can't you sleep now?"

"No."

He heard her let out a long sigh. "Me neither. Want me to help you out?"

"Help me out?"

She laughed under her breath. "Your eyes, Connor, they're always following me. It's natural at your age. You're curious. Want me to help you out?"

"I don't know what you mean," he said.

She said nothing to explain. He felt a movement beneath the blankets, then her hand at his waist. Her fingers slipped across his bare abdomen and under the waistband of his pyjama bottoms.

"Oh," she said, with another little laugh. "I see you're

ready."

"It... it just happens," he said, flustered. Her hand had begun to move. "When I'm asleep. It just happens."

"I know that, Connor. Don't worry. It's perfectly natural. Want me to stop?"

"No, I..."

"Does it feel all right?"

"Yes. It feels good."

"Come here. It'll feel better like this."

She lay back and drew him towards her, her hands sliding his pyjama bottoms over his hips. She wore a thin nightdress which she hitched up above her waist. In the dark she was all limbs, moving and clutching at him. Reaching down, she guided him with her hands. And she was right, it did feel better like this. They sighed and moaned and pushed and clutched at each other. But then, feeling a swell of guilt, he stopped.

"I can't," he said. "I can't do this. You're Lewis' wife."

"I don't have to be," she said. Her voice had an odd waver in it. "You can imagine I'm someone else. I can be anyone you want me to be. Honeybun, no one's going to know. Just—oh! Yes, just keep going. Just keep going. Don't stop! That's it! That's good! Oh, sweets, don't... don't stop."

~

When next he woke the room was bright with light. Lifting his head from the pillows, he saw Della splayed out next to him, sleeping still. Her nightdress was bunched up around her rib cage. The blanket covered her middle, but her long pale legs were spread out across the mattress. Guilt washed over him. Half turning, he yanked at the waistband of his pyjama bottoms which was still down around his knees. And that was when he saw them. The door was open and they were stood in the door space. They were staring straight at him, their faces pale and stunned. Then his mother turned with a frown and vanished. His father remained.

"Pa? You're back."

"Get up, son. Get dressed."

"Where's Lewis? Is he—?"

"We couldn't find him. He must've gone in too deep. Get up. Rae's here."

"*Rae?* What's she doing here?"

"We met her on the path by her house. She wanted to come by and surprise you. Guess she's the one who got the surprise."

"Pa, I'm sorry… it just…"

Pa said nothing. His face was downcast. Connor could tell that his father was suppressing his anger and disappointment. He would not let it show whilst they had company in the house.

Della now woke and lifted her head from the pillows. Seeing Pa in the doorway, she sat up with a little yelp, pulling the blankets around herself.

"I get scared when I sleep by myself," she said. "Connor was kind enough to let me sleep here next to him. Weren't you, Connor? Tell him."

"Get up, both of you."

Reaching forward, Pa brought the door to a soft close.

Connor dressed, went downstairs to the kitchen where his parents waited, and sat down at the table. He kept his head lowered. Whenever he risked a glance at his mother, he noticed how she avoided his gaze. His father was stood at one end of the room with his hands on his hips, looking about himself as if he didn't know quite what to do next. His mother passed by where Connor was sitting and placed a plate of toast on the table in front of him.

"I thought you said Rae was here," Connor said without looking up.

"She's out in the yard."

"I suppose it was her," Connor's mother said to no one in particular. "We know what she's like. We shouldn't have left her alone with him."

Connor, feeling his face begin to burn, covered it with his hands. "Then you didn't find Lewis?"

It was his father who answered him. "No. He's gone too far in. We couldn't get there."

"Why? Why couldn't you get there?"

"You don't know Sutter's, son. Is *madam* coming down? You two have got some explaining to do. Where're you going?"

Connor had stood up from his chair. "I'm going to see Rae."

"Didn't you hear me? We want an explanation."

"Let him go," his mother said. "It wasn't his fault, I'll bet."

Connor traipsed out into the yard where he found Rae sitting on a coil of rope. It was another grey day, but muggy.

Rae looked up, squinting, as he approached. Then she looked away. She said nothing. Connor leaned against the house wall and looked at her. He couldn't think of anything to say. He kicked idly at a bit of wood. Some minutes passed. At last Rae glanced around, looking at him as if she hadn't noticed he was there before, and said: "Then they didn't find Lewis?"

"Nope."

"You should go."

"What?"

"You should go and look for him. It's the least you could do."

"You think I should go into The Wilds?"

"Yes, I think you should go find him."

Connor huffed. "And what if I get lost too?"

"You could leave a trail or something. I could help you. I'll come with you if you like. I'll come with you to the edge anyway."

"And hold one end of a piece of string?"

She looked at him with such disappointment in her expression that he wanted the ground to open up beneath his feet. He waited, but nothing happened.

"I would've, you know," Rae said. "I just wasn't ready the other day, that's all. But I would've. I wanted to."

"Wanted to…?"

"But I suppose you couldn't wait."

Connor righted himself and looked around the yard. He couldn't look at her now. "I've got to get away from here. I'm going down to the beach."

"All right."

"Want to come with?"

"No, I've got to get home."

"Fine," Connor said, then without further pause he began striding away from the house. Rae said something to his back, but too softly for him to catch. He kept on walking.

~

It was dark when he returned to the house, and all the lights were out. He had spent the day walking on the beach and hiding in the long seagrass, mulling things over. By the time he saw the sun sinking down into the sea, he had decided Rae was right. The thought terrified him, but he had to go to Sutter's to try and find Lewis. It was the only way he could make up for what he'd done. It was the only way he'd be able to look his parents in the eye again, if he found Lewis and came out a hero. Still, he kept thinking about old Earl telling him: *I went in and then I got the hell out as fast as I could.* What could be in there that had so spooked the old man? There was a part of Connor that wanted to know. Nobody would ever talk about Sutter's.

He'd thought many times too, as he walked on the sand, about what had happened during the night with Della. His mind returned to it over and over no matter how he tried to prevent it. His shame, when he thought about what they had done, was mixed with something else. His cock would begin to stir and press against his pants. He tried to turn his thoughts away, but they just kept going back there.

He entered the darkened house like a thief, taking a torch from the yard and using it to find his way instead of turning on any lights. First he made and ate a sandwich. Then he made four more and packed them into a backpack. He filled a canteen with water, then sat at the table and thought about what else he might need. Unable to think of anything, he got up and grabbed his waterproof jacket, threw the backpack on his back, turned out the torch, and sneaked out of the door just as quietly as he'd entered. He crossed the yard with his heart racing, thinking about the journey ahead of him.

Only once had he visited the estate where Lewis lived with Della and her family. This had been shortly before the two were married, and the only way he knew to get there was to follow the coastal paths around to the opposite side of the island because that was the way his parents had taken him. This was the way he set off walking. To one side of him the sea was a great black void in the night, and on the other side he had sporadic sights of boatyards and houses. After about an hour's walking, the path climbed steeply up a rocky cliff face. Strong, cold winds whipped around the summit of this cliff, but he enjoyed being there in the darkness, feeling like he was on top of the world. Here, the stars were spread out ahead of him rather than above. He sat down to escape the wind behind a knuckle of rock and ate one of the sandwiches he'd packed. Mesmerised by the vastness of the heavens laid out in front of him, he rested there until he became too cold, then got up and grudgingly picked his way down from this high place. He walked on, stopping only once more to eat another sandwich and finish off the water in his canteen. He was feeling weary when he saw the lighthouse, one of the landmarks familiar from his previous visit years before. He knew that if he took the path that forked to his right he would come across the little village of Childerbury, Della's village, the village that stood on the borderlands of Sutter's Wilds.

The village was like a ghost town at that time of night. The houses were dark and shuttered up, the stony dirt streets silent. He tried to use what landmarks he could remember from his previous trip to find the house of Della's family: the little graveyard, the single street of stores and public houses in the centre of the village, the wooden schoolhouse. Then there was Della's father's large estate house, within the grounds of which was the small, two-story home that had been given to Lewis and Della as a wedding present. Entering the grounds, Connor saw that some of the windows in the estate house were lit. He thought about going there and knocking on the door, but he was unsure if anyone there would recognise him so he went straight to Lewis and Della's house instead. His brother's home was in darkness, but when he tried the front door it opened at a touch of his hand. He took the torch from his pack and directed the light ahead of him.

"Lewis?" he called as he entered the house. "Lewis? You here?"

There was no answer. He went about the modestly furnished downstairs rooms before starting up the stairs. On the first floor there were three rooms, the bathroom, a small room with a few crates in it, and a larger room with a bed. Lewis was not in any of them. In the last room, Connor sat down on the bed and kicked off his shoes. He had already decided that he would sleep here before beginning his search for Lewis in the morning. He was not going to walk into Sutter's in the dark. When he lay back on the bed, he couldn't help but think about Della. He wondered what it was like for his brother, lying here beside her every night. Then he remembered Della saying: *Hon, just lately Lewis didn't want me anywhere. Not in the kitchen, not in the dining room, and most decidedly not in the bedroom. You get me?* And he wondered what Lewis could have found in Sutter's that could have taken over his thoughts and made him forget that he had a beautiful wife at home. Then he thought that perhaps there was something here, something that could help him find Lewis. He sat up, but then realised that his parents had been here before him. Pa would have thought to look around for a sign or a clue as to what exactly Lewis was up to. And if there had been anything, anything useful, Della would have mentioned it. Wouldn't she?

Perhaps not, he thought.

Della said Lewis had been walking in Sutter's before she met him. And if Connor knew his brother, Lewis wouldn't have just been walking. He would have been making notes, writing things down, perhaps making a map. Somewhere in the house there had to be notebooks, or drawings, some kind of guide.

He lay back on the pillows, his thoughts buzzing. First thing in the morning, he decided, he would search the house for Lewis' notebooks, if any existed. If he found them, then he would not have to go into Sutter's blind.

He had only been lying there for a few moments when he heard a sound from the floor below. There was a creak of the front door opening, then footsteps. At once he got up, grabbed his torch, and hurried out of the room and down the stairs. Someone was standing in the downstairs hallway. He heard the sound of feet turning on the floorboards as he rushed down the stairs. He directed his torch light toward where the sound was coming from. He was about to shout out his brother's name, thinking, hoping, it was him standing there, returned, but then another voice beat him to it.

"Lewis?"

The voice was female. Peering forward, he saw a young blond woman shrinking away from his light. For a moment he imagined it was Della. And he thought wildly: *She must have followed me!* But when the young woman lowered her hands and glared at him he saw that it was not Della, but someone who looked very similar. She was smaller than Della, though, younger-looking, and softer somehow. Where Della was lean and long-limbed, she was more full-bodied. Where Della's eyes contained humour and mischief, hers were wide and startled. It took him a few seconds to remember her name.

"Paige?"

"That's... Connor? Connor? You scared me half to death rushing down like that. I thought you were Lewis."

"I thought *you* were Lewis."

"What're you doing here? Why didn't you come to the main house?"

"I didn't like to. It's late."

"I was at my window and I saw someone crossing the grounds. I thought it was Lewis. I thought he'd found his way home at last. Suppose you came to look for him too, eh? Your parents were just here. They went to the edges of The Wilds, but they couldn't go in. Just couldn't. Not even for Lewis' sake. They came back to the house looking real shaken, said they were going back home again to speak to Della, see what they could work out. And now you."

"They don't know I'm here. I'm going in, and I'm going to find him."

Paige's gaze shifted away. Her face looked doubtful.

"Why don't you come up to the house? Everyone's in bed. I'll fix you something to eat. And we can talk."

"I was planning to sleep here, then take a look around in the morning. I'm thinking there might be some of Lewis' notebooks around somewhere. Maybe even a map."

Paige looked concerned. "You mean, like a diary? I don't think Lewis kept a diary."

"I don't mean a diary exactly. More like notes, drawings, directions. Stuff he wrote down when he was out walking in Sutter's."

"Walking?" Her eyes fixed on his face. "Lewis never walked in Sutter's. He went in for the first time five days ago and he never came out again. He knew nothing about the place. He was curious, but he didn't want to go there. It didn't interest him."

"What're you talking about? Your sister told us he's been walking there for years, since before they even met."

He saw Paige's eyes widen. She glanced away again. "Della...?"

"Are you telling me she lied? Lewis never walked in Sutter's before?"

Paige remained thoughtful. "He never went there."

"Then there aren't any notebooks? There isn't a map or anything?"

She returned her gaze to him. "Oh, there are. There are notebooks. But Lewis didn't make them."

The main house was in darkness. Instead of turning on any overhead lights, Paige found an oil lamp by the entrance and used that to light the way, saying only, "Daddy's sleeping," in a hushed voice by way of explanation. The hallway walls were hung with huge painted portraits and Connor shifted his eyes away from the stern faces that leered at him out of the half-dark like hovering spirits. She led him to a large kitchen area where a fire burned low in the grate and sat him down at a broad table in the centre of the room. Taking the light with her, leaving him in near-darkness, she fussed for a while at the stove on the far side of the room, then returned and placed before him a plate of what looked to him like broth.

"You are hungry, aren't you?" she said when he only stared

at her.

"You said that there are maps. Of Sutter's."

She sighed and said, "Yes." Then she crossed to a set of drawers, crouched, and routed in the lowest one. "I've tried to understand them. Honest, I have. But it's hopeless. Only she knows what they mean."

"She?"

Paige returned, placing a pile of notebooks on the table in front of him. "Della."

Connor took one of the notebooks and began to leaf through it. Every page was filled with jottings and doodles. There was nothing that looked like a map.

"Della made these?"

"Della has been walking in Sutter's for years. She's been doing it ever since she was a child. The first time she went in on a dare. She must have been about ten years old. I asked her if she was scared and she said she was at first. But she said she saw something, something other people hadn't seen. And after that she wasn't scared at all, and she went back in again and again."

"What did she see?"

Paige glanced away. "I don't know. She wouldn't tell me. It was her secret."

Connor went on turning the pages of the notebook. He read a note that said: *Here the winds start.* He had no idea what that could mean. He looked at Paige.

"You think I could use these books to find Lewis and get

him out?"

Paige shrugged. "I think she took him in real deep." Her eyes flashed then, as if she'd said more than she intended. She made to get up from the table, but Connor caught hold of her wrist.

"Took him in? She *took* him in? On purpose?"

Paige said nothing. She tried to wriggle her arm free but Connor held fast to it.

"Tell me," he said. "Did she take him in on purpose or not?"

"She was angry, I suppose, because of what she saw."

"What do you mean 'what she saw'?"

"She wasn't supposed to see. She wasn't supposed to be there. She was supposed to be at the stables, but she came back early."

"And she…?" Connor was now starting to grasp her meaning without her having to explain further. "You mean… *you and Lewis*? Something was going on between you two?"

"We're *in love!*" she burst out. Then, glancing up at the ceiling, she quietened. "It wasn't 'something going on.' He got married to Della, but then after he came to live here he fell in love with me. He told me he loved me. He said he wasn't interested in Della any more. He wanted me. We tried to keep things quiet. Daddy would have hit the roof if he found out, and Della, well Della's got quite a temper too. Don't you see?"

Connor nodded. It had all become clear. "So Della saw you together. And then she took Lewis into Sutter's and she left him there? And he went with her, willingly?"

"He wouldn't have known. He thought they were going on a picnic. After Della caught us together that day, we lied and told her that it wasn't how it looked, that it was an innocent mistake. For a while we thought she believed us. She seemed her normal self. But she must have been plotting. Then, a few days ago, Lewis told me Della wanted to go on a picnic, and he said he was going to try and explain to her, to tell her that it was me he loved and not her. He promised me he would tell her. He wanted it out in the open. But Della must've tricked him. She led him into Sutter's. She knew the pathways. And she abandoned him there, so that he couldn't find his way out."

Tears had sprung up in her eyes, and her face looked stricken, so he knew she was telling the truth. He felt a sudden rush of anger at himself, realising that Della must have planned to seduce him from the moment she set eyes on him at the house. Or maybe even before that. It had nothing to do with him of course. It had just been another part of her revenge on Lewis. Lewis had bedded her sister, so Della bedded him out of malice.

"We have to get Lewis out of there. Get this mess cleared up once and for all."

"Only Della can get him out," Paige said in a small voice.

"But we've got her books. The two of us can find him."

"The two of us? Oh, no. No."

"I thought you said you loved him."

Paige was silent a moment, gazing at him, her face pale in the lamplight. She closed her eyes for a few moments, then opened them again and drew in a deep breath.

"All right," she said. "All right. We can try."

~

He returned to Lewis and Della's house and slept there. He spent much of the night either lying awake, wondering what it was about Sutter's Wilds that brought such a look of fear to people's faces, or sat up in bed examining Della's notebook by torchlight. Early the next morning, Paige appeared at the house and woke him. She looked paler still in daylight, and avoided his eyes. He guessed that she did not want him to see how scared she was. He could see though why Lewis might have been drawn to her over Della. She was more composed, more buttoned up. You knew everything you needed to know about Della within five minutes of meeting her, but her sister kept to herself more and gave the impression that there was more to discover.

Carrying the notebooks in his backpack, he followed Paige out of the grounds of the house and, eventually, they walked along a dirt track overgrown with wildflowers that wound along the slope of a hill.

"How will we know when we're inside Sutter's?" Connor asked.

Paige only glanced at him with an expression of derision as if what he'd actually asked was: how will we know if it's raining? After about half an hour's walking, he discovered why. The landscape became wilder, with ancient trees bent low to the ground and uncertain tracks between them. They also began to see slabs of white, furrowed rock. As they walked on, these rocks began to take on strange and eerie formations. Connor could imagine how, at night, or from a distance, these formations might look like hunched, human forms. He could remember how he'd read something in one of Della's notebooks about standing stones. Stopping in his tracks, he took the pack from his back and routed for the book. Paige walked on ahead a little until he stopped her with a shout. Seeing that she had left his side, she hurried back.

"What're you doing?"

"We're there, aren't we? We're inside Sutter's. I read something about these rocks in here." He opened the notebook. On the first page there was a sketch of one of the rocks which he'd seen some way back along the path. *The white stones mark the way in*, Della had written.

The wind suddenly picked up and turned the pages of the notebook. A line of trees on a ledge above them began to sway. Connor thought he heard another sound, and Paige must have heard it too because she looked around in alarm and pressed against his side. The wind became fearful and though they were relatively sheltered from it in the valley where they stood, the trees above began to bend with the force of it. Watching them, Connor's heart leapt up as he thought he saw the grey figure of a man standing beneath the trees. He had thought it might be Lewis, but it was not. The man was oddly tall, and like the trees he swayed back and forth, but he was swaying with laughter. Connor realised that this was the sound he'd heard, a kind of mad braying laughter coming to him from far away. With his heart pounding, he flicked to the start of the notebook again and scanned Della's notes, but there was nothing written about this laughing figure. He saw a line he'd read before. *Here's where the winds start.* And there was a drawing of three trees, much like the ones now swaying above them.

"Keep walking," he said to Paige. "Keep going. It'll be fine."

She stared at him, distraught. Then with only a sob and a shake of her head, she darted past him and ran back the way they had come. He shouted after her but she didn't stop. Consulting the notebook again, he pressed his hand against the pages to keep the wind from turning them. Before he could read anything the book was torn out of his hand and it was then, as he bent to retrieve it, that he saw the people emerging from behind the slabs of white rock. From behind one rock came his mother and father, from behind another came Rae and Earl, then behind them Della. At first, though he was stunned at their appearance, he was overjoyed to see them. Then he saw that they all had a black, murderous look on their faces. And they were carrying things. His father carried a mallet, his mother what looked like the poker from beside the fire in the kitchen at home. Rae carried a fish-gutting knife in each hand, and Earl and Della each had a length of knotted rope. He knew immediately they meant to do him harm. He'd never seen such a look on any of their faces before. Terror-struck, with heart hammering, he began at once to run. He left the rough path and made to lose himself amongst the trees and boulders. When he stopped, panting, to look back, he saw that he was alone. A black hawk floated in the sky overhead, but apart from this there wasn't a soul around. There was only silence. Even the wind had died down. The trees up on the ridge had ceased to sway and there was no sign of the tall man who had stood there laughing.

I imagined it! Connor thought as he crouched behind a boulder and tried to regain his breath. *Something about this place, it makes you see things. That must be it! I was seeing things! Ma and Pa ain't here. They're at home, Della too. Rae's with her grandfather. They're not here. How could they be?*

He glanced over the boulder to make doubly sure and to see if there was any sign of Paige, but anyone—real or imagined—who might have been there was now gone. He was alone.

If this is only the start, he thought. *What's it like when you go deeper in?* And he thought of Lewis. Today was the fifth day Lewis would spend alone in this place.

He thought of Paige saying: *Only Della can get him out*. And, at that moment, he knew that she was right. He also knew that if he went deeper in, Della's notebooks or no, he would most likely not be able to find his way out again. He would see things. He would run and try to hide and lose the path and lose himself. That was what Sutter's did to you. It dragged you in, and kept you there.

"I'm so sorry, Lewis," he said aloud. Then he turned and looked for the path, beginning to pick his way out from that place. On his way out he heard crazed laughter again from the ridge overhead, but he ignored it and broke into a run.

~

Arriving back at Lewis and Della's house, he found Paige sitting alone at the kitchen table. She flashed her eyes at him when he entered, but seemed unsurprised to see him. It took him a moment to understand what she was doing. She had one sleeve of her blouse rolled up and her bare forearm was flat on the table. There were thin red marks on her exposed skin. In her other hand she held a knife which she must have taken from the nearby drawer that she had left open.

"What're you doing?" he said, snatching the knife from her hand.

"It helps!" she said, in sudden distress.

"Cutting yourself? Is everyone mad in your family?"

"It helps me get the pain out. I feel so bad, so guilty about what happened to Lewis. He's lost in Sutter's and it's all because of me. And I'm too scared to go in and look for him! He's lost in there and no one can get him out!"

"That's not true," he said. "You said it yourself. She can."

"Della won't!"

"She will. She will. We'll make her."

"No one ever made Della do anything she didn't want to do."

"I will," he said.

"How? How will you?"

Connor was silent a moment, thinking. "I'll talk to her. I'll make her see what she's done."

~

When he arrived home with Paige in tow, his mother rushed out into the yard and embraced him. When she drew back, though, he saw from her expression that she was angry and upset.

"Where the hell have you *been*? We were looking all over for you! Then Rae said she thought you might have gone to Sutter's to find Lewis. She said she might've put you up to it. Did she? Did she put you up to it?"

"None of this is Rae's fault, Ma."

"What do you think you're doing going out to that place on your own? Do you think I want both my sons wandering lost in The Wilds? I told you never to go near that place! What did you think you were doing? Your poor father's gone off this morning to see if he can find you, to stop you going in there. Pretty soon, the whole family's going to be lost. Is that what you want? Is it, Connor?"

When he didn't answer, her face softened and she went on in a subdued voice, daring to hope. "Did you go in? Did you… find him?"

"No, Ma, but I found out some things that might be useful to us."

His mother now noticed the girl standing behind him with her face lowered.

"Paige? What brings you all the way out here? You're looking for your sister, I suppose."

Paige nodded. Connor said, "Della's still here, isn't she?"

"Of course she's still here."

"Great."

Marching into the house, he found Della sitting in the wing-backed chair in the lounge with one foot resting on his mother's sewing box. Just as she had the day she first arrived, she shifted around in the chair and grinned at him as he entered. Her smile melted away when she saw her sister walking behind him, and her eyes filled with scorn.

"What's *she* doing here?"

"You have to go into Sutter's, Della, and get Lewis out. You're the only one who can."

"What? What's she been telling you?"

"Everything. About what went on between her and Lewis, about how Lewis never walked in Sutter's, but you did, and about how you took him in and left him there to punish him."

Connor's mother, who had come last into the room, said: "What's this?"

"Della lied when she said Lewis liked walking in Sutter's. He never went there. She did though. She's been walking there since she was a child. Paige showed me her notebooks."

Della sat suddenly upright in her chair and looked savagely at her sister. "How dare you touch my books!"

"I thought they would help me find Lewis," Connor went on. "But I guess I got scared. That place, Sutter's, it plays with you. It shows you things, things from your own mind."

Della fell back in her chair, laughing under her breath.

"Don't worry, sugar, Lewis will find his way out. One day."

"No, Della!" Connor said, fused with anger. "You have to go in and get him out *today*! You've had your fun! I know what Lewis did hurt you, but you've had your revenge now. Enough's enough! You're not just hurting Lewis and Paige; you're hurting everyone! Can't you see how selfish you're being? Pa probably won't look me in the eye ever again, and Rae will probably never want to speak to me! Paige cuts herself because she feels so bad about everything. My mother's out of her mind with worry! And Lewis... you can't leave him in there, Della. He'll go crazy in that place. You have to get him out and you have to get him out today! You're the only one who can."

When he finished, he could feel his face was flushed and he was breathing heavily, as if he'd just been running. Della sat back in the chair, contemplating his face. She was no longer smiling. Her face showed nothing, except a hint of surprise. After a long drawn-out moment, she lifted herself up from the chair.

"Well," she said in a casual tone. "I guess it's time."

"Time for what, Della?"

She looked straight at Connor with a wan smile. "Time to bring him out, silly. Like you said."

"You're going into The Wilds to get Lewis?"

"Guess I got no choice. You told me. I'm a selfish girl."

Unable to stop himself, Connor stepped forward and took hold of her arm. "What's the secret, Della? All those things in there. How do you not let them frighten you?"

Della laughed, drawing away from him. "There ain't nothing in there, sweets. How could there be? There's only what you take with you. That's all."

She began to shift towards the door. Connor noticed that she was no longer hobbling on one foot.

~

They waited on the edge of The Wilds, where they could see the white rocks but not be drawn in by them: Connor, Ma, Pa, and Paige. The sky had just begun to darken when Connor noticed two figures climbing up the path from below. One was Della. The other was Lewis. Della led Lewis up the path and without a word presented him to his mother. Connor hardly recognised his brother. Lewis had always taken pride in his appearance, but here he was with his hair wild and his clothes torn. His eyes were wide and staring, his face streaked with dirt and his lips dry and sore looking. He was shivering.

"Ma?" he said, softly. "Ma, that really you?"

"It's me, son."

"Oh, Ma. The things I've seen."

He fell forward and his mother embraced him. Connor caught Della's eye. She had remained silent, but had a cat-like smirk on her face. Connor leaned forward so that only she could hear him when he spoke.

"How's it possible? How is it you're not affected by that place?"

"I ain't afraid of what's in my head, Connor."

Connor faced forward, scanning the entry way into Sutter's as the sun disappeared from the sky overhead.

"Want me to take you in?" Della said, her eyes shining, reflecting the last of the light. "You'll be safe with me."

He didn't answer. He only looked at her for a long moment, until she shook her hair back, laughed, and moved forward, brushing past him and continuing on along the path towards home.

Mousetrap

Robert G. Ferrell

It was a lot like other home-grown VR rigs, except that the components were semi-permanently attached to a large, comfortable chair. The computer-controlled headgear, gloves, and forearm/ankle cuffs were mounted on flexible shafts anchored to appropriate sections of the chair frame. Attached to a rack slung on the underside of the chair itself were the CPU and multimedia processors, plus some blackbox circuitry Mix had conjured up to control proprioceptive feedback and the like. Rane was a little unsure about the whole setup, but Mix finally convinced him to give it a try.

"All you have to do," Mix reassured him, "is sit there. The shafts will get more or less stiff depending on what's going on in the VR world. They're full of electrically-actuated nanotubes designed to provide you with some realistic physical feedback. Don't worry: this isn't like *The Matrix* or something—you can't be killed or even injured. It's just a way of making surfing a more immersive experience."

"Too bad. What's the cap thingie for?"

"That has some electrodes that respond to changes in the electromagnetic field on your scalp. I got most of them from one of those brainwave biofeedback units, and added a few others that I sort of invented myself. They're experimental; I'm not really sure if they have any effect or not. They can't hurt you, anyway. It's a totally passive process."

Rane shrugged and sat down. The sensors and cuffs were well-designed; after a few seconds he hardly noticed them at all. Mix fired up the CPU and a short interval of neutral gray-white noise gave way suddenly to a roomful of color and sound. Floating in the air about six inches out from his chest, Rane saw the familiar Web browser menu.

"See the little mouse in the lower right-hand corner?" he heard Mix's voice ask from somewhere, "just grab it and click on any of the choices, the same way you would if you were sitting at a normal keyboard. The system is voice-activated: start by saying 'U-R-L' followed by an actual Web address, or 'search' if you don't know the exact string. You can also click on that infinity symbol, which will send you to a randomly-chosen site from my proxy cluster. I've got about two million in there right now."

Sounded a bit loopy, but Rane gave it a try. He reached for the semi-translucent mouse (it looked like a real rodent, because Mix had that sort of sense of humor). His fingers closed around it and he actually felt the diminutive furry beast in his hand. The sensation was so real that he dropped it in alarm when it squeaked at him, but instead of falling to the ground and running away it floated serenely there in midair, waiting patiently. He grabbed it gingerly and poked at the infinity button. The blue and gold 'home page' background dissolved and was replaced by what looked like a movie screen, on which was displayed a rather pedestrian Web page for some bank. He walked around the screen, which appeared about half an inch thick. Behind it he could see the same Web page in reverse. The rest of the space was a tasteful light blue, with no features except a photo calendar on the far wall featuring a gorgeous red drop top 'vette for the month of August, 2001.

As Rane was puzzling over this, Mix clarified. "Right now, almost all Web pages are two-dimensional. That's because they're coded that way, and *that's* because no one had invented any reason for them to be coded in *more* than two dimensions. Until now. I'm not talking about lame crap like VRML, either. If you want to see what sort of potential the system really has, surf over to 'Local file demo dot eye ess ell.'"

"ISL?" Rane asked.

"Impact Simulation Language. Has all the info needed for 4-D simulation of the experience. Coming up with that was actually the hardest part of this project."

Rane shrugged. "Local file demo dot eye ess ell," he said. Nothing happened.

"You forgot to say 'URL' first. That's the key phrase that triggers the address parsing routine. Eventually, I'll map shortcuts to make it less cumbersome."

"You are ell local file demo dot eye ess ell."

The movie screen and light blue room faded to solid black, a close stifling black that almost gave Rane an attack of claustrophobia before it resolved after a few seconds into a mind-bendingly familiar childhood memory. It was the Melon Island amusement park, exactly as he remembered it. Sights and sounds were both reproduced in excruciating detail. Rane was not a computer geek, but he knew enough about the digital world to realize that something was amiss. There was simply too much data being displayed here—it would take a massively parallel supercomputer with hundreds of thousands of processors to reproduce a scene with this level of fidelity.

"Psychoreflective surfaces," explained a voice that appeared to come from a potted plant at the end of the bench where Rane sat, taking in as much of the spectacle as he could manage.

When the plant seemed disinclined to elaborate, Rane frowned and addressed it, trying to keep in mind that this was just a Web page, albeit a spectacular one that made even the most sophisticated Flash animation look like a kindergarten flip book. "What does that mean?" he asked the plant, trying not to feel silly.

"It means," replied the tree behind him, "that I've discovered a specific combination of visual and audio stimuli that encourages the brain to fill in missing details from memory —a sort of 'psychological green screen' in effect. That's why you see what you see. If I were standing there with you, I'd see a somewhat different set of details. In a way, this is kind of the ultimate electronic manifestation of solipsism."

"Wow." That was all Rane could think of to say. It seemed

apposite enough. He got up and walked around; could feel the rough ironwork of the bench frame, and chip off bits of peeling paint from the ticket booth with his fingernail. The air was redolent with a mixture of popcorn, diesel fuel, and the faint salt tang of the nearby bay. Suddenly a thought struck him.

"What if you've never been to the place?"

"You just fill in with scenes from the nearest analog in your memory. It can lead to some weird déjà vu-type experiences, but they're sort of interesting in their own right. I've only tried it a couple of times, admittedly, and then with pretty primitive renderings."

Rane noticed that some of the structures had areas that were glowing faintly. He pointed to one and raised his eyebrows interrogatively at the empty air, which obligingly responded.

"Those are hyperlinks. Click one."

Rane reached for the mouse. He was beginning to enjoy the feel of its warm fur in his palm. It squeaked but offered no resistance to his grasp. He chose the glowing sign that said "Roller Coaster Rides" and clicked. Instantly he found himself in a somewhat cramped and rickety wooden car, a padded steel bar across his lap. He was being hauled slowly up a steep incline, the rails clacking rhythmically beneath him. He could see the shimmering bay off to his left and the tree-lined boulevard that ran the length of the island to his right. He even felt the first faint stirrings of the minor nosebleed he habitually got on rides of this nature. After the car reached the crest and executed its screaming plunge towards the ground, he groped for the mouse and clicked the 'back' button.

Standing in front of the ticket booth with a trickle of blood on his shirt and his hair sticking out at odd angles, Rane had to admit he was impressed. This rig definitely tacked 'reality' onto 'virtual' with significant aplomb.

"Okay, how do I get out?"

"Just click the 'x'."

Rane grabbed the mouse once more and followed Mix's instructions. Melon Island faded back to light blue, then suddenly Rane felt a slight jolt and the goggles went dark. He uncuffed his arms and legs, swung back the headpiece, and stood up in the real world once again.

"That was seriously cool. I have questions, though."

Mix was standing there with his arms crossed. "Shoot."

"How do the brainwave electrodes interact with the psychoreflective surfaces?"

"I haven't worked that out yet. There may or may not be any interaction between them. That's gonna be part of the next phase of the project."

"Is there any other way to get out than using the mouse?"

"I don't know. I don't think so. I hadn't really thought about that. Suppose I should design some sort of manual emergency exit, huh?"

"I think it would be a good idea, yeah. I need to split now."

"Got a date?"

"Sort of. There's someplace I need to…go later tonight."

"New club, I'll bet. Let me know if it's worth the trip."

"Um, I will if I can."
"Cryptic, as always."

Mixolydian Oscar Gray was the only son of two tenured professors at a small liberal arts college. His father was a musicologist and his mother taught English literature. Together they concocted Mix's name as a sort of inside joke. In contrast to most children who are named at parental whim, Mix hadn't suffered greatly under the onus of his odd moniker. Few could pronounce his full first name; 'Mix' was the obvious diminutive and Mix is, after all, a fairly cool label. It's easy to remember and easy to spell. He rarely told people about the Oscar, as he didn't think it would lead to anything but lame wiener jokes.

Today Mix was 'bouncing'—alternating between Vspace and Mspace (his names for the VR and conventional computing environments; M for *meat*). He was working on improving and expanding the interface, and tweaking his runtime code for better performance. The project, or at least parts of it, was accessible via the Internet using SSH so he could share with certain close friends, but he'd kept it pretty much under wraps for the most part. A chance mention of it on a predominantly blackhat forum by a friend who was in his cups had led to unwanted attention, so Mix had as the next item on his "to-do" list a revamping of his packet-inspecting stateful firewall rules and some additional ingress filtering parameters.

The first inkling that something sinister was afoot occurred as he was sitting at the programming console making changes to a dynamically-linked library. On another screen just at the corner of his vision a window suddenly popped up with a log file displaying in it. He had set his intrusion detection system to trigger this action if certain attack signatures were seen. He clicked his tongue in irritation because the alert destroyed his concentration at a particularly bad moment, when he was deeply involved in the intricacies of unraveling some rather awkwardly nested calls drilling down to a delicate inline assembly function.

He rolled over to the DMZ box and surveyed the screen briefly. Looked like a port scan, and nothing more. Odd—the IDS shouldn't be triggering for such a low-level threat. That was doubly frustrating, since it meant he'd lost his train of thought for no good reason. He'd need to review his triggering rules. He sighed and mentally added that to the list of future security-related tasks.

What Mix hadn't noticed was that two of the ports being scanned in detail were the pair of high-numbered ports he'd configured for future use in communicating between Internet-linked ISL servers. The ports were non-consecutive, a feature he'd designed specifically to make any activity surrounding them stick out, but he'd failed to realize that this was the reason for the IDS alert. Right now he just dismissed the alert screen and went back to coding. The incident kept nagging at him, but Mix was determined to finish this bit of programming prior to hitting the sack.

Before work the next morning, Mix noticed that the alert

screen had returned. He didn't have time to sit and analyze it, but to be safe he turned off the router before he left. That would prevent anyone getting in while he was gone. It occurred to him as he was driving away that he should have just shut the whole system down. Oh, well. No harm done.

Mix had a tough day; he was exhausted and cross when he got home. He had a nap and some supper, and then got back to work programming, relieved to be doing something he enjoyed for the first time today. After a few more tweaks he was ready to launch the ISL server again. He strapped himself into the VR rig and clicked.

He was still working with the Melon Island module, but he'd added some elements that were, quite frankly, right out of puerile fantasy. They involved a password-protected 'Tunnel of Love' with enthusiastic denizens who leapt right into the boat, and a 'House of Horrors' stocked with a variety of weapons he'd shamelessly appropriated from his favorite single-person shooter computer games. He, of course, had the benefit of 'god' mode, so the slaughter was widespread and wholly unilateral.

Before he ventured into any of the attractions, though, Mix had some surveying to do. He wanted to add a third component to the module, but there were spatial and aesthetic considerations. The best way to work them out, he felt, was *in situ*, so he walked around the park area using his developer's toolbar, on which was located an icon that, when clicked, generated a small polygonal wireframe that could be scaled to size and shape on demand as he scouted out suitable locations.

All of this could be done using raster graphics in the developer console, of course, but he found this method to be more satisfying and definitely more engaging.

Near a small stand of pecan trees (one of his favorites, although not strictly botanically correct for the area), Mix stopped and framed a likely spot with his avatar's hands. He plopped a three-quarter-scale wireframe in place and slowly expanded it to full size with a virtual slider poised conveniently in midair at his right hand. Suddenly one section of the wireframe near the front entrance began to deform strangely. Mix stared in puzzlement and consternation as the deformation took on the appearance of a face, which evolved itself into the countenance of a demon of some ilk.

The demon's face stayed wireframe except for a few shreds of decidedly rotten-looking flesh that flapped stiffly from the cheeks and temples. He could almost smell the decay. The face turned and looked straight at him. The mouth opened, and Mix suddenly realized he didn't have audio enabled. He grabbed for the mouse and clicked on the sound control panel.

"What a nice little playground you've built here," said the demon. It was a heavily filtered voice, with most of the upper frequencies compressed to give it a low, rumbling quality that seemed stereotypically correct for the species. The demon looked vaguely familiar: maybe he'd seen it in a game. Probably someone just snagged the graphics files from some game disc and superimposed a composite over the wireframe matrix. Minus ten for originality. That failed to explain how the unoriginal construct came to exist *here* in his private world, however.

The demon laughed hideously and said, "I will pose you a riddle, mortal; if you can give me an answer I like I may let you live. For now." The construct glowed a dark scarlet that was presumably intended to suggest freshly spilled blood—although it looked to Mix more like cherry lollipop red—and seemed to get larger. It might be comical if Mix knew a little more about what was going on. It was certainly clichéd.

"What has four legs, a wide grin, and a tail at both ends?" asked the demon.

Mix was unsure what to do at this point. He decided to erase the wireframe and see what effect that had on the intruder. It seemed to work—when the model disappeared, the demon face vanished along with it. He turned around and walked back toward the main part of the park, but as he did he noticed that the plants and other ornamental landscape features were taking on the demon's visage. In a matter of seconds he was surrounded by dozens of copies of the face, all animated in unison.

This episode had crossed the line into downright annoying, and he was going to put a stop to it now. The best place to do that, however, would be from the console. He reached for the mouse. It wasn't there. In its place was a bright blue cat, grinning ear to ear, with a mouse's tail hanging limply from one corner of a very well dentally-equipped mouth. As Mix watched in dawning concern the cat faded from view (teeth last), taking the remains of the mouse with it. The demon head bellowed out possibly the most evil laugh he'd ever heard.

The worst-case scenario Rane had proposed had now unexpectedly come to pass. Mix was trapped in the VR simulation. Any motion he used to try to tear himself out of the goggles or harness was interpreted within the simulation rather than as actual muscle movement. He had painted himself into a digital corner. To recreate the mouse would require console access, but he couldn't get to the console without using the mouse to exit ISL mode. Meanwhile, the demon intruder was gradually taking control of his entire module.

The realization hit him like a falling safe. Those alert screens he'd been seeing were telling him that someone scanned for and subsequently accessed his system from the outside. Via what mechanism, he didn't yet know. Worse, he didn't have a viable means for finding out from in here.

He passed by that same bench where Rane had sat and plopped down on it himself to sort out what action he should take next. The tree directly behind the bench suddenly sprouted a long, sinuous demonic tongue that twisted and undulated its way over his shoulder and down one leg. Mix jumped up in mingled alarm and disgust and ran for the nearest building. He'd never tried running full speed in ILS mode before; it seemed awkward and jerky somehow. His peripheral vision blurred and distorted as he sprinted, giving him glimpses of objects that he knew should not be there.

He didn't have time to think about what that meant, because

demon heads were taking over the park, each sporting a powerful, agile tongue that jabbed and slapped at him if he passed too close. He dodged them as well as he could; one thing he could say for the experience is that it was teaching him a lot about the limitations of his proprioceptive feedback system.

Puffing along, Mix racked his brain trying to think of some place to escape the ubiquitous invaders. He was getting tired— while it didn't take as much of his physical energy to run in ISL mode as it did in real life, he did still have to pump his legs— and he knew that sooner or later he'd give out. If that happened within reach of several of those tentacles or tongues or whatever they were, he might not be able to get loose. In that event he could theoretically starve to death, or die of dehydration, unless someone came along and released him from the harness in time.

The demon heads were getting more and more plentiful as he ran. He couldn't help but wonder how long it would be before his system ran out of RAM. He had 64 gigabytes installed, but these things were rather complex and at the rate they were multiplying it wouldn't take that many more to overload the memory.

Something occurred to him. He put on a burst of speed and suddenly reversed his direction. As he ran back the way he'd come, a wave of new heads followed, but the ones he had passed earlier were no longer there. The attacker was using clipping to get rid of any heads not in Mix's immediate environment. That meant the CPU could continue generating them forever, since each new head merely replaced one that had just ceased to exist somewhere behind him. Frustrated and disappointed, Mix turned around and continued on his original course. He had to find some sort of refuge before his strength gave out. None of the park buildings or rides was safe from the infestation, however.

Suddenly he had an idea. At the dead center of the module map was a small cubic structure he'd termed 'the bunker' just big enough for his avatar, built of read-only components and used as an anchor to the underlying software application layer. It was the first element of the module he'd coded, and it was marked read-only because he wanted to be able to add and remove structures around it without worrying about accidentally modifying the anchor.

In that bunker was a small 12-key keyboard that he used as a quick way to access certain critical console functions in the early phases of the build (since a crude avatar was functional before the floating toolbar). If he could get to the bunker and remember the last set of key mappings, he might be able to accomplish something.

Unfortunately, he'd chosen to hide the bunker by covering the outer surface with a granite block texture and making it the lower section of a fountain in a fair-sized pool in the center of the park. The pool itself was surrounded by small trees which would, naturally, make perfect substrates for demon heads. This wasn't going to be fun.

Mix decided that the best approach would be from the side opposite where he was now, down a narrow cobblestone path leading to the pool. The path itself was lined with trees, but he figured that with careful timing and a bit of luck he could evade the demon tongues long enough to get into the cube. The bunker looked solid, but he knew that one side sported a false front. If he could get through it and to the keyboard, he could solidify the wall to keep the invaders out.

He circled the central park area, looking for the path. He'd slow down to a walk every so often, until the tongues homed in on him and started interfering with his movement, then accelerate back to a jog. Once, a tongue managed to trip him, and he fell headlong into a short railing near the walkway. Although Mix knew there was no hard-wired connection between his avatar and his physical nervous system, there was also no doubt that the wind got knocked out of him and his knees throbbed.

Behold the power of suggestion.

He scrambled painfully to his feet, kicking at a couple of the encroaching tongues, and hobbled on his way. Finally, the entrance to the path hove into view. There was an unavoidable copse of trees between him and the target, but he'd just have to run the gauntlet, as it were. He would have felt a lot more confident about the prospect before he hurt his knees, but there was nothing he could do but damn the torpedoes at this stage. The pain was tiring him out more quickly and his reserves were running dry.

Mix decided it was prudent in his injured condition to skirt the trees to the right, rather than plunging right through the center on a direct course to the fountain, as he had originally planned. He didn't feel strong or agile enough to fight off the barrage of tongues he knew would be waiting for him there. There was a nasty moment as he swung around to the front side of the copse near where the tree line split to border the fountain approach path. Demon heads sprang up all around; tongues shot out from either side simultaneously and met in mid-air, prompting him to slide under them: limbo at a dead run.

He'd made it to the edge of the water, but now Mix had to contend with thirty feet of faithfully programmed 2X viscosity fluid before he could reach the safety of the fountain. He had a shortcut that enabled him to walk across water as though it were a solid surface, but as it was on the console it might as well not have existed at all. He jabbed at a nearby demon tongue in frustration; the sensation was not unlike punching a wall of gelatin, although there did appear to be some minimal physical reaction.

There was nothing for it but to plunge right in. He hadn't yet worked out the algorithm for swimming, so wading was his only locomotive option. Thirty feet was a long way to slosh under fire, but at least the pool was a uniform three feet in depth. He accelerated to full speed coming down the path and leapt as far as he could towards the center of the fountain.

Just slightly after mid-jump, Mix noticed that the water

seemed to be moving rather oddly: the part nearest his feet was receding, while the pond a few yards ahead of him was building vertically. He couldn't tell what was happening, exactly, but he felt certain he wasn't going to like it.

The entire contents of the pond had formed a huge, grotesquely misshapen parody of the demon head, and Mix was headed directly into its gaping maw. He twisted violently in midair trying to change trajectory, but he'd done too good a job of modeling real-world physics. He was irrevocably committed to his course, which took would take him directly down the throat of the monstrosity. It was just (simulated) water, though, so what was there to be afraid of? All he'd programmed it to do was slow movement by 50%; it had no other properties. Of course, he hadn't programmed it to morph into the top part of a hell-spawn, either.

Inside the mouth the intruder had done a pretty good job of texturing reddish, shiny, and slimy. All trace of anything that looked like water had disappeared. As he landed on the jiggling, squelching surface of the demonic glottis, the jaws snapped shut. He ran to the nearest wall and plunged into it. By the time he'd pushed his way through to the other side, however, the throat had shifted in the same direction and reformed around him. The end result was essentially the same as if he'd been caught up in a tangle of tongues: he was trapped.

Mix realized he was cut off from the rest of the park visually, and that if he kept thrashing around he'd lose all sense of direction. His only chance was to find the bunker before that happened. He stopped, calmed himself, and tried to recreate mentally all the moves he'd made since his last glimpse at the outside world. The fountain would have been directly at the rear of the larynx in his initial orientation; he'd moved three or four yards to the right and rotated clockwise about 45 degrees, so that would make the bunker just about in...*that* direction.

He stepped over to a pharyngeal wall and pushed carefully, trying not to lose his orientation as he passed through the heavy pudding-like structure. Emerging on the far side the enclosure began to reform around him, but when he swung his arms and failed to encounter the fountain he realized he had miscalculated and stepped back in the direction he'd come to more or less his starting point. The throat obligingly followed.

Mix took two steps to the left and plunged through once more. Again he found nothing. Repeating the process for a third time, his left hand encountered something solid. Since the program that had converted the pond water into a giant demon head was overwriting the park's native topology as it moved, the fact that he'd found something solid strongly suggested that it was a read-only structure. The intruder could change the textural overlay of the fountain, but not the underlying wireframe. Now he just had to locate and figure out how to get inside the bunker without being able to use any of the visual reference points he'd been counting on. Piece o' cake.

He started slapping the avatar's hand against the solid structure, looking for the false partition. It wasn't the one facing him, so he moved around the pedestal to probe another. As he did, the walls of the throat began to surge, trying to sweep him away. Apparently the intruder had at least some inkling of Mix's intentions.

He could resist the flow, of course, but doing so made it difficult for him to continue with the pedestal exploration because just staying in one place was keeping him pretty busy. If he allowed the intruder to force him away from the fountain he might never find it again, so he struggled to keep his place.

Fortunately, the effect algorithm for the water object was fairly simplistic, as he never intended for there to be this sort of interaction between it and an avatar, and so the force exerted by water was constant regardless of mass. In other words, a six foot-thick column of water didn't exert any more force than a two-foot column. The program logic just said *if the avatar is in contact with water, slow avatar movement by one-half.*

Finally, Mix managed to force his way around to the opposite side of the fountain's base and was rewarded when the avatar's hand disappeared into it. He waited a moment for the latest wave of pressure from the water to pass, then dove straight through the seemingly solid fountain wall. Once inside he grabbed the small rectangular keypad floating serenely in the otherwise unadorned space and jabbed at one of the keys. The wall through which he had entered suddenly solidified, cutting off part of an invading tongue as it did. The slimy reddish fragment writhed slowly for a few seconds, then faded away as the garbage collection routine claimed it.

He had two rows of six keys to work with. One of them (fortunately) toggled the permeability of the wall, which function he'd included in case the three-dimensional vector mapping of one of his creations didn't behave as intended. That left eleven mappings from which to choose. He tried to remember what functions he'd last assigned to which keys. His usual procedure was to make the leftmost keys, starting with the upper left and proceeding clockwise, Load, Select, Unselect, and Unload. Since there was no object menu available, though, none of these should do anything under the current circumstances. Mix verified that this was the case. Usually he assigned the bottom right key to 'exit,' but that wouldn't do him any good here because there were no compartmentalized subroutines running from which to exit.

He resisted the urge to just start pressing keys willy-nilly because that could have wildly unpredictable consequences; he had enough variables to deal with as things stood. He would have to choose one at a time and try to deduce what, if anything, was the result. He started with number three from the left, top row. Nothing happened. Not surprising, really. When he had that luxury, Mix customarily left a 'buffer zone' between active key regions to minimize accidental operations. On to number four.

The pale gray interior of the bunker grew increasingly saturated the longer he held the key down. "Chroma slider," he mumbled. Key five created a translucent sphere in the air in front of him. He hit the exit key and it disappeared. He punched the first key again and a solid cube shimmered into existence. *Primitives generator.* That meant the next key and the corresponding one on the lower row were probably x-y and z adjustor toggles, which left only two keys on the lower row unaccounted for. Things were starting to look a little grim. Mix crossed his fingers and proceeded to the next key.

Two groups of hex digits arranged in columns popped up, one on either side of the tiny bunker. He stared at them for a moment and then realized they were dynamic memory dumps: one from the stack and one from the heap. They were changing spasmodically as the invader tried to gain entrance to the bunker. Mix blinked in surprise—he didn't usually enable hex dumps unless he was actively troubleshooting memory leaks. This combination of keys didn't make much sense: hue adjustment, object creation, memory monitoring...what had he been doing?

His concentration was disrupted by a sudden pinpoint of brilliant light that broke through the bunker wall in front of him. He stared at it in alarm and two more appeared near the first. The intruder had somehow managed to defeat the read-only protection! That was impossible, so far as Mix knew. On the verge of panic for a few seconds, he managed to calm himself and reason things out. The sole way to modify the read-only flag would be gain access to the administrator account for the module, and if the intruder had somehow managed to own the box totally, he could just wipe out the bunker altogether and be done with it. This had to be some sort of vulnerability in the bunker code he was taking advantage of.

More and more pinpricks were dappling the walls all around him now, and light entering through them was much brighter than he remembered the ambient module illumination to be. The wire framework of the bunker was beginning to be visible, contrasted by the intense backlighting. The intruder had figured out some way to replace the texture of the bunker, albeit one random pixel at a time. Mix glanced up at the memory display and noticed that it was almost completely obscured by the glare. At that moment he finally understood his enemy's tactics. As with the mouse, Mix couldn't manipulate what he couldn't see.

He had very little time remaining before it would be too bright to resolve anything at all in the bunker. He had to do something. It crossed his mind that his opponent wanted him to panic and hopefully make some foolish mistake in the blind rush of trying to take action, however, so he focused on ignoring the light and went to his happy place. In an extreme act of concentration, Mix formulated a plan for defense and counterattack. Step one was to find out what that last key did.

He pressed the final key and the hexadecimal digits stopped changing. He pressed it again and they changed only once. It was a debugger for stepping through module execution, one function call at a time. It didn't affect the bunker, which ran in a dedicated memory partition. As long as it was initialized, the intruder was helpless to take any further action. Unfortunately, so was Mix. He could move about in the bunker, but little else.

It gave him time to think, though.

He considered just leaving the bunker while module execution was paused, but quickly dismissed that because he wouldn't be able to move at all on the outside. The intruder couldn't get him, true, but he'd be trapped all the same, unable even to return to the bunker. He had to terminate the program altogether or somehow block the intruder from further interfering. He remembered the IDS alert bitterly and mentally kicked himself for not paying more attention to it.

The intruder seemed to have gotten in using the inter-server communications link, which meant that he had to have exploited some weakness in a network daemon. Mix didn't have any way of investigating that at present, unfortunately. He racked his brain for something, anything, he could use to his advantage here. If only he had some way to halt main program execution. To crash the system, he'd need to violate datastream integrity or perform an untrapped illegal operation or overflow...the...

Mix stopped and cocked an eyebrow. The bunker was running in a separate thread, true, but halting execution there would more than likely crash the whole system because that thread hooked directly into the kernel. But how to orchestrate an overflow from here? Injecting code seemed beyond the realm of possibility without any sort of I/O device available. All he had was the bunker keypad. He was pretty sure the buffers for the keypad weren't overflowable, but there was a small possibility that one of the ad hoc control functions he'd hotkeyed to it might not do comprehensive bounds checking.

He took a deep breath and unpaused the module. Almost immediately the pixel replacement attack resumed. Already he could barely see the keyboard; he had very little time left. He jabbed at the keys until he found the primitives generator, then toggled the axis controllers until he had generated a rotating dodecahedron sheathed in tiny spectral hexagons, the most computationally-intensive primitive in his library. All but blind now, he repeatedly pressed the generate key as rapidly as possible before the light intensity totally overwhelmed him. He knew that if he lost track of the keyboard, he might not be able to find it again. Shimmering, revolving dodecahedrons began filling up the bunker, overlapping in ever-more complex layers.

It took about 500 milliseconds to generate each object. He could press the key much faster than that, so he knew he must be filling up the instruction buffer. The real question was, what would happen when it reached capacity? If he had coded it correctly, it would simply start to erase the oldest renderings and reallocate their memory on a first in-first out basis. However, Mix also knew that he tended to take shortcuts when he was creating sandbox utilities like the primitives generator. In this case, sloppy coding was his best chance for salvation.

The light intensity was completely overwhelming now. Almost all of the bunker walls had dissolved, leaving huge gaps through which he could feel the demon tongues beginning to intrude. All he could do was close his eyes and keep jabbing at the keyboard, hoping against hope. His fingers were cramping and he was developing a splitting headache from the extraordinarily intense light and constantly increasing noise level. He felt himself slipping away, and wondered if he lost consciousness now if he would ever wake up. It took him a few groggy seconds to realize that the noise had ceased.

Mix opened his eyes. He was sitting in the VR chair. He ripped off the goggles and found himself staring at a blank monitor. He'd done it! He sat there for a moment, trying to reorient to the real world. His eye wandered to a dangling wire, and he realized that in thrashing about he had pulled the mouse cord loose from the USB port hub. That explained how the attacker was able to make the mouse disappear completely. A coincidence, or was he so good and so familiar with Mix's physical setup that he was able to manipulate him into pulling the plug?

He was about to unstrap and reach over to plug the mouse back in when the monitor suddenly flashed to life. The system was rebooting itself. Mix was puzzled for a moment until he remembered that he'd set that option himself to save time during debugging. Time to clean up after the attack and build some better walls around the project. He slipped the goggles back on and relaxed in the chair.

The virtual world rebuilt itself around him. He surveyed the damage. Not every change the attacker had made was persistent after the restart, but enough of them were to be distressing. He reached for the mouse and then realized he'd forgotten to reconnect it. Sigh. He headed for the bunker.

The bunker was very different. It was encased in something that had a texture like solid bronze. Must have been installed by the attacker. He walked around it. No way in. He tried his old secret entrance. No longer there. Mix rolled his eyes and cursed himself for not making changes to the code before he came back in. He'd have to break down the barrier around the bunker one pixel at a time. He picked up a virtual rock and started chipping.

Before he got very far, Mix noticed an odd sound coming through the headphones. At first it emanated mostly from the left channel, but as it grew louder and more shrill it took over the entire sonic field. Concerned, he looked up from his deconstruction to see that every visible object had morphed into an even more threatening version of the demon head from before. His tormenter had returned with a vengeance.

Mix realized that he had to get out as soon as possible, but once again he had no way to do that without the stupid mouse. He couldn't believe he had blown the chance to fix everything. He leapt up on top of the bunker to gain a little temporary breathing space and tried to formulate a plan. The previous solution was denied him this time around unless he could break into the bunker while dodging the seemingly infinite number of imposing demon heads now converging on him from every direction. Think, think...He dodged a vicious thrust from a demonic tongue covered with stout, razor-sharp barbs. As he ducked, another one clipped him from the opposite side. Time was running out. Again.

It was obvious that his best shot was somehow to regain control of the mouse and use it to click the "exit" button shimmering tantalizingly in the air in front of him. The only way to accomplish that, unfortunately, was to reattach it physically. Since his movements were interpreted within the game environment, he had to work out what action to take in the virtual world to result in the correct motions in Mspace to reconnect the cable. It was not a trivial exercise, especially given that the kinetic transducers amplified arm and leg movements by a factor of at least five.

His first order of business, though, was to find someplace to get away from the new, improved demon heads assaulting him from every direction. The top of the bunker had ceased to provide any sanctuary at all, so he waited until one of the heads was in mid-attack and leapt between it and its neighbor. He ran flat-out broken field, dodging and weaving among the heads that popped up along his path.

He wasn't even certain the destination he had in mind was actually there. It was a ravine he'd created by accident while mapping landscape textures to the wireframe world model. The thing which made it attractive as a potential refuge was that the clipping algorithm seemed to have some sort of issue with the particular areas where the coordinates and meta information attached to the ravine were stored in memory. Even though the ravine itself appeared to be accessible, it really wasn't except via one very narrow non-intuitive approach. Mix hoped he could find that entrance while avoiding the lacerating tongues.

Running full speed, he suddenly tripped over something invisible and fell to the ground, sliding uncontrollably as the physics engine took unexpected liberties with the visually abrasive surface texture. He flailed haphazardly for a moment before it occurred to him that the demon heads were being triggered by motion. As he slid to a stop, Mix ceased all movement. The barbed tongues thrust and slashed all around him, but made no contact. So long as he didn't move, they couldn't detect him.

Unfortunately, remaining motionless was not a reasonable long-term strategy as it interfered with his goal of reattaching the mouse cable, but he wasn't sure where the threshold of detection lay. He started inching his left hand down while visualizing his position in the VR chair and the relative location of the dangling mouse cable. So far, so good.

Best he could remember, he'd need to execute a rather dramatic extension down and to the left until he could feel the cable, then somehow guide it into the USB slot. To be honest, he wasn't even sure if that was possible from the VR chair, given that he was semi-restrained, but it was his only real option. He also knew that as soon as he moved more than a few inches the tongues would resume their jabbing.

There was no point in putting it off. He jumped up and started straining in the direction he imagined the mouse cable to be, swatting madly at the demon tongues with his right hand. They couldn't actually injure him in Mspace, but they could throw him off balance or trip him up here. Since damage was cumulative even in demo mode, they could also cripple or eventually 'kill' his avatar—which would, maddeningly, require the unobtainable mouse click to respawn.

The assault seemed to pause, and suddenly he became aware of a tingling sensation in his fingers, which rapidly worsened. His arms began to cramp, then his feet. Somehow the attacker had taken control of the limb actuators of the rig and was closing the clamps on him. He hadn't anticipated this attack, or even considered that it was possible. He wasn't sure if the clamps would restrict far enough to cut off his circulation altogether, but it wasn't an experiment in which he was prepared to engage under these circumstances.

His range of motion now severely limited, Mix had to swing his torso back and forth to effect any real extension which, he couldn't help but speculate, probably looked rather peculiar. Odd or no, he now had even greater motivation to find some way to reconnect his only conduit to normalcy. The demon heads evolved into elongated snapping jaws as he struggled, irritatingly complicating an already nigh-impossible task.

He resumed running, stumbling, toward the ravine. His avatar's clothes were beginning to tatter from all the snapping and tearing. He didn't even remember the avatar module supporting apparel degradation, but he must have coded that feature in there at some point. Mix kept pushing on, leaving a trail of wardrobe as he ran. Fortunately for modesty's sake, certain core elements of his ensemble seemed to be respawning as soon as they were lost. The snappers were left with infinite undergarments in their slavering jaws, which he found grimly amusing.

Finally, he reached the ravine. It was only accessible from one certain angle; it took a minute to maneuver around until he could slip in through the narrow opening. The snappers were hot on his heels, but they possessed the wrong wireframe geometry to squeeze in after him. Secure for the moment in his dark little cubbyhole, Mix concentrated once more on the mouse cable quest. He wasn't making any tangible progress with normal movements, so he decided to ramp it up. He stuck his restricted left arm out as far as it would go, flexed his wrist to the point of pain, and threw his whole body up and to the left. He was rewarded by contact with something that felt gratifyingly similar to the elusive cable. He slid his fingers down the plastic sheath and closed them around the USB plug, keenly conscious of the fact that if he lost track of it now he might never find it again.

Even though he had the mouse plug, locating the slot and inserting it properly were far more difficult propositions. He strained to visualize in his mind the exact spatial relationship between the dangling cord and the USB port hub into which it fitted. As he sat quietly concentrating, Mix felt a little tickle on his right leg. Alarmed, he opened his eyes to see a strange eel-like manifestation wriggling in through the narrow opening above him. The tenacious bastard had figured out how to gain access to his little fissure using mini-tentacles.

The tentacles seemed to be ignoring him completely. Instead, they were intent on dismantling the surrounding infrastructure in an apparent effort to trap Mix's avatar using his own clipping algorithms. Effing great. This son of a bitch just wouldn't give up. Mix redoubled his efforts. He'd made contact with what felt like the USB slot about the time the first tentacle slithered across his leg. Maneuvering an unseen plug to line up with an invisible hole was going to be a freaking challenge in and of itself, never mind the race to get it done before the ravine collapsed in on him.

Since this wasn't a real geological formation, but rather a matrix of computer-generated polygons, the deconstruction was more akin to taking apart a jigsaw puzzle than an actual sapping operation. The tentacles were proving quite adept at removing a chunk of wall and then reintegrating it with the wireframe in such a manner as to trap one of his limbs, though. He had to get some wiggle room fast, so he kicked one of the tentacles as hard as he could, damaging it until it withdrew, and then slid into that newly-vacated space.

Working feverishly, he strained at the very limit of his mobility to get the plug back up to the vicinity of the USB port. Once he felt contact, he tried inserting it. No good. He backed off, twisted his hand a bit, and tried again. He sensed partial insertion, but it wouldn't lock in place. Damn these asymmetrical sockets; he'd need to rotate the plug exactly 180 degrees. Mix tore away one of the tentacles and rolled over on his side to get more room to maneuver. As he was feeling once more for the port, several new tentacles suddenly slithered in and made a beeline for his arms, as though the intruder had divined his strategy.

His only chance now was to rock continuously, to prevent the tentacles from completely encasing him. Trying to keep that up while simultaneously working on reinserting the USB plug was a decidedly challenging exercise in solving three-dimensional vector equations. To top things off, his arms were cramping fiercely now from the limb actuators having been restricted to their maximum stop. Mix realized with sudden catastrophic clarity that in his effort to create a realistic virtual experience he had totally ignored security. The price he was paying for that oversight was steeper than he would have imagined possible.

He was almost immobile now, having lost the battle to keep the tentacles at bay. He stopped struggling against them and concentrated on winning just enough movement to try again for the plug. He wasn't sure how much longer he could keep this up; it occurred to him that the constant constriction on his arms and legs might cause some sort of blood clot. It was pretty much now or never.

Mix took a deep breath—fortunately, the intruder wasn't able to control his breathing—and kicked his legs spasmodically to draw the tentacles away from his arms for a few seconds. Once he had gained a small, albeit temporary, measure of freedom for his upper torso he closed his eyes and focused every atom of concentration he could muster on the task at hand. He had heroically managed to keep the mouse cable in his hand throughout his struggles. He inched it up carefully, straining to discern subtle contact with the USB hub amidst the thrashing the tentacles were giving his avatar. He bumped up against something, felt the rectangular shape with his finger, rotated the invisible plug just so and inserted it smoothly until he felt a definitive click.

There was a pause of several seconds while the USB controller located and loaded the appropriate driver, then the cursor appeared magically on the screen at dead center. He knew he only had a very short time before the intruder figured out what had happened; he had to get out of the tentacles far enough to grab and move the mouse while he still could. He began thrashing and bucking wildly, trying to overload the tentacles' tracking algorithms. Gradually they loosened their grip so that he was able to grasp the mouse then inch it over, one jerk at a time. With one mighty final spasm he slid the pointer squarely over the Exit icon and clicked twice so that he could skip the "Are You Sure?" prompt.

He was back in the chair, VR goggles off, programming screen quietly flickering in front of him. At long last the nightmare was over. His first order of business was to wriggle out of the incredibly tight arm and leg cuffs and let the circulation back into his extremities. He sat there rubbing his forearms and calves, wondering who the intruder could be and why he had gone to all this trouble to mess with him. He suddenly realized how dead tired he was.

He replayed entire episode while in the shower the next morning. There was some salient piece of the puzzle missing that he couldn't quite put his finger on. Standing in the bathroom in the nude toweling off, Mix thought he saw something snake-like slide furtively across his peripheral vision in the hallway. Frowning, he wrapped the towel around himself and went to investigate. There was nothing there. He got dressed and wandered the house, looking for anything out of the ordinary. Eventually he dismissed the incident as just imagination and made his way to the kitchen to scarf some leftover beef stroganoff for breakfast, then headed off to work.

That evening, Mix examined every detail of his logs, looking for clues as to the intruder's origin and intentions. The connections were fairly easy to track, but they led to an IP address in South Korea that almost certainly was itself a compromised box. Unless he could get a look at the logs for that ISP, tracing the attack vector any further would be difficult if not impossible. *C'est la vie.*

He decided to err on the side of caution in fixing Vspace. Rather than work inside the live program as he usually did, he pulled submodules into his external development environment: code on one monitor and wireframes on another. The damage done by the intrusion was simple enough to identify, but the way the code was written and implemented seemed eerily familiar. The intruder exhibited little programming quirks and shortcuts that were almost identical to his own. A coder's overall style is unique—like a fingerprint—and these two fingerprints matched almost perfectly. It spooked Mix to the point he had to stop and go to bed early.

That night he dreamed about his virtual world. Rather than demon heads and tentacles, though, the electronic landscape was populated by near-forgotten childhood figures: his favorite storybook characters, animated cartoon celebrities, and fragments of his own personal whimsy. They were all innocuous, even friendly, at first, but as time went on they grew more and more menacing. Mix found himself ducking and weaving as myriad beloved icons of his formative years slashed viciously at him. He ran full speed through the hostile park grounds toward the towering wooden roller coaster. He ducked into the tangle of support beams, looking for some safe haven. As he reached the central area of the coaster, the superstructure itself began to wobble and deform, collapsing in on him, smothering him under an enormous mass of twisted steel and splintered board.

Mix awoke sweating and in a panic. He thrashed wildly at the bed linens in which he had become entangled, threw off the pillow covering his face, and sat bolt upright in bed, breathing hard and trying to sort reality from dream fantasy. Even after ten minutes of reorienting himself that line was still blurred in his mind. He wandered aimlessly around the house, watched television, and played video games looking for distraction, but the dream refused to fade. The symbolism was eating at him, and he realized the only way to deal with it was to face it head on. The only possible explanation was that he had been a victim of his own dark machinations.

The idea that a jury-rigged biofeedback helmet could possibly be harvesting his memories and that his own program had them used them against him was so ludicrous he was almost embarrassed to entertain it, but he didn't have any other scenario that fit the facts. He had rigged the sensor web to feed into the computer via a 9-pin serial to IEEE 1394 converter. To consolidate the signals into something he could compress and interface into the game he'd hit upon the idea of using 5.1 surround sound audio channel multiplexing in reverse. Essentially Mix synthesized a complex digital waveform from the discrete data channels. He intended at some point to develop an algorithm for incorporating that waveform into Vspace, but at the moment the data just got dumped into a dynamic volatile RAM buffer and ignored. Or so he thought.

He spent the rest of that evening and far into the wee hours analyzing the output from his "brain scanner." It was still very difficult for Mix to come to terms with the fact that this little mesh of electrodes was actually capable of capturing and encoding visual representations of his private mental constructs. As with any digital device, the output was just ones and zeroes. It occurred to him in a passing moment of insight that the world was increasingly under the control of ones and zeroes. Human culture had manufactured its own binary control channel.

Regardless of whether or not he personally was able to decode the brain scan files correctly, it seemed that his program had somehow accomplished it. Maybe he could reverse-engineer the decoding algorithm: it was worth a try, anyway. He took a series of frames containing the demon heads and tried to correlate them one-on-one with the brain scans. Startlingly, the initial unscramble attempt he made was apparently successful. That in itself was quite disturbing, because it meant he'd guessed exactly right on every aspect of the process the first time—almost as though he'd designed it himself. The increasingly recursive nature of this investigation was beginning to unnerve Mix. He was trying very hard to squirm away from the conclusion that he somehow was responsible for his own ills, but the jaws of logic were clamping more tightly with every passing minute.

Mix decided to try Vspace once more. He disconnected the network altogether, taped the mouse cable firmly in place, and didn't even fasten the limb restraints. Just for good measure, he pointed the exit function to two different keys in the bunker and added a timeout: the system would automatically shut down after sixty minutes unless he clicked on a new button in the heads-up menu. *Not going to get trapped in there this time.*

Thus armed for battle, he headed back to Melon Island. It was absolutely, completely, ineluctably normal. No trace of the demon heads or the destruction caused by them was in evidence. Mix blinked; he must have reloaded an archived copy somehow. No matter. He would back it out and restore the most recent core.

Inexplicably, this *was* the most recent core. A quick check of the last three autosaves showed no evidence at all of the corrupted load. The proliferation of mysteries was starting to fatigue him. He needed to take a break from this project. Just get away and decompress.

He had a buddy who lived down on the coast, in a condo. He gave him a call. He was out of town this week, but he'd leave a key for Mix. Toss a few things in a bag and jump in the car. In a few minutes he was happily on the road.

Sitting on the balcony of the condo with the salt air filling his lungs and beer mellowing his psyche, Mix reflected on recent events. There were too many fragments of uncertainty floating around to put together any coherent picture. Mix decided to concentrate on what he did know, or could reasonably surmise.

He got hacked via a network vulnerability. The attacker had access to information about him that seemed at first glance to be a little more intimate than should have been possible, but he comforted himself with the idea that all of that stuff could have been harvested from social networking or from files the hacker had gotten off Mix's own system. That was the explanation he felt most comfortable with. It still left a lot of unanswered questions, but at least he was making progress. The eight-hundred-pound gorilla on the balcony with him was why anyone would go to all that trouble on his account.

That evening, he went for a walk along the beach. The warmth, the moonlight, and the gentle wash of the surf proved a most pleasant and relaxing ensemble. A deep breath and he closed his eyes, letting the sea take possession of his senses. He drifted there, half-aware, for a long while, feeling rather than seeing the ocean and the gibbous moon. A sudden movement, an unidentified sound, brought him back. He opened his eyes and a terrifying tsunami of cognitive dissonance flooded him.

Mix was disoriented and dizzy, but the reason wasn't immediately obvious. The sea was still there, as were the moon and the beach. Something had changed, though: he could sense it. He turned back toward the condo; it wasn't there. In its place was a towering wooden roller coaster. The Melon Island Screamer, to be precise. He walked toward it as though in a dream. The sand crunched and slid convincingly under his feet. He couldn't remember programming that particular detail into the module. The smell of fish and seaweed was still strong in his nostrils, but that could be a reflected memory. Was he still in Vspace? Was he somehow actually on Melon Island (over a thousand miles away and long since closed)? Was he dreaming?

It abruptly, violently, occurred to him that he might not be equipped to tell the difference any longer. He crouched, wild-eyed, for no reason, suddenly feeling hunted and desperately seeking refuge from encroaching insanity. Dawn was breaking off to the east; an early-rising seagull wheeled over his head, chattering.

He crept toward the wooden behemoth. He could see the white paint peeling and flaking on the lower sections of the superstructure. The realism was almost too much for him to bear, but even under that enormous psychic strain some part of Mix was calculating polygons and ray-tracing angles, and marveling at the rendered detail. It was pretty impressive for a simulation, if that's what it was.

He wandered the park for a good three-quarters of an hour, touching, smelling, and listening. In the end, he had no real option but to admit to himself that it really was Melon Island. The fact that this was physically impossible he decided he would deal with later. For now he needed to sit down. There should be that fountain at the center of the park with stone benches surrounding it. He loved sitting there as a child, watching the water cascade into foam.

The benches and fountain were just where they were supposed to be. He sat on the cool stone and smelled the water swirling around him. He was a good programmer, but he wasn't this good. No one was. This had to be real. But how could it possibly be real? He had driven over two hours to the coast, but that coast and the one where the real Melon Island was located were over a thousand miles apart. There was simply no way to work this out logically. Something he had experienced in the past day or two had been false. That was the only explanation that would allow him to remain sane, if sanity was even an option at this juncture.

Mix was getting hungry. He wondered if the funnel cake booth was open yet. As he stood up to go investigate, he glanced at the fountain centerpiece, a trio of stylized water-spitting dolphins. The base of the sculpture was a moss-encrusted series of granite blocks fitted so tightly together that no seams were visible. Except that there was a visible grout line around one of them. Odd. That must have been the result of some repair or construction since he'd last been here. Ironically, it was in exactly the same location and orientation as his 'secret' bunker entrance in the module. A tiny nagging voice he'd been suppressing for some time now suddenly became a shout he could no longer ignore.

Hesitantly Mix lowered one foot, then the other, into the shallow pool. He waded to the fountain and reached out to touch one of the blocks. The stone was hard, cold, and slimy. He slid his hand around to the portal block and held it there for a second. It passed through the seemingly solid rock as though it were thin gauze. Heaving a sigh, Mix swung himself into the hidden compartment. He found a keyboard and pressed the emergency exit buttons. Nothing happened. He pushed all the keys, with equal effect. Puzzled, he crawled back out and waded across the pool to the promenade. He made his way to the beach and walked along it for a while, pondering this freakish turn of events.

When he reached the path leading back up to his condo he took it. The building was there now; Melon Island was not. It was becoming increasingly apparent to Mix that he was going crazy and the VR rig was the cause. Had it given him some sort of brain damage?

He stayed there for three days, walking along the beach in the morning and evening. Melon Island did not reappear. On the way home he had a waking vision that very nearly resulted in an accident. It was filled with demon heads sprouting from roadside objects, but in a less realistic way than the VR rig generated, making it easier to distinguish them. It did not render them less startling or distracting, however. Mix pulled over at a rest area to let the phantasms spend themselves. He now had a new worry: could he trust himself to drive safely any longer?

He made it home, finally. The demon heads did not haunt him overtly for the rest of the journey, but he imagined he saw them innumerable times, in every roadside object and passing cloud. He sat in the bathtub that evening and stared at his wrists, fantasizing what it would be like to slit them and watch the warm red blood seep into the foam that swirled around him. Mix sloshed the water with his knees until the bubbles grew larger. One rose up out of the lather and floated past his face: a demon head grinned back at him. He stared at it in revulsion and leapt out of the tub when he realized the grotesque visage he beheld was his own reflection.

Mix found himself having to come to terms with the deep fear he now harbored of the VR rig. At length he decided to face the beast once again with the hope of conquering it and thus regaining control over his mental faculties. The problem had evolved beyond the technical and spilled over into the realm of psychopathology, a realm totally unfamiliar to Mix. He had no idea how to navigate here, other than by the seat of his pants.

He modified the code so that he could exit the program a dozen different ways, and made certain that no wires or plugs could experience motion-induced disconnection. As he sat in the rig mentally preparing himself, Mix wondered again about the odd coincidences he'd experienced in the simulation. Had he really somehow sabotaged his own project without his conscious knowledge? The evidence was strong in favor of that theory, but he just couldn't bring himself to accept it. Why would he do such a thing? He loved this project. He thought it was a great idea, and that it might even eventually make him rich. That prospect seemed dim now.

The VR engine flickered into life. Mix plunged straight into the Melon Island module, eying everything warily, regarding each piece of the environment as a potential enemy combatant. He no longer thought of this place as his creation, his child. It was now quite definitely a hostile alien landscape, to be explored with due caution, weapon drawn. This was not simply a metaphor: Mix had grabbed one of the hardcore military gun models from his arcade sub-module and programmed it to trigger a memory dump for a certain radius around the coordinates of the ray-traced impact point of the projectile, which he'd made appear similar to the 'photon torpedo' of the old *Star Trek* series. He wasn't taking any flak from the demon heads this time. The memory dump would cause the wireframe models to display as their hexadecimal components and thus render them nonfunctional as manipulable objects in the simulation.

He walked the length of the fully-rendered portion of Melon Island without encountering anything untoward. He sat at the fountain, rode the rides, shot things up in the arcade: nothing happened. No demon heads, no strange voices, nothing. Discouraged but secretly hopeful, he exited the program, but not before blasting a few innocent landscape features just to test the gun's effectiveness. The resulting devastation was deeply and strangely satisfying. It occurred to him that now would be a good time to continue diagnosing the original network intrusion incident.

After a few minutes he concluded that he might not be able to get any useful information from his intrusion detection system logs after all, because the settings were obviously hosed. All external network traffic stopped getting recorded shortly *before* the first intrusion incident should have taken place, which really made no sense because he had seen the intrusion alarm pop up while he was in Vspace that day and traced it back to an obviously compromised box in Southeast Asia. Mix sighed heavily as he realized this was not going to get him any closer to identifying the mystery attacker. He switched over to the security event logs for the firewall, expecting them to be essentially blank. They were instead filled with hundreds of probes and expressly targeted custom packets that hallmarked a sophisticated attacker. Their origin IP address was 127.0.0.1.

Mix sat and stared at the screen for quite a while. This had to be a mistake, of course: no one could have sent those attacks from the local loop without direct access to his system. He spent the rest of the evening mapping out each hostile action in detail. The sequence matched the events he had experienced in Vspace perfectly. It just wasn't possible. The attacker must have figured out some way of hiding his tracks that Mix had never before encountered. A zero-day, in other words. How he could have accomplished this was a puzzle. It meant he had somehow either modified the logs after the fact—and in this case why not just delete them altogether—or talked the log daemon into replacing the attacker's IP address with the machine's own.

On a hunch, he pulled down all of his system configuration files and went over them, one by one. None of them reported being modified recently, although not even file modification dates were necessarily trustworthy under these circumstances. Mix put all of the relevant evidence up in windows side-by-side on his two monitors and stared at them until an unmistakable correlation became apparent. Every attack could be matched to corresponding inputs from a particular hardware driver: the biofeedback headset. That eight-hundred-pound gorilla suddenly reared up, beat its chest, and roared. There was no intruder: *he* was the attacker, via his own brainwaves.

It took quite a while for this to sink in totally. He had created these monsters in his own mind; somehow those creations had been harvested from his thoughts and encoded into the module. There were many things deeply troubling about this theory, aside from the technical aspects, one of which was that the demons were really not at all familiar to him. They were nothing he had seen before, or even dreamt of, unless it was in passing in some mostly-forgotten video game. Nor was he aware of harboring any prior self-loathing or self-destructive urges.

There was something nagging him about the timing of the incidents, too. He created a timeline and stared at it. The inflection point—where all the weirdness started—was the key. Since there was not in fact a network intrusion involved, there had to be some other precipitating event. Mix searched his logs over and again, looking for anything that could possibly have triggered that chain of actions. He was deep in concentration when his cell warbled the theme song to "Lost in Space." He ignored it and let it go to voice mail. He was not going to be distracted until he figured this thing out.

Mix wandered over to the VR chair and stared at that for a while, as a change of pace. He played with wires, pushed buttons on the keyboard, and finally ran some diagnostics. Suddenly he noticed that the data feed log for the headset had zero content all the way back to a certain date that was very near his magic inflection point. Odd. He opened up the entire archive and scrolled through it. There was a flurry of data input for a few minutes that, he noticed comparing logs, corresponded with a lot of CPU activity: more than he would expect for simply collecting serial data, parsing it, and dropping it into the database.

That evening, he decided to take a break from the VR incident and do some housework. He had a stack of boxes to go through that his parents had insisted he take away before they threw them out. There were a lot of memories from his childhood and teen years in there. Mix wasn't certain if he wanted to keep any of this stuff, but he felt obligated to rummage through it nonetheless.

He found some yearbooks, programs from the plays and concerts he was in, and even his old art portfolio. There was a trip. He'd gone through so many phases: pencil, pen and ink, pastels, watercolors, acrylics…Mix smiled as he found a thick manila envelope with the art for a Halloween door contest entry he and Rane had made together for their dorm in college. He leafed through the drawings until one stopped him cold. It was the demon head from his VR module, in exquisitely faithful detail. It was drawn by Rane. With an icy jolt, Mix realized that the headset stopped collecting data right after Rane had tried out the rig.

Rane did not respond to his page, so Mix called: voice mail. He phoned Rane's mom. She hadn't heard from him in a few days. Mix tried several of their mutual friends. No one had seen him for at least forty-eight hours. He wasn't entirely sure why, but Mix had a deep need to confront Rane in person with the demon images. He jumped in the car and started hitting every spot he thought Rane might be.

At midnight, his need for sleep began to overtake his desire to find and question his friend. Mix reluctantly headed home, hoping he could actually get to sleep once there. On the way, he passed the little mini-airfield where he and Rane flew their RC planes. There was a familiar-looking car in the parking lot. He pulled up: it was quite definitely Rane's. Mix got out and peered through the windows with some trepidation. It was unoccupied. He searched the area, but there was no sign of Rane.

He tried the car door, which proved to be unlocked. In the front passenger seat there was an envelope with one word on it, apparently written in blood: "Mix." Mix sat in the seat and folded back the unsealed flap with trembling hands. Inside was a crude map of something that he almost recognized. He turned it this way and that until suddenly it clicked: Melon Island. His head started spinning; he leaned back against the headrest and closed his eyes. The demon heads swirled around him, taunting. He remembered the phone call he'd ignored and checked the caller ID: Rane. No message.

When he finally felt recovered enough, Mix got out of Rane's car and walked over to his own. He drove to the exit of the lot, but found that someone had padlocked the gate. He was trapped. There were no cell towers way out here, either, so he'd have to hoof it to someplace where his phone worked. He sighed and started to walk the fence line, hoping to crawl over somewhere. About a hundred yards from the gate there was an odd trail he'd never noticed before that veered off to the right into the woods. Maybe there was a pocket of cell coverage in that direction. It was worth a shot, anyway.

The woods weren't particularly thick or tangled, but in the darkness they still seemed to be closing in on him. *Given my current mental state, that's hardly surprising.* A mist had arisen from somewhere, as well, and this added to the otherworldly atmosphere. He was jumping at every little sound now, real or imagined. Still no bars. He thought about turning around when a clearing appeared in the distance. He almost sprinted for it.

It was all wrong. The soil in the area was a rocky loam, but this clearing was composed of fine white sand. Must be making a volleyball court or something. He walked on a little further and the wind shifted. He swore he could smell salt. Suddenly an owl flew across his path and brushed his face. Mix instinctively slapped at it and made a glancing contact. The owl screamed in response, but it was not the screech of an owl: it was the cackle of a laughing gull. He stopped dead in his tracks.

There in the distance, was a grand painted archway emblazoned with the colorful name "Melon Island." He jolted himself around to look back from where he'd come. The woods had vanished. There was only a line of brushy scrub there now. Mix stood for a moment, considering his options. He finally shrugged and started walking toward the amusement park grounds. "So," he said aloud as he trudged through the sand, "I'm officially insane. I always wondered what that would feel like. Not a lot different, really, except I see entire landscapes that can't possibly be there. The flying monkeys should be along any minute now."

No flying monkeys appeared, but caramel apples did. They were in a booth just inside the park entrance. He bought one and ate it. The caramel was warm and runny. For a figment of his imagination it tasted pretty good. He even dribbled some fictitious caramel onto his shirt; watched it hit the fabric, spread, and congeal. If he was going to live an insane life, he figured he could at least enjoy it. He wandered for a while, taking in the various textures, surfaces, odors, and visuals. They were all perfectly normal and as expected. At least his insanity was internally consistent.

Finally, he reached the fountain. He sat on one side of the round concrete bench that encircled it and splashed his hand in the water. It was much more realistic water than his VR rig generated. He wondered idly what algorithm was being used and felt a pang of anger that his insanity had a better frame rate and more sophisticated programming than his VR module. If only he could download this stuff directly from his imagination to the code base. He wondered if being insane would affect his programming skills. Probably not.

He got up and began to circle around the fountain when he noticed someone sitting on the other side. Mix instantly had a peculiar warning feeling about getting any closer, but decided that insane people don't care about things like premonition. He walked over and realized that it was, inevitably, Rane. Well, he *had* been looking for him. Nice of his insanity to accommodate, at least.

As he approached, imaginary Rane stood up to greet him.

"Looks a little better in real life, doesn't it, bro?"

"Hi, Rane. *Is* this real life?"

"Sure. What else could it be? It's not one of your simulations."

"Not a computer simulation, no. But it is a simulation from my mind."

"Funny, that's the sort of thing you'd think I'd notice."

"Since you're part of the simulation, I don't think you would."

"One of us is the Red King, then. Is that what you're saying?"

"No, I'm quite definitely the Red King here. Except I'm not dreaming."

"What are you, then?"

"Bat shit crazy."

"So that demotes me from a friend appearing in your dream to a mere manifestation in some insane hallucination. Am I assessing the situation accurately?"

"If you're a manifestation of my insanity, does it matter?"

"Deep. Depressing. Well, since we're here, let's hit the rides. Remember the old mine train? It's still running."

"The old mine train closed down years ago. So did the whole park, in fact."

"Then it's reopened. I just saw it a few minutes ago. Let's check it out."

Mix looked up at the night sky full of brilliant stars and shrugged. "Okay, I'm in."

They rode everything in the park except the Ferris wheel, which they were saving for last. Sitting on a bench across from it, eating cotton candy, Mix felt the warm salt air flowing through his hair and closed his eyes.

"Rane, do you think there's a God?"

Rane munched on his confectionary for a few moments.

"You mean one who exists independently of human cranial activity? Probably not."

"So you think man created God, rather than the other way around?"

"I think they were both involved in the act of creation."

"How would that work?"

"I think the essence of God is woven into the fabric of the universe, but it requires sentience to tease it out, as it were."

"In other words, God only exists for creatures to which God would make any difference."

"That's one way to put it. Since each person's 'brainwaves,' if you will, call God into being, God is never exactly the same for any two people because no two people have identical thought processes."

"Isn't that the same thing as saying that no two people perceive a statically-defined God in the same way?"

"Yes and no. What it really means is that divinity and the intellect are inextricably and somewhat chaotically intertwined. Even God is subject to entropy."

"I never really considered the relationship between thermodynamics and the Almighty before. Interesting."

"Well, I think it's Ferris wheel time." Rane stood up and strolled over to the loading ramp. He sat down in a car with a dancing number three painted on it and closed the door behind him.

"What, no room for me?" asked Mix, puzzled.

"Not this time. God wants to see me alone. I'll check you soon. Bye."

With that, the Ferris wheel leapt into creaky motion and Mix watched as Rane circled to the apex, eyes closed serenely. Somehow he knew that when the car came back around, his friend would not be in it.

Mix wandered along the deserted beach for hours. At length, he encountered a long jetty and walked all the way out to the end. He suddenly felt overwhelmed by sadness and sat down on the rocks to cry. He sobbed so hard he had increasing difficulty breathing, and then everything went dark.

When he opened his eyes, the world had changed dramatically. He was in a hospital bed. His mother was there, watching him with red, puffy eyes. She was holding his hand. "Mix," she sobbed, "we thought we'd lost you."

He was confused and tore the oxygen mask off his face. "What do you mean, 'lost me?' How did I get here? Where, for that matter, is 'here?'

"You're in Sisters of Mercy. A security guard found you on the edge of a parking lot, unconscious and barely breathing. They brought you here and you've been in a coma for three days. The doctor said it looked like a drug overdose, but they couldn't find any drugs in your system."

"I don't take drugs."

"I know that honey, but that seemed like the most reasonable explanation. Then we thought you may have had a heart attack or a stroke, but you don't have signs of either of those, either."

"I didn't have a stroke, mom. I went crazy."

"Well, I'm glad you're not crazy anymore."

"I wouldn't bet on that."

The next day they let him watch television. There was a news story about the body of a young man that washed ashore in a popular east coast beach town, across the bay from the old abandoned Melon Island resort. It was Rane. Mix felt empty, sad, but strangely at peace with the tragedy, as though he had already done his grieving beforehand.

Two days later they were ready to discharge Mix. His mom brought over a paper sack and handed it to him.

"What's this?" he asked.

"The clothes you were wearing when they brought you in. I took them home to wash them."

"Were they that dirty?"

"The pants were pretty grimy. The shirt had a big stain on it: streaks of brown sugar or something. Where did that happen?"

Mix stared at his lap for a moment, and then shrugged.

"On Melon Island."

Mom thought for a minute. "The amusement park? On the east coast? Didn't they close that down?"

"Yes."

"When were you there?"

"Just before I got brought in here."

"How is that possible?"

"It isn't."

"I... I don't understand."

"Neither do I. It has to do with God and thermodynamics, apparently."

"You just sit here and rest, honey. I'll be right back."

He knew she was going to tell the doctor that he needed to be psychiatrically evaluated. He put on his clothes and slipped off down the hall in the opposite direction. Mix had a sudden urge to ride the Ferris wheel.

Witchy Man, Woman Skin

Anna Yeatts

The Witchy Man's ancient rocker creaked beneath the pin oak trees. The rocker, so old it had glossed over like pitch, was dark as the Witchy Man's hooded eyes, and its creaking echoed like a second heartbeat in Froggy's scrawny little girl chest.

Always the rocking. Back and forth, dusk 'til dawn, until Froggy thought she'd scream and pull her hair out in great clumps.

Thunderclouds rolled in from the east, low grumbly things hunched over the marsh, pushing the waterbirds down into their nests and rippling the reedy water into dark folds.

The Witchy Man's faded black clothing flapped in the rising wind, his head leaned forward like a dog scenting for the fox. The same sulfur-bitten wind carried the creaking to where Froggy clung to the pin oak's high branches. Sweat beaded her upper lip, but she caught it with her tongue before it could fall and sucked the salty bead into her mouth.

Across the clearing, the underbrush rustled. The rabbit tobacco swayed, white blooms parting then swishing back as the snake slid out. His tail churned up dust before he disappeared beneath the pin oak.

The heavy ripeness of the air nudged Froggy. She shinnied down to a lower branch. Her bare arms and legs were nut-brown, scabbed and gnarled as the tree trunk itself.

With his face withered and dried until his eyes'd disappeared into the creases, the Witchy Man stared out toward the place where the hardwoods thinned into the marsh. His shriveled tongue touched the corner of his mouth.

Froggy wanted to slink away and hide.

But there was only the snake and the marsh. The pin oaks atop the hill, the scrublands, and the fistful of hardwoods.

And the old Witchy Man with his sun-faded black clothes, and that rocker of his, always a rocking.

The snake twined about the Witchy Man's ankle. It lifted its flattened head and flicked its tongue at her. "I see you, girl," the snake said. "Can't hide from the Witchy Man."

"Not hiding when I'm not trying." Froggy kicked her feet and jumped down out of the pin oak tree. Her hair fell over her face in lumpy tangles that smelled of clay and sweat and scalp.

"Witchy Man be wanting," the snake said.

The Witchy Man's tongue brushed his upper lip. The back of Froggy's knees tightened. One day, she'd be free of this, she told herself. One day, she'd find a way.

The snake wound up the Witchy Man's thigh, curving between those stick-thin fingers.

"Witchy Man don't like your games, girl," the snake said.

Froggy imagined the snake's neck between her fists. One thick snap of his back. That's all it'd take.

The Witchy Man's lash came from nowhere. No sound. No warning. Conjured out of the air itself, it caught her across the shoulder blades. Froggy pitched forward, her back filling with heat. The second strike took the back of her thighs.

She fought the tears. Squeezed her eyelids together and sucked in the choking marsh air.

And always the hateful rocker in front of her, creak-creaking. Waiting for her to break, flattening her into the dirt.

She held out long as she could. The third lash struck her mouth, below her nose, and fat teardrops spattered onto the dirt.

The creak-creaking stopped. The Witchy Man had turned. He was looking at Froggy. Thunderclouds boiled over the treetops, stinger winds whipping the hair 'round her neck. She squeezed herself tight, wishing she could fold away entirely. The Witchy Man knelt in front of Froggy. He held her by her upper arms and she shuddered.

The snake coiled 'round her bent knees. "Lift your eyes, girl."

She did as told.

The Witchy Man's breath was sweet, like honeysuckle in the spring, but there was a wrongness to it. A bloated corpse tucked 'neath the brambles where nobody could reach it.

Froggy made herself still when the Witchy Man lapped up her tears.

When he suckled the saltiness from the corners of her eyes, her breath came in shreds. But still she didn't move.

The lash struck the back of her neck. Fresh tears made the Witchy Man sigh. Thunder rumbled, and she tasted lightning on the back of her tongue, prickly and thick. *No-no,* her heartbeats thumped out, *no-no, old Witchy Man.*

He licked her eyelids, his tongue an old slug sliding across her skin. The hair on Froggy's neck stood up and her whole body tingled from tip to toe.

A fork of lightning speared overhead. Froggy shoved her hand into the Witchy Man's mouth. His teeth scraped her fingers. She grabbed a hold of his wrinkled tongue, dug in her nails.

The smell of scorched earth was bitter in her nose. From deep in his creased eye-sockets, Froggy saw her own death looking back, her flesh pulped from her hide easy as fruit from a berry. She yanked all the harder.

The winds howled. The snake hissed underfoot. Froggy shoved away from the Witchy Man, her hand and face sticky with his saliva. She fled through the fat spatters of rain with her rabbit-racing heart trying to climb out through her ribs.

But the Witchy Man's power was thick, thick as a fallen log flattening Froggy to the ground. Her knees wanted to buckle and her spine cried to snap.

Froggy ran, slip-sliding through the brush and brambles, farther than she'd ever gone before. Far enough that she couldn't feel the pressing silence of the Witchy Man no more. Only the slippery remembrance of his tongue under her nails.

She collapsed under a stand of longleaf pines, digging in

pillbug-tight among the roots. Rivulets of rainwater turned into fat runnels, all siphoned into her little earthen nest. A rounded surface shifted in the mud beneath her. She sat up and dug around her knees, muddy pools slurping wider and wider. Froggy tugged loose a skin rolled tight and fastened with rawhide strips.

The strips were old and knotted, but with teeth and nails, Froggy worked them loose. Her belly griped at her to hurry, the Witchy Man would see, but her legs were tired of running. With shaking hands, she unrolled the skin, flattening and setting it to rights.

She rocked back onto her heels, lightning cracking overhead.

The skin made a woman.

There was no mistaking the sunken curves, the hollowed belly, the flattened breasts. A full-sized woman, skin nut-brown as Froggy's own, but sliced open from chin to belly in a jagged strip.

She touched the sunken eyelids with their curling lashes. Her own eyes itched for her to do the same.

The woman's lips were thick, chewed upon, tough. Bowed down at the sides like they had known sorrow.

A chill wind moaned through the pines. Froggy shivered. She ran her palms over the woman skin, drinking in the feel of another like herself.

Now it wasn't just the snake and the old Witchy Man. But Froggy and the woman skin, too.

Froggy grinned 'til the corners of her mouth about split. She leaned her head against her own shoulder, rocking on her heels.

Froggy wrapped her hand around the woman skin's wrist, liking the way the skin felt against the circle of her palm.

But the woman skin's head didn't lay right. It had a lump above the left ear, knotted and wrong looking.

Careful-like, Froggy lifted the skin and wriggled her hand inside.

The voice itched like a mosquito inside her ears.

I's a... I's a... I's a...

Froggy snatched her hand out, the skin folds slapping against one another.

"Who you be?" Froggy croaked out.

The woman skin didn't answer, but Froggy could feel those lips straining to speak.

Froggy slid her fingers into the woman skin's empty throat. The mosquito words lit up her mind.

I's a... I's a...

A fat bloom of aching lit up inside Froggy's head.

I's a... I's a...

The woman's words buzzed over and over in a loop, like she couldn't jump over that aching to reach the thought on the other side.

Froggy squeezed her eyes together against the blinding pain. Her fingers wrapped around the lump in the woman skin's head, a tough ball that felt like rock, only it didn't.

Froggy tugged. The lump wiggled.

I's a... I's a... I's a... I's—

Words skittering, the woman's face wrenched up on one side like she was screaming. Froggy twisted back and forth, working at the lump until it started to give. The woman's mouth split open showing a pink tongue. Froggy yanked. With a sickly rip, the lump tore loose. The ache in Froggy's head disappeared.

I's a... lost.

Froggy slid the lump free. The voice faded.

The color of old bone, the bulging growth was like nothing she'd ever seen before, fat ropey tentacles reaching off into nowhere like a giant spider living in the woman skin's head.

Froggy pitched the lump into the pines, far as she could throw it.

The cold wind walked icicle feet up Froggy's spine, made her rain-spattered flesh shake. The Witchy Man's silence settled heavy in her lungs. Froggy lifted her chin, eyes sharp as flint. "I know you done found me." She bared her teeth. "But I come back when I wants to. Not before. Not after."

The wind blew colder, deeper into her bones, until Froggy's teeth chattered. She crawled deeper into the grove, but these were just bitty pines, not the great old ones with deep nests of fallen needles at their roots.

His anger burned like bitter snow on her bare skin.

"I said, you not making me!" Snatching up the woman skin, Froggy wrapped it round her scrawny self. She huddled in the pines. "Go way, old Witchy Man."

The woman skin held her tight. The storm hissed and spat and sputtered. But Froggy leaned her forehead into the earthen blanket of the woman skin's neck. "We even now, whoever you may be."

Froggy's breathing slipped and slid, her scrawny self sinking into that warm woman skin. Soft hands nudged her down into a tight little ball. Froggy hugged her arms about her scrawny chest, yawning so hard her jaws cracked. The woman skin wrapped her tight, with its humming voice vibrating through her.

I's a lost... lost my baby...

"Never seen no babies 'round," Froggy said. Warm as a cocoon, she wanted only to sleep now. But the skin was holding her tighter, her elbows digging painfully into her hips.

Froggy tried to open her eyes, but there was only darkness. Wet rasping darkness and nowhere to move.

You's a lost too...

The voice moved into her head, painting pictures behind her eyes.

The woman pressed her palms over her swollen belly. Already, her baby was pushing to get out, hands and feet stretching her skin parchment-thin, palms and heels ready and reaching for the bright world, not knowing that only death waited outside.

She called out to the Witchy Man up top of the hill. "Look down here," the words burned like poison in her heart but she didn't have any more choices. "I done brought your baby."

It was the snake between her feet who answered. "I'm a listening. What you want of the Witchy Man?"

"Witchy Man's baby going to die," she said.

The snake chuffed, his scales tickling past her ankles.

"Baby's safe," the snake said. "I see it swimming round in that great belly of yours, a froggy I could swallow in one gulp. It's you needs saving."

Those words climbed right up the woman's spine and curled into the base of her skull, wrapped round the knot bulging into her brain that was march-stepping her to her grave just as fast as it could.

"Can you?" She kept her eyes on the old Witchy Man. "Take the knot out?"

"No," the snake said. "But you already knew that."

And she knew it was true, just the way she knew her baby didn't have any choices either. Her fingers dug tight into her belly, her throat dry as ashes.

"Save the babe." Her voice was no more than a whisper.

Up top, the Witchy Man's black clothing rippled, face upturned into the wind.

The woman shuddered. Maybe he smelled death a coming for her.

The knot's fat roots reached deep into her skull, sucking her dry. Skinny fists pounded her insides, trying to rip her apart. She licked her chapped lips. Her eyes were heavy.

"Even the Witchy Man has to care for his own blood," the woman said.

The Witchy Man stopped his rocking.

Silence washed through the marsh and the pines and the loblolly trees, clamping down the bird calls and the clicking cicadas, hushing the woman's whimpers; silence unrolling in front of the Witchy Man like a carpet of his own making. Even the snake stilled, hunching lower into the road dust, tongue flicking.

Sweat pooled beneath her swollen breasts, knees tucked up either side of her great heaving belly.

Tumor grasping, baby fighting.

The woman covered her face with dirt streaked arms. But she couldn't hide from the Witchy Man. Her baby kicked and thrashed, fighting to stay inside a little longer. The snake popped open its jaws. The woman screamed as white hot needles unsewed her belly and the old Witchy Man took his baby right out of her.

"I kill you," Froggy screamed. In the sticky darkness, she curled tight, cradling her belly. The woman skin squeezed so tight she couldn't breath.

I found you...

Froggy lurched, shoving against the taut arc of the woman's swollen belly. The skin stretched and stretched until it should have burst. A sour taste slunk up Froggy's throat, but she swallowed it down.

Hush, baby...

The woman skin was pleading with her. But Froggy's heartbeat came in short knocks, and the only fear she cared about was her own.

Inside the massive belly, her arms and legs thrashed.

Skin hands slapped the belly's outside, sliding off like dead things.

You killing us both...

Froggy clawed with her nails.

He promise to keep you safe...

Feeling no stronger than a mewling kit, Froggy pushed feebly at the woman skin. The skin tightened. Froggy sucked in tiny mouthfuls of dank air.

Snake done found us... Tell it to leave us be...

Froggy felt the woman skin try to drag them backward, but Froggy's weight was too much.

"Witchy Man wants his girl," the snake said.

"Here," Froggy cried. "I's in here."

You belong with me...

The woman skin writhed. The snake hissed. The woman skin shrieked inside Froggy's mind.

When fangs broke through the woman skin, Froggy grabbed a hold and ripped with both hands. She shoved her head through the gash and elbowed her way into the night air, kicking and churning and fighting.

Froggy's back legs slid loose. The woman skin collapsed behind her. But the voice echoed in her ears like a clap of thunder.

Froggy half crawled, half ran, not looking back.

Not stopping until she heard the creaking of the Witchy Man's rocker.

The sulfur breezes from the marsh made the back of her

throat sour. Froggy sucked in a lungful and spat it out again.

Weeds rustled. The snake slid into the moonlit clearing. "Thank the Witchy Man right, girl. He done saved you twice now."

The snake slithered closer, forcing her towards the Witchy Man, his chair creak-creaking.

"Do it," the snake said. "Else I put you back where I found you."

Mouth dry as cotton, she forced herself to pick up her foot, set it down, one then the other. Her whole body coiled tight, waiting for the lash.

Stuck between the snake and the lash, the old Witchy Man and the woman skin who claimed her.

The scent of rain lay heavy on the back of Froggy's tongue so she wanted to lick it from the air. Like the Witchy Man did to her tears.

But always that burning in her veins, her heartbeat tapping out its *no-no, no-no, no-no* in her ears.

"Leave me be," Froggy said. "I got no more tears for you."

The Witchy Man didn't stop his rocking but his spine straightened against the back slats. The snake's tail whipped sideways in the mud.

"Always more tears for the Witchy Man," the snake said.

"Not mine," Froggy said. "Not when he can't make me."

The lash cracked out of thin air, catching Froggy across the forehead. She wanted to yell out. The tears shoved against her eyelids but she shoved right back.

Her voice shook but she ground out the words. "I'm part Witchy Man just like him."

The rocker stopped its creaking. The old Witchy Man was staring at Froggy now, his eyes boring straight into her gullet.

Froggy held her ground. "I brought the woman skin to life. She showed me her secrets. Your secrets."

The snake wriggled between them lightning fast. Froggy stomped onto the snake's belly. Fangs slashed for her calf. But Froggy squatted, wrapped both hands tight around that snake's old neck, looked him in the eyes and wrung its neck.

"Told you, I did," Froggy said.

She flung the snake's body at the Witchy Man, hard as she could.

His silence poured back, but Froggy wouldn't bow her back. She hightailed it back the way she'd come, back toward the stand of pines.

The woman skin frightened her near as much as the Witchy Man. But sometimes the fox needed a boar to bring down the hound.

Vacant eyes staring upward, the woman skin lay with her belly shredded open. Froggy dropped to her knees. She put her palm on that torn up belly. The belly she'd lived in twice now.

"Mama?" she asked, her throat dry as dust. "It's me, Froggy, your baby."

The woman skin shuddered.

Froggy yanked out a great clump of her hair. She didn't know if her charm would work but it felt right. She scooped up a handful of mud and spit in it. Balling the hair and the mud and the saliva all together, she opened the woman skin's chest and put the fist-sized lump where she thought the heart should go.

She closed the skin up and rocked back on her heels.

"You come on back now," Froggy said.

Groaning, the woman skin shivered. Froggy scuttled away and wrapped her scrawny arms 'round a pine lest she get sucked in again.

Wide-eyed, the woman skin looked ready to gobble Froggy up.

Froggy snatched a fallen branch, sticky with sap, thick as her wrist.

The woman skin looked down at the ripples of sagging skin falling around her naked hips. She threw back her head and opened her mouth, sucked in a lungful of silent screams and let 'em out again. She slapped her chest and belly and thighs with boneless limbs then the ground she was laying on.

"No time for that." Froggy held tight to her stick as she picked up the woman skin. "He a coming."

The Witchy Man's silence washed over the forest. Drove the insects to ground. Even pushed the thrum of Froggy's own heart down too deep in her belly for her to hear. He stepped into the grove and the pine trees stood a little smaller. The grasses withered on the stalks and the moonlight darkened.

Froggy waited, clutching the woman skin. The Witchy Man grabbed a hold of Froggy's arms and lifted her up, the woman skin trapped between them.

Froggy's insides quaked. She shoved the woman skin against the Witchy Man's chest. Flattened arms clung tight around the Witchy Man's ribcage. The woman skin's head lolled back to watch him with sunken eyes. The woman skin's empty lips twisted open, half smiling, half sneering.

The Witchy Man dropped Froggy. The woman skin had opened herself wide, the same way she'd done to Froggy, and now she was trying to wrap her great sliced open belly around the Witchy Man.

But the Witchy Man opened his shriveled mouth and the cold silence rushed out, peeling the woman skin off of him. He tossed the woman skin down, no more than a gutted earthworm wallowing in the dirt.

Turning to Froggy, the Witchy Man lifted both hands, palms flat to the ground. The solitude rippled out, threatening to shake them both apart.

Froggy struggled to her feet.

The Witchy Man opened his mouth. His cracked lips were twisted tight, his tongue a shriveled black slug lashing the cold into suffocating waves.

A glint in his eyes as he smiled and the breath rushing out of his chest like bellows. That power of his came a tumbling. Shoving. Making way.

The ground rumbled. Living trunks shuddered and groaned. Branches splintered, the air thick with pine dust.

His silence forced Froggy inward on herself. Her flesh cried to slide off her bones, her body crumbling.

The woman skin's fingers slid into Froggy's, twining up her wrist, reaching. Froggy pulled the skin overtop of herself, huddling underneath.

The woman skin lay open over her back. Not swallowing. Not taking.

Just protecting.

Froggy shoved her arm into the woman skin's chest, wriggled her fingers down the empty arm. Her head lit up with her mama's voice.

Save my girl... save my girl...

Froggy worked her other arm into the chest, putting the skin on like a coat while the sawdust-filled air settled.

Witchy Man got to pay the price...

Froggy wriggled in one leg. Then the other. She pulled the woman skin's head overtop her own, blinked open those long-lashed eyes, chewed on the sorrow worn lips.

'Fore you even drew breath... didn't have no choices but wrong choices...

"Reckon I can understand that," Froggy said.

The woman skin sagged off Froggy's smaller body. She clutched the rolls of extra skin, pulled tight as she could in her arms, and went to make her reckonings.

He waited for her in the clearing he'd made. Upturned pine roots clawed out of the earth like the lump Froggy had ripped from her mama's head.

Froggy and the woman skin and the Witchy Man, all

together and no one else.

Silence poured from the Witchy Man, thick as clotted blood.

Can't kill what's already dead, child...

Froggy smiled inside the woman skin. The woman skin tightened around her.

He owe you a price...

The nut-brown skin merged with Froggy's own, the pink weals left by the lashes fading into pale ghosts. Her muscles filled beneath the newly taut skin that wasn't her own.

As do I...

But it was Froggy's skin now.

Do I... I... I...

The voice slid deeper into her mind until Froggy's thoughts swallowed those up too.

The old Witchy Man sunk to his knees. His skin was ashen, eyes sunken deep into his hollowed skull.

"Cry my tears," Froggy said.

But the old Witchy Man only stared out toward the marsh.

"I'm a giving you a chance."

His thin lips twisted.

Froggy wrapped her fist in the Witchy Man's hair. "Lift your face."

A dry rustle, the rattle of autumn leaves tumbling over stones. The old Witchy Man was laughing.

But he lifted his chin.

Froggy pried open the wrinkled lips. Dug her hand into his mouth until the Witchy Man's laughing turned into choking.

Froggy yanked. She opened her fist and looked at the blackened tongue on her blood slicked palm.

The scent of honeysuckle filled the air, pure and sweet.

She tossed the tongue into the brush.

His eyes were still laughing when Froggy took hold of his head. Her fingernails dug in tight under his chin.

In silence, she tore his head from his shoulders.

His withered body collapsed into the dust, already breaking into ash as the marsh winds came to claim him.

Froggy used her nails to peel back the soft folds of her belly. The empty softness of her insides welcomed the old Witchy Man's gnarled head before she pushed the skin closed again. She winced as the wound closed itself back up, a bright pink scar like the welt from a lash running down her belly.

Froggy's bloated belly swayed uncomfortably as she walked. The Witchy Man's power already seeped through her body, an alive feeling like the smell of mint crushed underfoot on a summer morning.

Under the pin oak's sprawling branches, the old black rocker sat motionless.

Froggy eased into the rocker and stared out to where the hardwoods thinned into the marsh. She began to rock, the creak-creaking of the rocker gentle as a mama's crooning.

Where Sheep Have Fangs When You Count Them

Gerri Leen

Eris walks the night, spreading discord in her wake. She is the goddess of unease, of quick slaps and hurtful words, of nightmares with no sense that leave the heart racing and the body shivering. Eris should not be out.

The man who let her out is following her, but he should not be. Eris haunts the souls of whomever she wills, but the haunting itself should not give her leave to wander freely. She should be trapped in this everyday man's mind, in his overly fast heart, in his slightly tarnished soul. She should not be walking the streets, feet hitting firmly as she looks into windows, searching for something that leaves her weeping—and she never weeps.

But Eris weeps now, and leaves fall from trees, crows peck out the eyes of the vagabond dead, and a prostitute turns the knife of a vicious customer against him, shuddering as she feels the blade enter soft, yielding flesh.

Eris feels that knife go in. And she laughs. And then she cries some more.

The moon goddesses gather. They're charged with watching Eris at night; others watch during the day, ever since that incident with the apple of gold: one petty moment that led to a most horrible of wars. One second of jealousy, of derision—none of the goddesses remembers who left Eris off the guest list. Or none of them *claims* to remember. There is a difference.

The guilty party knows. Eris may know. The gods point and whisper and pretend they know, but they don't. But the moon goddesses know it wasn't them, so they worry about keeping Eris contained, not about who left her out so long ago. And until now, until she inhabited the dreams of this common, rail-thin man with his wild dark hair and even wilder eyes, she was held fast. She could haunt dreams, but she could not haunt the world.

Artemis and Hecate slip from the moon's grasp and follow Eris and the man. The moon dims as they leave, until Selene invites Apollo up to keep her company. They make love, and Artemis shudders with revulsion, and Hecate shivers with nostalgia, and the earth shakes to keep her daughters company. And as Selene and Apollo celebrate their union, the moon brightens and the goddesses move on.

The man following Eris has a notebook in his hand. He is writing, but his words make no sense. He tries to hold them in his mind, tries to make sense of them, but they shift like sand rolling under the waves.

He realizes he is asleep, sleepwalking after the errant spirit who has haunted his dreams for so long. Or maybe he is still in bed and just imagines that he is chasing this figure who smells like smoke from an opium pipe.

He decides he is not sleepwalking, is still lying in the big bed he shared with his lost Virginia. Or is he in Providence? Is he in bed with dear Sarah, before her mother turned her against him?

But... did he ever sleep with Sarah? He can't remember what is fantasy and what is reality—and that has always been a problem for him. He chases after this ghoul who drives his dreams because he thinks she may know the truth, may know what it is inside him that makes his thoughts take such dark turns, that make liquor and drugs the only things that deaden his pain.

Eris feels the man behind her, but she does not turn. She senses what he wants from her. She will not tell him that she is as trapped as he is. He has captured her. The darkness inside him, the pain, the discord between a mind that loves to elevate and a heart that loves to frighten drew her in initially and now holds her faster than any prison her sister goddesses could ever devise.

Not that they've ever tried to imprison her. They know better than to attempt what this fool of a man, with his stories of ravens, sisters and brothers, and lost loves under the seas is doing so easily.

She feels the others coming faster than the man, one on either side of him, careful not to cross the cord uniting him with her. She knows the man can't see the cord, but she sees it glowing in the night as silvery as the bells he immortalized, can hear it thumping like the heart that told all, can smell it filling the air with the scent of spoiled amontillado, can almost taste it —she imagines it tastes like absinthe.

She sees a black cat cross her path; the animal hisses, its back up, tail puffed to an unimaginable size. The cat casts a shadow that blocks her way, and she shudders and she feels the man shudder, too.

"Why do you wander here?" It is Hecate, and she casts no shadow at all. The crossroads approach, and she smiles with loving devotion.

Eris looks at the street signs. Unlike the man, she is not delirious. She can read the letters. Broadway and Fairmount. They pass a hospital, and Hecate shivers and sighs.

"You feel something?" Artemis asks her, blending with the night in her deerskin clothing, only her silvery hair giving her away—the same color as the bell-like cord.

"Death," Hecate says. "I feel death."

For a moment, Eris feels the cord tighten. The man is getting closer, and he sees them and smiles as if they are his heart's desire. He looks at Artemis first and murmurs, "Virginia."

Artemis nods, but Eris knows this is not a tribute to Artemis' chastity; it is the name of his lost wife.

He names Hecate Sarah. Names Eris that as well, but she can feel through their connection that the Sarahs are two different women. He runs toward them and the cord between them all feels like a noose.

"What is he?" Artemis murmurs, and she reaches for her bow, but her hand stops short, and Eris realizes that she, too, is now trapped.

The moon above dims, and Hecate looks up and whispers, "Help us."

The moon brightens, the earth shakes again, and Eris imagines what Selene is doing instead of paying attention to the trouble her sisters have gotten into.

The man laughs as he catches up to them. He takes first one and then another in his arms, feels their soft skin, their warm breath, their silken hair. He laughs and murmurs names he thought never to utter again.

There is no jealousy among them, and he smiles in joy. There is no spite or envy. No fear, either, in their eyes as they look at him. They love him. They all love him. He won't be alone.

The bells ring. He hears them again. The bells and the sea and the raven above him. He hears a wall being built, the sound of a rock falling into a bottomless pit. He pulls the women to him and laughs and laughs and laughs.

Hecate shudders with fear. Hecate, the darkest of the gods, the crone that even Hades walks to the other side of Olympus to avoid—this man has made Hecate afraid.

The man whispers to Hecate, then to Artemis, who this time tries to pull out her dagger. She gets it only as far as half out when the man begins to cry.

Artemis begins to cry, too. She pushes the knife back in its sheath and follows the man down, kissing a face now sweaty with night fever—or with the sickness that comes from drink and drugs and other things that leave their mark after giving pleasure and oblivion. Artemis, who has never touched a man in kindness, is soothing this man's brow, brushing back hair that is streaked with a gray that mimics the silver of the cord that has grown into a net.

"What is he?" Artemis asks again.

"A writer. He dreams stories from nightmares. He pulls my world into his own." Eris feels another piece of her go as, even in his delirium, this man thinks of a new horror to set to paper. Her heart breaks at the thought that he will write no more tales.

"Virginia," he mutters, and Artemis leans in, saying, "What do you want?"

If he asks her for the right thing—peace—they will be free.

But he asks for nothing, and Artemis shudders with distaste as the man lapses into a fever-dream sleep.

"We are trapped," Hecate says as if it is Eris's fault.

"I did not ask for your help." Eris feels her temper rising, and in response mirrors break, babies cry, and rats scurry away. Hail falls from the sky, then lightning cracks.

"Calm yourself," Hecate says.

It is a good thing Hecate is older, better controlled. If she let go the way Eris just did, nothing would be left alive on this street.

Artemis is not so contained. She sends out a piercing scream, a mix of wolf and hawk. The street comes alive with the sound of hounds baying. Two break out from their yard—huge, black dogs with saliva running down their jowls—and rush to them but are stopped by the net that holds the goddesses to the man. Something lunges out of the sky, diving down and almost hitting Eris. Then it is gone, a silver-white arrow in the night.

The man twists and seizes on the hard street. Hecate lays her hand on his forehead, murmuring words that were old even when the Olympians were born. For a moment, he lies still and the net is not so solid.

Artemis is the first to break away.

"Virginia, come back. The man sees her moving away with two black dogs at her side and is broken hearted in his nightmares. He sees her going, his young, beautiful cousin-wife who keeps shifting into a deer-skinned huntress.

He forces his thoughts to his wife, but his mind stops at the night when she coughed and coughed, and it seemed a life's worth of blood came up. She spits up much more in the months after that. So much blood—on sheets, on her nightdress, on the hundreds of little handkerchiefs. More blood than in all his stories.

Artemis holds her hand to her mouth, then spits. Even in the dark, Eris can see that her mouth is full of blood. With a howl, Artemis leaps into the air, catching a silver ray of moonlight and climbing it back to a safer place. The coppery tang of blood seems to fill the spot where she stood.

Hecate moans and starts to chant, the ancient words filling

the night, and Eris can see them written in their shared language, golden letters on the hard surface of the street.

It is powerful magic. And for a moment, nothing happens.

But then a man rounds the corner, and he sees them—or their man, anyway—and he rushes over, calling out, "My God, sir. Are you all right?"

And their man murmurs something about hearing the bells, bells, bells. The mystical net around them disintegrates as the stranger, who carries the bag of a doctor, lifts their man up.

Hecate is gone as soon as the cords release her. A group of crows in a nearby tree rise as one, even though Eris knows crows don't fly at night. They follow Hecate, and Eris imagines them landing all around her as she rolls safe and free in her crossroads dirt and sings in a crackly voice to her ghosts and jackals of the man who dared imprison the Dark One.

Eris sees the man—she knows his name but didn't want to share it with the others; it was hers alone and so little ever is—open his eyes.

"Who are you?" he asks her softly.

"Sarah."

His smile is heartbreakingly sad in its momentary lucidity. "No, you're not."

"I'm your muse." And she leans in and kisses him and for one moment lets him understand fully the power of discord.

And it is too much. It pushes him all the way into his fantasies of women who never forsook him and fathers who loved him no matter what and a life where he walked straight and tall and never fell.

"Dream of sweet things," she murmurs, even though sweet things have never been her domain. But a man who can imprison darkness and savagery and discord into a twistedly beautiful tale is worthy of the effort.

She touches his forehead one last time, making the doctor flinch as if he can feel her near him.

The man opens his eyes. He sees his women. Lovely Virginia. The two Sarah's sitting behind her. And in the background, a little, hunched woman. She smiles, and he expects to see rotted pits of teeth, but her smile is straight and white.

"My muse," he says, finding her beautiful.

And for that moment, Eris is.

Nevermore

Jay Seate

I could sense a storm coming. The sky was filling with angry clouds, the kind of weather that suited my dour thoughts. Loneliness surrounded my heart like a thick fog. I poured a glass of wine and settled back in my easy chair, expecting nothing more than a search for a ballgame on the boob tube. At this point in my life, fifty-five going on eighty, I was desperate to fill a hole left by the death of my wife. Not feeling up to playing the dating game, I occupied myself with nature photography and long walks during available daylight hours.

But then came the nights.

I'd watched Mary wither and die from breast cancer. The bereft longing that began at the bedside when her eyelids closed for the last time deepened when her casket was lowered into the ground. Looking forward rather than back was good advice, but the door to my past apparently had no lock to keep it closed.

After the initial shock, the guilt and remorse phases were handled pretty well, but twenty-five years of marriage still left a load of *what if*s, and *why didn't I*'s to sort out. They sometimes spun in my head like an old, scratchy 33 1/3 LP. Had Mary and I appreciated each other enough? Had she picked the right man to share her shortened life with? Had I picked the right woman? These were questions that had crossed my mind in recent months, and there occasionally seemed to be attempts to provide answers—a message from spirits running in and out of unfocused dreams.

As the storm outside gathered strength, I set the bottle of wine next to my chair and lost myself in some mindless TV program. Up the street, a neighbor's dogs began to howl. They didn't bother me. There was something primal and beautiful in the chorus of their cries. Just as I was pouring a second glass, I heard my doorbell. "Crap, a neighbor with belated condolences, no doubt," I muttered, and struggled out of my comfort zone.

A young woman stood on my porch. Her arms wrapped around her shoulders fighting off the biting wind. "I'm so sorry to bother you," she said, "but my car died on me around the corner, I saw your light and..."

In today's world, the old saw about strangers just being friends you haven't yet met seems incredibly naive. One must be skeptical of any intrusion, but this woman possessed a face to which almost any door would have opened. She had full lips beneath a pert nose and unbelievingly piercing gray eyes, so unlike my dead wife's languid pools of blue. There was something in her expression that was hard to tear away from, and following a pregnant pause I finally said, "Come in, by all means."

She was dressed rather formally, I thought, and without a jacket. Instead of offering her use of the telephone, I asked if she would like have a seat and a glass of wine to warm up. She looked at me with a friendly smile to complement those penetrating eyes and raven hair.

"Yes, that would be very nice."

Had I known the consequences of this pivotal moment in my life, I can only speculate if I would've had the willpower to turn her away.

I retrieved a second glass from the kitchen. She accepted it and sat on one end of my sofa. I turned off the television and poured her wine.

She looked at the label on the bottle. "Mr. Duncan, you have excellent taste."

I didn't remember telling her my name. "I know this sounds silly," I heard myself say, "but you look very familiar. Are you a student?"

"I used to be a student, but not anymore." She took a sip and seemed to be reflecting. "They say one never forgets a face."

Her brilliant eyes were as riveting as if they were mirrors in the water, offering an ocean of desire only dreamed of, and I was unabashedly staring.

She must have noticed and rescued me by saying, "So you're a teacher?"

"A professor at the university."

Tilting her head as if observing some new curiosity, she quickly finished her wine and I just as quickly poured her another before planting myself on the other end of the couch. A child lurks inside most men, alert to an opportunity to cast the drudgery of routine aside. Pushing ahead, feeling rakish, I told her, "Maybe I've just seen you in my dreams."

"In your dreams?" She said it with humor, not in a mocking way, thank goodness, her words ending with another winning smile.

She seemed in no hurry to deal with her disabled vehicle. She told me her name was Laura Masterson. She was twenty-five years young. She claimed to have been finishing a graduate program before some unexpressed fate interrupted. As we spoke, I felt a thread of familiarity—a look more sensual than a touch, a tone more meaningful than words. Of course, I fell in love instantly.

Observing the heartbreaking grace of her neck, she reminded me of a model out of a L.L. Bean catalog. She was a great deal closer to the age of my son than to mine, thirty years my junior, to be exact, but a father figure was definitely not the image that toyed with my mind. Still, I hadn't lost my total grip on reality. I knew once the wine bottle was empty, she would ask to use the phone and then walk out of the house and my life. But as it turned out, she allowed me to open a second bottle and tell her about myself. Not having just fallen off the turnip truck, I weighed the possibility that her *problem* might be more than a broken-down car. She might be someone planning to take advantage of my obvious interest in her. *I won't be taken in by any sort of scam, pretty girl or not.* That's what I told myself, anyway.

Whatever her motives, I wished I could have cast off twenty-five years of my life for one night. Laura's long raven hair framed her youthful face and spilled over her shoulders, perfectly setting off her cocked head and impish smile.

"I'm so, so sorry, Mr. Duncan. Here I am taking up your time. I should probably think about letting you do whatever it is you need to do."

"My only desire at the moment is to help you. I can go have a look at your car."

"I wouldn't ask that of you. It's raining cats and dogs."

"Well then, let's just visit some more, unless you're sick of an old man's company."

She looked aghast. "You're not *old*. You're a very handsome man. It's only the unfortunate death of your wife that's pulling you down."

"Old habits die hard."

"That's so true, Mr. Duncan. So true."

"Okay. We're going to get over this 'Mr. Duncan' stuff." She looked at me with either delight or curiosity. "Welcome to my house," I said. "And from here on, it's Robert. All right?"

"Yes, sir. Robert it is," she said with a theatrical flair, giving me a mock salute.

Laura kicked off her shoes and languished on my sofa. A stirring beneath my rocky strata of abstinence ensued. I could see an epistle written in stone: *Here lies a beautiful twenty-five year old woman with the face and body to make the heavens weep, holding her third glass of wine, preparing to tell me her trials and tribulations.* I felt like a schoolboy getting his first hard-on at the blackboard, and a stitch of what could only be envy toward every young man in her age bracket.

We talked for some time, my concerns drowning in a cocktail of wine and youthful company, the moment frozen in time with no right to expect it would get any sweeter.

Then a new journey began as Laura stretched her arms above her head. Her breasts rose beneath her dressy garment. I wondered where the hell she'd been going before this curious auto breakdown. "Robert, could I stay with you tonight?" she suddenly asked.

Almost choking on a mouthful of Cabernet, I cleared my throat and tried to keep my cool. "Why would you want to stay here? Are you in some kind of trouble?"

"Sort of." Her voice trailed away and her eyes grew distant. Then she said, "I have a problem with the place I'm at right now. It should be worked out soon."

I poured us another glass and drank in her story along with the wine.

"Someone needs my help and being away from where I usually stay is important. It sounds silly, I know, but…"

"Why me?"

"Quite frankly, I felt so at ease when you came to the door… There must be some connection between us."

"I think we can work something out," I said, accepting her praise and letting it go at that, not about to analyze the situation by using common sense.

I watched the play of light and shadow upon her face. She seemed forthright, just a young girl in need of sanctuary. And yet, there was that familiarity about her. It was more than the fact that she'd mysteriously appeared. She wanted to hear about my deceased wife, my son, and past relationships. She told me how brave I'd been and how she admired me. All this flattery with two and a half bottles of wine consumed between us would have been more than enough. But then I told her to take her pick of the guest rooms.

"I hope I don't embarrass you, but I'd rather sleep with you."

I stopped playing with my wine glass. *Red flag. Red flag.* My thoughts were a pendulum swinging between emotion and common sense. "Are you absolutely sure about that?"

"Never more sure of anything since my return."

I moved next to her on the sofa and tenderly kissed her parted lips. We kissed again, then fondled, and then we took the remaining wine into my bedroom.

Once undressed and in bed, we became like children, intoxicated not by drink, but by requited pleasure, cuddling and giggling. Then with the urgency of a man and woman too long bridled, we began our passionate dance. In one night, this young woman had captured both my heart and soul.

~

Each of us live in a small lighted space surrounded by the dark unknown. My little space was suddenly lit with new expectation. For the first time since Mary's passing, I'd tuned my entertainment center's radio onto a classics station. Tunes from the great composers softly wafted into the bedroom as Laura and I became lovers. The next morning, she lay with her head on my chest, her naked breast against me, older flesh pressed against younger flesh in a liaison I would have previously thought impossible. Music still drifted in from the living room, but it was pop tunes playing. She must have gotten up during the night and changed the channel.

As her breathing rose and fell, I reviewed the events of the evening and her story for stopping at my house. Truth seemed available only on a need-to-know basis. Still, a young woman had ravished me; we had ravished each other. What a wonderfully delicious night it had been. How long since lust and inebriation had accompanied me to bed? This beautiful young creature was mine for the moment and I dared not dwell on the fact that it could end as quickly as it had begun. Slowly, gently, I touched my new lover's face, wishing my entire being could somehow crawl within her. I was mesmerized by this lovely girl's bold, unleashed sexuality. She'd seemed as hungry as I for the closeness, as if there might not be another chance for our bodies to become one. But I prayed that wouldn't be true.

At this moment, life seemed good. Very good.

Consummation had been satisfying, but no more so than admiring Laura from afar on my couch the night before. As corny as it may sound, watching this delicate creature sleeping softly next to me was the richest moment.

I looked at my ceiling and noticed its rough texture. I thought of how it contrasted with the silkiness of Laura's skin. On this morning, everything seemed tactile, vibrant, and more alive.

When she awoke, she looked up and smiled with an astonishingly familiar expression. "Hi, guy."

"Hey, you."

She snuggled against the crack between my arm and chest.

"Robert?"

"Mmm?"

"How do I feel when you make love to me?"

This is where men often concoct a glorious tale of ethereal bliss beyond the physical pleasure they've enjoyed. But, in this case, any words I might have strung together would ring hollow compared to the joy I had experienced in Laura's arms.

"Baby, you're the greatest," I said.

She looked at me, through me, then pinched my cheek and laughed.

"Is that the best you can do? Quote Jackie Gleason?"

"I'm surprised you know who Jackie Gleason is."

"I know a lot more than you think." She absentmindedly ran a finger along my appendectomy scar. Mary used to do the same thing. "If you're not going to describe romantic thoughts of lust, I might as well get a move on." Laura crawled over me. "I need a shower. Do you mind?"

"Mi casa es su casa."

"Want to join me?" Her eyes sparkled with the promise of mischief.

I was tempted, but it almost seemed too much of a good thing. "I think I'll just lie here, relax, and think about last night a while longer."

She laughed, gave me a kiss, and dashed to the bathroom. As she walked away, her bare bottom swayed with each step. I'd almost forgotten how beautiful the movements of a young woman could be. My mind strayed back to the front seat of my dad's car all those years ago, the mind-boggling sight of the creamy white torso and thighs belonging to a complicit female under the yellow glow of dashboard lights.

While Laura showered, I heard her humming happily, which pleased me. The picture on the nightstand next to the bed caught my eye, the one of Mary, the sunlight on her face, smiling into the camera. She wouldn't begrudge me a little pleasure, surely. I had my failings over the years, God knows, but my love for her had never wavered.

Laura emerged from the bathroom wrapped in a towel and began to gather her clothes.

"Will you be back?" I asked while wishing I'd showered with her.

She sat next to me. "Robert, you are a caring, tender, unique man. Your age means nothing to me. You're as vital as men half your age, and I think you proved it last night."

I brushed the loose strands of hair away from her face.

"I hope you don't think this is an act I'm pulling to get a place to stay?" she continued, looking into my eyes.

"I'm not sure I'd care if it was," I answered, trying to control my emotions.

"Well, it's not." With mock anger she stood, removed her towel, and swatted me.

Lunging for her, she danced out of my reach and wiggled her finger. "No, no. No more for you, young man. You had your chance at the shower. I've got to get myself together and go check on something."

"Can I come with you?"

"I'm afraid not, but I hope to be back just after dark."

She dressed while I watched. Wrapped in her discarded towel, I saw her to the door. How long had it been since I'd seen a woman off in this manner? That would take some serious thought.

I watched her saunter down the walkway and admired her shape as she rounded the corner. I wondered if the poor thing was without any car. We'd made no arrangements for a tow. I didn't even know what the problem was, and actually didn't care. I would have gladly loaned her mine. At this point, I would probably have given her anything.

She was as strange, unknown, and illusive as the banks of the Amazon. I could still smell her strange scent which sent a shiver of excitement through me. Feeling like a college boy after conquering the homecoming queen, I strutted into the bathroom. The radio was playing *You Sexy Thing* and I sang along. Whatever type it might be, music could touch something basic and pure, sounds blending to produce an emotional effect. My most intimate fantasy had been brought to life, my most secret of dreams made flesh. If I *was* dreaming, I didn't want to wake up. It was all too beautiful and grand.

The face that looked back at me in the bathroom mirror was somewhat drawn and world-weary, yet still handsome. There was a renewed twinkle in the eye; a gleam accompanied by a surging feeling not experienced since my early dating days when I nervously waited on some girl's doorstep. Or later in life when a woman first entered my bedroom. But then doubt began to sneak around the corners, a tendril of concern penetrating my euphoria. In less than twenty-four hours, my existence had shrunk to the confines of my heretofore lonely house. My desperate union with Laura almost seemed like something beyond myself. She had been a presence which soothed a barely remembered need until the need was met. As I walked from one room to another waiting for Laura's return, the walls themselves seemed to press upon me, closing in like a coffin, a prison of my own making, devoid of the magic of a new beginning.

"She'll be back. She has to come back."

~

That evening, I had a fidgety reluctance to go to bed. Every sound was exaggerated: a slight wind around the eaves, the infinitesimal creaking of the wood within the walls, the sound of by breath soughing in and out. Even my skin seemed more sensitive against the texture of my clothes since the previous night.

Around nine o'clock, I dozed off on the sofa, the previous night of drink and frivolity catching up with me, I suppose. Swept along on a wave of darkness, sleep descended like an unfolding shroud, bringing with it a lurid dream. I was walking alone in some dark place. I heard the rustle of footsteps in fallen leaves behind me. When I turned, a robed figure stood in the gloom. It was the Grim Reaper, I believed at first, but this apparition carried no scythe, and as I got closer it proved to be the opposite of my first impression. The shape was that of a woman, a statue of a hooded Virgin Mary, maybe. When I was near enough to reach out, I realized it was neither the Reaper nor the Virgin, but a mannequin with Laura's porcelain-like features, cold and still like a frightening death mask. I tried to back away, but my legs were paralyzed as the creature's lips parted slightly and the face seemed to change shape, almost folding in on itself.

I looked over my shoulder and saw a second figure behind me—Mary. Her shroud was open, revealing an autopsied torso ravaged by cancer, a vision so horrifying I didn't know whether to scream or run. I was caught in the middle, not knowing if one or both of these revenants had come to help me, or to pull me into the depths of retribution. I felt like a child cowering in the darkness, praying for this dread to pass. The scene had a despairing atmosphere of moral failure.

The ringing of the telephone pulled me back into my living

room from some abstract stasis of half sleep. I sprung from my makeshift bed like a kid on Christmas morning. The caller ID read *Unknown*. Has to be Laura, I thought, and grabbed hold of the device.

"Yes?" I said hopefully.

A slight pause and then, "Mr. Duncan?"

"Yes," I said again.

"I'm Detective Carmine. I'm afraid I have some disturbing news." Another pause. "There was an incident at Rose Hill Cemetery. I'm sorry to tell you that graves were desecrated and remains disturbed."

What he said took me a moment to grasp. "Graves vandalized? Bodies disturbed?" I asked incredulously.

"A couple of bodies. Your wife's and that of a woman buried next to her. It appears their caskets were broken into a couple of nights back." A third pause. "Damned kids and their pranks."

My mind raced at the idea of Mary's eternal rest being disrupted.

"No employees had been in that part of the cemetery for several days. The grounds crew found them this morning. I'm terribly sorry to have to tell you this, Mr. Duncan. We'll, of course, be investigating, but there is nothing for you to do. The remains were resealed and covered."

"What was the name on the other grave?"

"On the other stone?"

"Yes, the other grave that was opened," I said on the cusp of uncertain discovery. "The name on the tombstone of the other woman."

"Mary Duncan on your wife's stone, and let's see… the other one is Laura Masterson."

My mouth went dry. I wasn't able to swallow or speak. It must have been what schizophrenia felt like with the random awareness of a world turned topsy-turvy. The air around me was as still as death. Was this some kind of bizarre game? Would Laura suddenly come on the line laughing? I swallowed the stone in my throat and asked the man for his badge number. He gave it to me along with his precinct and his captain's name in case I wanted to check him out.

When I said nothing more, the detective added, "Who can figure what goes on in people's heads these days? You have to wonder what makes people do the things they do."

An old itch niggled along my scar. What else might happen when the fabric of reality rips open? I simply said, "Thank you," and stared at the phone like it owed me money before finally setting it back on its cradle. My world struggled to remain in focus. I put my hands on my ears as if to block out the detective's words, or to force my brain to understand, but it didn't help. I thought of Laura again, silhouetted at my doorway, her figure outlined, her hair shimmering. I walked to my door and opened it onto the night. The dogs were silent. There was no young woman passing by, nothing but the wail of a zephyr that sounded like a thousand hearts breaking. The chilly breeze blew a plastic bag along the curb, as forlorn and empty as I. Had Laura been an illusion, a sad trick on a lonely mind? Maybe she was an onset of madness. I felt withered, sapped of spirit. A thought kept going through my head like a repeating guitar riff: *Dead is dead. Dead is dead.* Then I imagined two open graves, side by side, two corpses covered only by moonlight, rising from death to… what?

The radio suddenly came on without my assistance. It was back on the classical station and was playing a piece by Chopin, one of my dead wife's favorites. I looked around the room halfway expecting to see Mary in the shadows, but it wasn't to be. It was too late for that. To the silent walls I whispered the tormented word, "Nevermore" while allowing the music to play on until the telepathic moment came to an end.

Paranormal activity assumes there is more to people than the organism in which they inhabit. Ghost sightings are reported regularly. Television programs are devoted to them. I'd never believed in the paranormal, but the facts seemed to state loudly that it was time to re-evaluate by beliefs. I poured myself a strong drink, but felt no relief as the hot trickle of liquor ran down my throat. I walked to the living room window and looked across the dark lawn. Laura's strange fragrance hit me. The night before, it had smelled sensuous and earthy, the bittersweet scent of an aroused woman. Now, it bore the hint of decay. My disquiet began to slip into terror, as if I was entering the graveyard where two people I'd known had been buried, and then reburied.

There was something in a horror novel about how our eyes and minds deceive us. Could something be real if it lived only in the mind? What we know to be certain never is. On one dark and stormy night, one event separated itself from all other experiences. Something was born out of my loneliness that contradicted the real world.

There was one final thread in the string of events. On the afternoon of Laura's visit, I had uncharacteristically cut a flower from a rosebush lovingly tended by Mary when she was alive. Laura had taken notice of it and, holding it by the stem, smelled it on our way to the bedroom. I didn't notice it again until shortly after Detective Carmine's phone call. The rose was dead, withered into little more than a black husk. I knew what I had hopefully waited for would never come.

~

I've been told that after the loss of a loved one, a sort of hypnosis can occur. Although God remains a questionable hypothesis, there is definitely another plane of existence, a perversity stitched into the fabric of the world that has modified my laws of spirituality. Since the night of the detective's phone call, my sense of reality has been dramatically altered. I would have expected nothing less after seeing, touching, and making love to a ghost.

I was destined to see Laura's name written in stone after all, but far from what I had imagined on our first and only night together. I visited the cemetery and placed a bouquet of flowers at the plinth of each headstone. Laura's held the inscription, GONE TOO SOON. I looked up her history. She had indeed been a student who'd been killed in an auto accident a year before my wife died. That meant I had stood next to her grave during my wife's funeral. Her return had been an accident too, I surmised, through some strange and ironic act of vandalism.

My wife used to accuse me of being *certifiable*. Now, I guess I really am. Although both women are little more than shadows, ghosts from my past, the evening and following morning with Laura floats on the surface of my memory like a beautiful, gliding swan, where her very much alive eyes and her youthful, eager body beckon to be taken again. She's a spectral whisper in time that comes back to haunt me on sleepless nights like the feature attraction in a paranormal movie.

Where does reality leave off and fantasy begin? Materially, all I have left of Laura is the memory. I look at Mary's picture and try to make some sense of what happened. I satisfy my parched body with my glasses of wine while offering a toast to the virtues of both Venus and Bacchus, and then dream about both women. Most of all Laura though, about her standing at my threshold with a golden halo of light from the porch light upon her, and later, about her body writhing with pleasure beneath mine. I sometimes think I feel the touch of a lingering, stroking fingertip and wonder if I can ever lie down again without thinking about our legs intertwined and feeling the heat of my unrequited desire.

I've heard it said that a good thing about being older is not worrying about dying young. Perhaps Laura felt cheated. Mary too, for that matter. Maybe some kind of collaboration between my wife's spirit and Laura's restored body created a specter capable of transcending time. And when the open graves were discovered and the disturbance rectified, Laura had to return from where she had come.

Time is a fleeting commodity all too scarce. It was as true with Mary as it was with Laura, twenty years together or just one night. If memories are all I have, I should hold on to the good ones as if they were fading postcards. There are times when I can feel them both, in the still of the night, or in the breathless throes of a passionate memory when an unseen hand will tickle my neck or tug at me. It feels as real as my pounding heartbeat. The two women taken before their time are more than ghosts to me.

Like a man caught in a piece of machinery and pulled into its grinding jaws, I am consumed by the ramifications of the detective's narrative. If only the disturbed graves had not been found so quickly. There is no remedy to resolve the incomprehensible, yet my devious mind wants to create a sliver of light into the swirling darkness, to step beyond the threshold into a world where bright eyes are not opaque in death. Longing loins infect me with a dangerous nostalgia as I lay awake with the thoughts of a haunted man. I wonder what would happen if the graves were to be opened once more?

Closure is a myth and religious dogma doesn't provide any meaningful answer. There are nights when the doorbell rings and no one is there, just a soft, unnatural stillness hanging in the air. And on some quiet evenings, it's Laura's voice I hear through some ethereal vortex like a single clear current in a river of turmoil, the sound of her words whispering in my ear… calling… calling, "Find me, Robert. Come to me."

And I listen.

Love The One You're With

Birney Reed

Beth Tompkins didn't care that the other people in the hot tub could see her. The water felt fantastic on her toned dancer's body; she never wanted it to end. She opened her eyes to see the man and the woman sitting on each side of her. Smiling at Beth, the woman asked, "Are you ready to be with us?" In answer, Beth reached up and kissed the woman.

Jane turned towards the other four couples sitting in the hot tub as she stood up, revealing her own nudity, and addressed the group. "Let's all go inside and get comfortable. There are robes in each of the bedrooms, but I assure you the house is warm enough so you won't need them." The four couples helped Beth to her feet, each person anxious for things to begin. Beth didn't know it would be her end.

~

Deputy Tommy Richards hadn't been with the department very long, if six deputies and one sheriff could be counted as a department. Being the rookie guaranteed him the graveyard shift most of the time. He didn't mind. He was just glad to have a job in law enforcement.

Parkinton County, east of Meigs on the Ohio River, was one

of the poorest in the state, and traveling down its 300 miles of roads could be the most boring job in the world at 3:00 a.m. Tommy's main task was to help stranded motorists, but the occasional drunk driver helped contribute to the county coffers. He enjoyed the late hours; it gave him time to think about working his way up to the police force in Columbus, where there was more action in one night than a year in the sleepy back-country.

Rounding the curve, his high beams caught a lump lying in the center of the two-lane road. The cruiser screeched to a halt ten feet short of the thing glistening crimson in its headlights. Illegal hunting had always been a problem in this rural Ohio area. The poorer folk didn't have a choice, it was hunt or starve. The department knew this however, and turned a blind eye to those situations. Sheriff Gilmore's stern voice repeated itself in Tommy's head.

"If you find somebody who's trophy hunting, by God, you bust them and throw their asses in jail."

He stepped out of the cruiser into a fall night air that smelled clean and pure. As he rounded the fender, he could see steam pouring off the carcass. The term 'fresh kill' popped into his mind. "Who in their right mind would skin a deer and leave it in the middle of the road?" He asked out loud just as the 'deer' turned its eyeless sockets to him and screamed a very human scream. Tommy's own scream rang in harmony with the skinned human writhing on the asphalt.

~

Sheriff Gil Gilmore and Deputy Tommy Richards stood by as Doctor Robert Sloan tried desperately to save the person lying on the gurney. The oxygen mask covering its face failed to muffle the agony. Tommy's mind had gone on automatic when he had picked it up and laid it into the back of the cruiser. On the way back to town, he intermittently vomited, spraying the passenger-side of the front seat while trying to relay the emergency over the radio to the twenty-bed county hospital.

As they watched, the muscles in the chest heaved one last time before the nameless victim expired. Tommy turned and walked out of the room, plopping down in the hallway with his head touching his knees, fighting the urge to throw up again. He jumped when he felt a hand on his shoulder.

"There was nothing you could do, son. The woman was dead before you brought her here. She just didn't know it."

Tommy stammered back, "It was female? What the hell happened to her?" He looked up at Doctor Sloan's faded brown eyes.

"She was skinned Tommy, plain and simple. There isn't a drop of epidermis on her anywhere. Not a hair or a fingernail, not even any body fat that I can see. All that's left is exposed muscle. That's what she died of, exposure. The human body doesn't work without its skin."

"What's Gil doing in there?"

The middle-aged physician looked down at Tommy and said, "The same thing I should be doing, searching for clues."

Later, the deputy walked into his one-bedroom apartment

above the hardware store and dropped down onto a worn-out sofa wondering if he'd ever be able to sleep again. A chill of terror ran up his spine as he recalled the agony of the poor woman's scream. He leaned back and closed his eyes. "Shit!" was the only word he could mutter as he stood and walked to the tiny kitchen and opened the fridge. A spoiled carton of milk and leftover pizza from two nights ago did nothing to quell his nausea. Instead, he reached for the half-full peppermint schnapps bottle from last New Years. He put the bottle to his lips and started chugging. A half an hour later he was hugging the toilet, relieved to be puking from drinking too much. An hour later he headed to the liquor store for something stronger.

~

The autopsy report arrived in Doctor Robert Sloan's office five days later. Having been a 'Friend of Bill W.' for five years, he couldn't help but mumble to himself, "Never in my life have I wanted a drink more," as he leafed through the six pages and read the summation.

Unidentified female had all epidermis removed. On close examination the nerve endings were severed within one thousandth of an inch from the muscle surface. By the amount of adrenaline found in the blood stream, it is believed the subject was alive during the entire process. At this time it is unknown what procedure was used to remove the skin.

Below, there was a hand-written note from Doctor Lawrence

Fishbein.

Rob, what in the hell is this? I'll have more for you later. God help us, she died of exposure and fright!

~

The skin that used to be Beth Tompkins looked at the man, amazed at the physical sensations coursing through her body. She reached for Rick's soft brown hair, glorifying in the richness of its touch. The skin that was Jane poked her head through the door, ignoring the coupling going on in front of her. She walked over to the side of the bed and spoke. "It's time to go back to the region."

Beth sighed in frustration but knew Jane was right. One question was on her mind. "Why is he not one of us?"

Jane looked down at Rick's smiling face. "He doesn't need to be. He's addicted to the pleasure."

~

Jane and Rick Ferguson loved sex. For them, nothing was out of bounds. They were rich in the only proper way to be wealthy—they inherited it. They were the last in each of their family lines. Rick and Jane could concentrate on the one thing they both loved, pure physical pleasure, and as licensed sex therapists the world was their playground. They believed sex had nothing to do with love; sex was a form of communication, a way of understanding. The search for ultimate satisfaction was their love, their binding force.

He looked like Ward Cleaver as he walked through the

mansion's massive oak doors. An older-than-ancient tome was tucked safely under his arm as Rick, sounding like the Beaver's father, shouted, "Jane, I'm home!"

From far away he heard, "Out here, honey!"

He followed the voice, shouting back, "Darling, I got it!"

Ten minutes later they were sitting cross-legged on a huge round bed, their heads bent over the ancient pages like two kids with their dad's *Playboy* magazine, turning each page slowly, trying to take in the various images and words as quickly as possible. Neither one could see the spirit floating off to the side of the bed, smiling in anticipation.

"We can't do half of these positions. I'm not a contortionist and you're not a gymnast." Exasperation filled Jane's voice as she looked up and saw the need in her husband's eyes.

Rick's voice took on a clinical tone. "The key to the book isn't in the positions; it's in the writing. We decipher the words, then we can achieve the positions. I know it. I just know it."

Each symbol in 'The Book' as Rick and Jane called it stood for a particular chant, to be said at the time of touching. Each touch was a step to the next level of pleasure. Rick had been right about the 'key'. A professor, whose doctorate was in dead languages from Ohio University, had told them, "I can write out the meaning of the words but I can only give you an idea of how the language is supposed to sound. The only way you can speak a language is to hear it. You can learn the syntax, but until you actually hear the words you can't understand how to say them. It's the same with all languages."

For two years they practiced, and every chant and position missed the mark. But the couple knew they were close. They could feel the power of total release; the way you know you're approaching the light at the end of a tunnel. For brief seconds they grew close, their bodies being fine-tuned by the pain, torture and pleasure of each sexual position. Where once there had been a little fat on their bodies, it was now replaced with hard muscle. Throughout the process, however, she never told him of the spirit invading her dreams or how beautiful it was.

Jane pulled away from Rick for the first time in their marriage. She saw the hurt in his eyes as she said, "Don't sweetheart. I'm exhausted, and I can't take anymore."

He looked down at the fiftieth page of the old book and cocked his head to one side. For the first time in two years, an understanding of the marks above the language made sense. His voice filled with religious awe. "Jane, these aren't musical notes. They're accents. I think they mean volume, not a tone. I want you to scream the words."

The confused and exhausted look on her face let him know she no longer cared.

"Please, we've come this far. Let's try one more time." He paused for a second and begged, "Please."

She thought about the last two years of frustration and how they had withdrawn from all of their friends because of 'The Book'. If lifestyles could be altered, their lives were a perfect example of an 180-degree turnabout. They never went out of the house. Food was ordered over the phone and prepared in the kitchen. He laid a hand on her cheek and she sighed at the softness of his palm pressed against her skin. "My skin," she thought, "it's filled with live wires."

His kissed her passionately. The continuing peaks of pleasure mounted as she sensed the tiny crevices in his lips. She found herself whispering the words "Tuhau Knolimau Tau."

Rick's breath touched her ear as he begged, "Please Jane, louder."

Rick knew she was too tired to do what he wanted. Jane needed spurring. He bit her shoulder, instantly drawing blood. This time she screamed, "TUHAU KNOLIMAU TAU."

Lightening flashed in her mind as her body released its pent-up frustration. Every nerve in her body felt awash in pleasure. She could feel the spirit of her dreams deep inside her and see her aura. She tried to close her eyes against the onslaught of light but her lids wouldn't lower. She raised her hand to cover her eyes and saw nothing but bone, muscle, and cartilage before she went blind.

~

Sheriff Gil Gilmore could smell the reefer the second he entered Doctor Sloan's private office. The good doctor, 'Doc' to his friends, didn't even try to hide the joint held between his fingertips. "Damn Doc, I wish you wouldn't do that when I'm around!" he said pointing to the half-smoked joint.

The Doc's bloodshot eyes smiled up at the sheriff. "Hey, at least I'm not drinking and driving anymore. And besides Gil, you know I've been diagnosed with glaucoma."

The sheriff eased himself into a smooth leather captain's chair, chuckling as he said, "You diagnosed yourself." Doc smiled his shit-eating grin and passed the joint to his friend.

The two men said nothing for a few minutes as their individual buzzes built in their heads. They knew business had to be handled but neither man wanted to jump into it.

"Have you heard anything more from Columbus?"

The doctor thought about his last conversation with Lawrence Fishbien, the medical examiner, before he answered Gil's question with a question. "Do you know why they call it practicing medicine?"

Gil didn't answer. Doc Sloan laughed softly. "It's because not one of us has it down." His laughter was replaced with a bitter tone as he added, "Sometimes we just don't know. Did I tell you someone had sex with the victim just before she died?"

"No." Gil found himself unable to imagine what kind of person could do this atrocity let alone someone having sex just before they peeled their partner's skin like an orange "Doc, what sick asshole could do this sort of thing?"

Sloan couldn't help playing devil's advocate. "What makes you think the person is sick?"

"You've got to be kidding me. It would take a seriously deranged individual to skin another human being."

Sloan didn't answer him right away. He opened his desk drawer and pulled out a lab report. He flipped to the page he was looking for. "The dopamine and tryptamine levels were through the roof."

"Could you put it layman's terms?"

"Her pleasure centers were in overdrive, Gil. In other words, she enjoyed what happened to her."

Gil shook his head in disbelief. He knew what it felt like to get cut, and he knew it hurt like hell. This girl had every inch of her skin cut from her body. "Any chance of identifying the woman?"

Doctor Sloan reached for a regular cigarette, lit it and inhaled deeply. As he let the smoke out of his lungs he sighed, "With no dental match or a missing persons? Yeah, slim and none."

~

Rick and Jane watched the doctor lock his office door and head down the street to the municipal parking lot. Jane turned to her husband and said, "It's time to get to know Doctor Robert Sloan." Rick started the car and headed in the Doc's direction. Jane shouted, "Hey Doc, Doc Sloan."

It took him a moment to recognize the woman leaning out the passenger window. He smiled at Jane Ferguson through stoned eyes. "What can I do for you on this beautiful fall evening?"

Her smile was warm and inviting as she answered, "Rick and I were wondering if you wanted to come to a cookout we're having tonight?"

Rob bent over a touch to wave a silent "Hello" to Rick. He thought of how stupid Rick looked staring straight ahead with an idiotic smile. "I'd love to! What time?"

As the car started pull away, Jane replied, "Seven will be fine. We'll fire up the hot tub. See you then."

Doc wondered what brought on the invitation. It had been over a year since the Ferguson's had been in town, before then they had rarely said hello to him. There were two reasons he accepted their invitation: he was stoned, and he hated his own cooking.

~

"Rob, how do you like your steak?"

The doctor took in the sight of Jane in her two-piece thong swimsuit, admiring the fine, highly toned shape of her body.

He answered, "Rare, please," before turning and heading towards the house to get another cup of coffee. Rick was standing in the kitchen staring out the window at his wife. He looked at Doc as he came through the door. "Get you something to drink?"

"Coffee please," Rob answered, wishing he could sneak off and smoke the doobie resting in his shirt pocket. His mind kept drifting back to Jane bent over the grill. "You have a beautiful place, Rick."

"Yes, I did have." The answer was morose, and it wouldn't be until later that night at home when it would throw Doc off center as he recalled it.

He woke the next morning to pounding on his front door with the final scene of an intensely vivid dream replaying in his head as his feet hit the wooden floor.

The garden had been beautiful beyond description. The blades of grass felt soft and lush against his bare feet as he walked through the landscape. Pushing aside a fragrant shrub, he saw thirteen of the most ideal specimens of humankind cavorting on the golden sand.

He saw himself as a worn-out copy of these gorgeous creatures. These were beings of sensuality, perfect in their feelings of lust, desire, and love; pleasure was their driving force. He was watching their history, their life together.

Two of the beings separated from the group. They were arguing about the purpose of their existence. It wasn't what they said, for there was no speech; the couple communicated with gestures and touch. Each movement spoke volumes. The woman flushed a dark, angry purple from her toes to the tips of her flaming red hair. The man was unable to understand her desire for change and, having no concept of violence, didn't bother to duck or step aside as her closed fist sent him sprawling to the ground, clutching his face in pain. The eleven others stopped their sensual cavorting, staring in horror at the man and woman who brought their end. Rob wanted to scream in horror as each person began to age. Tears ran down their collective cheeks at the loss that now destroyed them. All thirteen beings withered and died.

Rob felt a deep residual sadness as he opened the door to see Sheriff Gilmore standing in front of him. "Doc, get your clothes on! We've found another one."

~

Beth Tompkin's skin locked eyes with him, ignoring the other men sitting around her tiny dais in the center of the strip club. Tommy Richardson's gaze was filled with lust and desire and it pleased her to see the smile on his handsome young face. The music changed as she stepped off the tiny stage, making sure her breasts brushed against his back as she walked behind his chair and dropped a note on the small table. He read the small, precise script.

Tommy walked out of Doogan's into the brisk night air and saw Beth leaning against his car.

Hours later, candles in every nook and shelf lit a room that seemed aglow despite them. The thing that had been Beth pressed her lips against his lightly furred chest. She looked up at him and returned his contented smile. It took Tommy a few seconds to realize he was staring at himself. He turned his head back and looked down at the muscles containing his rib cage and screamed. Deputy Sheriff Thomas Richards screamed himself to death never knowing why the people gathered at the foot of the bed did nothing to help him. His last image was their leering faces.

~

"Lawrence, were you able to find anything at all on this body?"

Rob heard his friend from medical school sigh in frustration on the other the end of the phone before he started talking. "Listen up, buddy. There is nothing to go on. I don't know what's going on in that Podunk area of yours but if you find one more person, you're local boys are going to have to call in the FBI. I've already sent my findings to D.C. Not that it's going to do any good but I didn't know what else to do."

"Did the guy have the same endorphin levels as the woman?"

"Higher," Lawrence replied then added, "I'll email the test results tomorrow morning."

He hung up the phone before the doctor could say anything else and walked over to his desk, pulling out the joint he had stashed in the back of the drawer. Four hits later, his head was nodding from the power of the county-grown pot. He lowered his head to his desk and promptly fell asleep. It wasn't a dreamless sleep.

~

Gil looked up at the man who had just quit his job. "What are you going to do?"

"I'm going to work security for the Fergusons."

Gil stood up and extended his hand to Tommy Richardson and said, "It takes a different type of person to do law enforcement. It's better you realize it now." The skin that was Tommy headed out the door, leaving Gil's hand hanging in mid-air as he said, "Okay, goodbye."

A part of Gil was happy Tommy didn't shake his hand. Another part wanted to know—why?

~

Jane's angular face and azure eyes twinkled with mischief as he moved closer to examine the small rash on her wrist. An urge to run from the woman hit Doc hard. Her blue eyes were taunting him. He turned his back to her, walked over to the mirrored medicine cabinet and pulled out a tube of analgesic cream. With the door shut and her reflection framed in the glass, she reminded him of his dream. She was the woman who struck the man on the peaceful beach. Her hand wrapped around his as he handed her the ointment. "Would you like to come over for dinner tonight? Rick's going to be gone for the evening."

Seconds passed before he answered. "I don't think I better. You're a married woman and it wouldn't look right."

"Don't doctors make house calls?" she chuckled and added, "I'll expect you around eight." She brushed against him and walked out of the examination room.

He walked back to the medicine cabinet. His reflection in the glass cabinet revealed the weakness of a lonely man. Doc opened the door and stared at the half-empty bottle of Jim Beam sitting on the lower left-hand shelf. He quickly shut the door. A whispered prayer crossed his lips in the hope he would never need his brown liquid buddy, all the while knowing he was going to do the wrong thing.

Jane sat in her Mercedez Benz staring at the office. She was looking forward to the night of pleasure with Doctor Robert Sloan, a soon-to-be kindred spirit.

~

Gil looked down at the manpower reports and wondered how he was going to fudge next month's numbers without

Tommy Richards. He picked up the phone, hitting the speed dial to his house. The look of concern deepened on his face as the other end rang four times. The voice mail picked up. Sue Ellen's throaty voice came on the line, "We're unable to come to the phone. Please leave a message and we'll get back to you as soon as we can."

Gil slammed the receiver back down and mumbled, "Damn that woman, she's never home when I need to talk to her."

He would have been shocked down to the tips of his rightfully moral toes if he knew his unfaithful wife was in bed with his former deputy. They were at the Blue Lake Inn, just on the other side of Pomeroy. If you were to ask Sue Ellen Gilmore why she was in a hotel room with a man she barely knew or why she had, throughout her marriage, carried on with men who were passing through town, there wouldn't have been a logical answer. All she really knew for sure was that the boredom of living in Parkinton County was unbearable, and these little trysts were a way to break the monotony. *Besides,* she thought to herself as she kissed Tommy's strong young chest, *when a forty-two-year-old woman is pursued by a handsome young man, I'd bet my long-lost virginity that any woman my age would take advantage of the situation. How often is this going to happen again?*

His hands stroked her graying brown hair, lightly applying pressure to the top of her head. Sue Ellen smiled to herself at the less-than-subtle gesture.

~

Doc refrained from smoking the joint he had rolled before taking care of the four S's. He was extra careful with the shaving portion, the face in the mirror let him know what a heel he was. That same face showed a small flush of excitement as he thought of Jane's tight body and her striking looks.

The rear view mirror, which always reflected his eyes, was turned towards the blind side of the car as he drove up the driveway. This way, he couldn't see the guilt that would be there in the morning. His car rolled to a stop at the base of the steps leading to the mansion's massive oak doors. As he climbed the stone stairs the doors parted, revealing Jane standing in the foyer, dressed in a black evening cocktail dress that accentuated every curve of her body. The smile on her face made his heart skip a beat in anticipation, and he returned it as best as he could.

"I'm so glad you were able to come, Doctor Sloan. You are the perfect remedy for my problem." Together they walked arm and arm through the house.

The sun was setting behind the hill that towered over the house, causing a chill in the air. Jane and the doctor didn't feel it though as the steam from the hot tub rose above them, creating a moist blanket of protection. They sat across from one another making small talk but not making contact. Doc was ignorant of the people in the room overlooking the hot tub, watching and waiting anxiously.

"What brought you to Parkinton County?"

"Sheriff Gilmore is the one who saved me from killing

myself. I came down here one weekend drunker than seven hundred gynecologists at a convention. From what he told me, I took out a picket fence and tried to run down old man Forester's prize bull with my Porsche. Gil was the one who arrested me and threw me in jail for thirty days. It gave me time to dry out and get a better perspective on life. But I still wasn't ready to go the straight and narrow. I remember telling him to mind his business and I took a swing at him. I spent another thirty days in jail for assaulting a police officer, thirty more days to clean my system and see the error of my ways. I moved here five years ago and I don't want to leave."

In the space of a breath her lips were less than an inch from his. She whispered, "You'll never have to leave here. You'll be mine forever." Her lips moved to kiss him for the first time.

She jerked away from him as if a wasp had stung her. At first Rob thought Rick had come back early and was at this moment getting ready to throw a plugged-in toaster into the bubbling water. It took him a second to see through the blanket of steam Tommy Richardson's face covered in what looked like blood.

"We need to talk."

"Holy shit Tommy, are you okay?"

No sooner had Doc asked the question than Jane was standing beside Tommy, touching his face and whispering in his ear. She turned back to Rob as she put a finger in her mouth with whatever was covering Tommy and said, "It's just strawberry jam. He left it in the microwave too long."

"Hell, woman, if it exploded he might be badly burned." Doc stood up, aware of his own nudity, but more concerned with the well-being of another person and added, "Let me take a look at him."

It wasn't what Jane said next, but rather the tone of her voice that froze Rob in his tracks. "Tommy, get your ass in the house and clean that mess up. I'll deal with you in a few minutes!" The way she said the world *deal* had finality to it. Tommy spun on his heels and did as he was told. Jane stepped back into the hot tub and put her arms around Doc. "It looks like we'll have to do this another night. I've got to take care of Tommy. I hope you don't mind?"

He realized he didn't mind at all. Driving out from the gate he started talking to himself. "What in the hell was that all about? That sure as shit didn't look like jam to me. Serves you right old man, you really ought to know better." The eyes in the mirror agreed.

He went to bed that night without smoking any weed, but once again he awoke to the heavy-handed knocking of Sheriff Gilmore. He opened the door; the grief in Gil's voice grabbed his attention. "I need for you to come with me," Gil cried. "Sue Ellen is dead."

Neither said a word during the eighty-mile drive to the motel. Doc made Gil wait outside the room as he ducked under the yellow tape. Bile rose in his throat when he looked at the thing that was Gil's wife lying on the blood-soaked sheets of the dingy room

Sue Ellen's face was frozen in a mask of pain. The skin on her forearms had been peeled down from the shoulder to the fingertips, the way one would peel a banana. Her calves, thighs, and buttocks had received the same treatment. Flaps of skin were bunched around her waist. The part-time coroner from Meigs County looked over at Doc motioning him to come closer to the bed.

"There's something else you need to see." He said while opening Sue Ellen's mouth. Every tooth in her head was gone including her tongue. "I've never seen anything like this in my entire life, have you?"

"Actually, I've seen worse, but this is close, damn close."

He didn't see Gil standing in the doorway of the hotel room.

Doc drove the patrol car back to Parkinton. He knew Gil wouldn't be able to handle the twisting curves through the Southern Ohio hills. Especially while sitting in the back seat of the car sucking on the joint Rob had brought with him and taking long pulls off the bottle of Stolies they picked up at a package store. Gil Gilmore had been a recovering alcoholic for twenty years. When he asked his friend to buy the booze, Doc didn't argue. He knew that sometimes you fall off the wagon and other times the gods throw your ass off. He heard his friend slur from the back seat. "Did you say something, Robbie?"

Doc looked longingly at the half empty bottle cradled in Gil's arms and replied, "No Gil, I was just talking to myself." Twenty miles down the road the doctor pulled the car over and held his friend's head as he threw up and thought about the 'jam' on Tommy's face.

~

Eleven people looked at the young man standing in the center of their circle. No one said a word as arguments flew around the room. When alone, they communicated with pure thought. "He should not have done this; we have come too far to be denied." Jane walked up to Tommy and stroked his unlined face. He smiled at her touch. The circle closed in on the young man; their love for him showed in the flush of their skin. The incident would be handled. They would move to another location, a place where they could *be*. The skin that was Jane communicated an order. They obeyed her thought.

~

When they got back to his office, Doctor Sloan was surprised to see Rick Ferguson sitting in the waiting room. This time there was no idiotic smile on his face.

There was anger mixed with embarrassment in Doc's voice when he spoke. "Rick, I really don't have time for you. I've got another murder on my hands and Gil's too drunk to help. So, if you don't mind, I'd like for you to leave."

The next words out of Rick's mouth changed his mind. "I know what happened to Sue Ellen Gilmore."

Six cups of coffee and two hours later, the doctor finished listening to the most amazing tale of his forty-four years. He looked at Rick, not knowing whether to call the loony squad on him for telling such a fantastic yarn or for himself for listening to it. "So, what you're saying is Jane, Beth, Tommy and nine others are dead, replaced by these 'beings' that only focus on pleasure?"

Rick looked down at the floor and nodded his head.

"If that's the case, what happened to Sue Ellen?" Doc didn't hear what Rick mumbled. "Speak up, damn it!"

"Tommy tried it by himself. That's why you found her partially peeled."

"So why come to me now? Why aren't you still with them?"

Rick's answer chilled him to the bone. "Because you're next and I don't want to share Jane with you. She's mine. When they take your skin, they won't need me anymore. They'll kill me."

The door to the examination room burst open and there stood Gil Gilmore, his eyes bloodshot from tears and booze, his .357 leveled at Rick's chest. Rob leapt in front of Rick, throwing the butt-laden ashtray at Gil just as Gil pulled the trigger. The slug whizzed past his head.

"Move aside Doc! I'm going to blow this asshole's brains out."

Rob took a step toward Gil. "Do you have any idea how crazy all this sounds, you don't really believe that spirits killed Sue Ellen or Tommy or Jane? Now, give me the damn gun before you do something you'll regret for the rest of your life."

Gil looked at the man standing directly in from of him. Doc Sloan could see the struggle going on inside Gil's mind, and for a second it looked like he was going to make the wrong choice and shoot his closest friend of the last five years. What stopped him was Rick yelling "It's true damn it!"

For the second time in two days, Robert Sloan found himself driving back to the Ferguson home. The conversation in the car between himself and the mirror was more animated than usual.

Like before, the large doors opened to reveal Jane standing in the entrance. Jane's warm smile was gone, replaced by a look of irritation. "What is it this time Robert? I'm getting ready to go to Columbus."

"What's up there, more recruits?"

"I don't know what you're talking about. What is it you want?"

"Let me start off by saying Rick was in my office this afternoon and he told me everything."

He watched the woman absorb his statement and saw her eyes widen for just a split second before she answered with, "Did he also tell you he's a serious cocaine abuser and prone to delusions?"

"No, but he told me you would probably say something along those lines. Pardon the pun."

Her façade crumbled a bit, but she recovered quickly. "Alright Doctor, why don't you come in and tell me everything my drug-addled husband told you."

Rob walked passed her then spun on his heels. "I'll tell you everything, including the fact that I gave your husband a drug screen and he passed with flying colors."

Doctor Sloan never felt the blow to the back of his head delivered by the skin known as Tommy Richards.

The pounding in his head made him feel like he had never stopped drinking. As his blurred vision began to clear, he strained against the straps holding him to the narrow bed in the center of the room.

Jane leaned in close to him. "Well Rob, it looks like you're still with us. For a moment there, I thought Tommy hit you too hard; then you'd be useless. That would be a shame, for you are the last one to be chosen."

He turned his head away from her and looked at the other people standing around him, bringing back the dream of the couples cavorting in that beautiful long-dead land. Doc felt Jane's touch and the passion inside him began to grow. No matter how hard he fought against his own arousal, her caress flamed his desire. He tried to conjure up images of the mutilations these beings caused, but the pictures in his mind were driven out, replaced by erotic scenes and the overwhelming pleasure he was receiving at her hands. One hand moved close to his mouth and he bit down on it as hard as he could. The finger that brushed his lips was now inside his mouth, severed from the hand. The creature, whose name he didn't know, screamed in pain. The other beings drew back at the terrible sound. Doc spat it out. "If one of you bastards comes near me again, I'll bite off another goddamn finger."

Jane moved in close but stayed out of reach of his mouth. Tommy and Beth strapped his head down with duct tape. In Jane's hand was the one thing that would take away his ability to fight. She grabbed his jaw and pulled his mouth open while lifting the bottle of Jim Bean to his lips.

Doc knew he'd been beat and swallowed, closing his eyes to the inevitable.

The smell of burning flesh and terrifying screams caused him to open them again. He saw Rick and Gil wielding handheld blowtorches, rushing and attacking the people standing over him. Huge gaping holes appeared in their bodies as the searing heat sliced through their stolen skins. Inside each bag of flesh was a brilliant aura of emerald and gold. Their inner light was blinding to the eye. Doc could see it rage every time a body was burned by the torches.

Seconds passed like hours as the creatures fought to keep their hold on the corporal plane, but Rick and Gil were not to be denied. They attacked and burned each creature with a vengeance until the skins the beings inhabited became useless for their purpose. The air was filled with the odor of charred flesh, but a charge of electricity replaced the terrible smell as a blinding flash covered the room. The spirits who had known only pleasure abandoned the skins they believed were rightfully theirs.

Jane's screaming voice could be heard as the brilliant light went out. "We'll come back. We will find a way."

Doc looked down at the bottle of Jim Bean leaking its contents onto the floor next to the bed that held him captive, twelve bags of burnt flesh were scattered around the room, resembling piles of melted wax. Gil was staring at the one they both knew as Tommy while Rick was kneeling and crying over his wife. A deep sadness filled Doc's soul as he realized what the spirits wanted.

As he lifted the bottle to his lips, he knew he would be sober again, some day. Until then, he would soak his feelings away and think about the twelve beings whose real crime was wanting to feel again.

My Little Babies

Brett Reistroffer

The day could not have been any more perfect for her to be outside in the well-kept garden. It was mid-summer, the weather was as clear as it was warm, and the roses Karen had given immaculate care to over the past season were in full bloom, displaying a deep red satin livery in all their beautiful glory. The roses were the love of her life and during the growing season they were the sole focus of all her spare time, energy, and consideration. Every year Karen strove to grow the most stunning specimens, depositing every ounce of love and care she had into their development. The end result of her labor never failed to reflect the effort year after year, and this season was no exception. They were simply gorgeous.

Gently nudged out of her reverie by a rustling at the edge of the small yard, Karen turned away from her work. Above the tall white fence that denoted the garden's border appeared the cheery-faced head of her neighbor.

"Hello there!" Mrs. Gunderman exclaimed, a never-absent smile stretching across her puffy face. The woman, a retired sixty-something, seemed to drip neighborly good will and elderly charm.

"Hello Mrs. Gunderman," Karen replied in polite greeting. "How are you today?"

"Oh, just fine," the jovial old woman answered. "You know me, I'd love to complain, but this weather just isn't giving me a reason!" Mrs. Gunderman never complained.

"Quite nice isn't it?" Karen commented, turning her head to the clear sky. It was, in fact, a perfect day; the sun was blazing away in its summer glory, unimpeded by a single cloud.

"Just perfect. You couldn't ask for a better day to get dirty hands in the garden." The woman nodded towards the lush rose bushes Karen was kneeling over. "As I see you already know!"

"Yes," Karen smiled warmly. "But I'm out here most days Mrs. Gunderman, rain or shine. I have to take care of my little babies, you know." The last was said quite matter-of-factly.

Mrs. Gunderman gave a sarcastic snort. "Well, this *is* the only place I ever see you, after all." She examined the flowers more closely and slowly shook her head in subtle disbelief. "But you can't say the results don't speak for themselves, now can you?"

"Beautiful, aren't they?" Karen beamed at her handiwork. She ever-so-softly ran the tips of her fingers around the side of a large blossom, careful not to disturb the velvet petals.

"I just do not understand it; my green thumb isn't too shabby itself, if you ask me, but I might was well be growing dandelions with what you can do with your roses."

"Why thank you, Mrs. Gunderman," Karen blushed as best

she could. "You're too nice."

Her neighbor narrowed her eyes and lowered her voice slightly, in mock seriousness. "Really though Karen, you have to let me in on your secret. How do you grow such gorgeous roses?"

"Oh, you're making it seem like a big deal." Karen waved dismissively as she turned her head back towards the flowers in front of her and seemed to consider them for a moment. "Just some tender, loving, care... Only the kind a mother can give."

Mrs. Gunderman cleared her throat, feeling awkward at the sudden change of mood in her generally reserved neighbor. "Yes, well, a shame the season is almost through. I don't suppose that means you'll be doing your disappearing act like you usually do in the winter, does it?"

"I do not disappear, Mrs. Gunderman, I just can't stand the cold, and there's no reason for me to be outside anyway if I can't be taking care of my babies." Her tone suggested the fact to be too obvious to need explaining.

Karen often did become a self-imposed shut-in during the winter months. Her work as a transcriptionist allowed her the freedom to stay at home and set her own schedule, which was also how she was able to spend so much of her time tending to her garden in the spring and summer months. Over the last couple of years she had grown quite adept at making herself scarce in the off-season, to the point that her neighbors, the Gundermans being the only ones she socialized with on any level, could go an entire five month stretch of time without so much as a fleeting glimpse of the reclusive gardener. Like the seasons, her absence came with the late fall and her reemergence with the first thaws of spring.

"Your babies," the elderly woman echoed, giving a *humph* of amusement. "No one can say that you don't have a passion for what you do."

Karen simply smiled politely.

"But I really must be getting back inside," her neighbor continued with an exaggerated finality. "I've got a slow-pot going with Mr. Gunderman's favorite stew bubbling away, and it needs more attention than my flowers do at the moment."

"Alright Mrs. Gunderman, it was good to talk to you." Karen waved a goodbye to the old woman and got up herself, having finished her tending for the day.

Later that evening Karen stood in front of a kitchen window which looked out across the small garden, idly sipping at a steaming cup of tea. Her neighbor's compliments, she knew, were not simply polite niceties shared between friends. The garden genuinely was a beautiful work of art, and she liked nothing more than to spend her free moments cherishing it. Her own words about it were no exaggeration either; the pride she showed for her garden was genuine, and caring for it in such a labor-of-love fashion bestowed something of a motherly self-image in herself.

Currently though, her thoughts were not so uplifting. The summer was past the half-way point, meaning the fall season would be quick to follow, and the thought of her roses browning and wilting with the first chills and frosts of the turning season left her with a bitter feeling. She knew it was all part of a natural cycle, but Karen could not help but think of it as the seasonal death of her surrogate children. Retreating to the confines of her small abode during the winter was, in small part, a way to avoid the grim spectacle.

Although it was a good length of time away, her mind was already eagerly drifting towards the next season. A more casual gardener would not put an ounce of thought into it until the time came, but Karen took her pastime seriously. Her gaze wandered lazily across her handiwork of the current season, taking it all in while she nursed her cup of tea just below her chin.

I need to get ready, she thought to herself.

~

The same evening, Karen found herself in a quiet cocktail lounge. She had made sure to pick the right one; somewhat upscale, clean, laid back. One that would attract her age and social group; mostly white, mostly affluent, and mostly oblivious. While she viewed the process of casual courtship as nothing more than a glorified child's game, she also knew one had to be picky and choose a decent match, even if it was all for one night. Not for the romance, or for the sake of finding 'the one'. Karen had never been one to put much stock into emotionally invested relationships, they seemed like a waste of time that could be better spent doing other things. Like gardening.

While she had not spent an exorbitant amount of time on her appearance, she had made herself presentable. Karen knew she was at least mildly attractive, and could therefore count on being occasionally approached throughout the evening. *It's so easy*, she thought to herself, *but you still have to be picky.*

Sure enough, it was not long into the night before the first man made a pass at her. It was in textbook fashion, starting with idle small talk of generalities, naturally nothing of genuine interest to either party. She humored his effort and allowed herself a few minutes to test the waters before ultimately advertising to him in polite, yet subtly obvious tones that she was not interested. He had been nice enough, but she thought she could do a little better.

Sipping conservatively at her drink as time passed, she hoped to be approached again before having to order another; she had never acquired too fond a taste for alcohol. Luckily, she was not left waiting long. A younger looking man, maybe mid-twenties walked casually up to her seat at the bar and engaged her.

"Looking for company, or just enjoying the night alone?" he asked her with a warm, but not over-bearing smile. He was handsome, with a young business-professional look, and came off with confidence. Karen liked that.

"I wouldn't mind some company," Karen responded, careful to sound slightly guarded and not too inviting, as that would give away an upper hand.

The conversation was casual and benign, but it was not boring by any means. The young man was intelligent and devoid of the cocky ego that so many men assume for approaching women, as if testament to their masculinity. From his warm demeanor, a more naïve woman might think he really was there for pleasant conversation alone, but Karen could guess he was after only one thing in the end. *At least he's polite about it*, she mused, allowing herself to fall for his charm by just the smallest fraction. *I think he will do just nicely.*

The idle chat and niceties drifted on for another half an hour. Karen humored all of the pleasantries and subtle advances in good form until finally allowing the man to casually suggest they end the night at one of their places. She candidly nominated her own domicile, for reasons of personal comfort, toasted the night with a last drink, and left the bar feeling a satisfying sense of accomplishment.

~

Once at Karen's home they continued the flirting over glasses of wine, more boldly now that the deal had been clinched. While not a drinker, she kept red wine around because men generally preferred it to white when they would drink wine at all. The deep red of a glassful also happened to remind her of her roses.

The physical introductions were pleasantly satisfying, and Karen was appreciative of his mindfulness towards foreplay. He was gentle, but strong and assertive when needed. While not an overly sexual person, she was practiced enough to know how to please a man likewise, and returned the attention with honest enthusiasm.

Once they were both ready, Karen pulled herself over him with her legs to each side. He stopped her movement, gripping her at her hips. "I've got one in one of my pockets," he said softly, nodding slightly towards the side of the bed where his discarded clothing lay on the floor.

"Oh, don't worry about it," Karen replied reassuringly. "I've got one." She leaned to the side and opened the top drawer of her nightstand, feeling her hand around the bottom, careful not to prick a finger on the small sewing needle next to the condom. As she leaned back over him, he smiled and held out his hand expectantly.

"Don't worry about that either," she said coyly, leaning down so that she was speaking seductively into his ear. "I can take care of that too."

While the assertive play was certainly enticing and erotic for the man, in actuality Karen simply didn't want to risk him noticing the tiny pockmarks that riddled the prophylactic's wrapper.

With the precaution out of the way, the two settled into the motions of making love. It was not at all unsatisfying for her, and she allowed herself to be swept up in the act, at least in part. After all, why not? She might as well savor an experience that, for her, was seldom explored.

After a time, the two of them lay silently in bed, side by side, Karen with her head resting on his shoulder and he with his arm under her neck, running down the opposite side of her body. Both were fully content with the ending of their night, though she flushed with an additional rush of fulfillment.

~

Some months later, with fall fully setting in, the garden was no longer the vibrant crimson beauty of the summer. The roses had gracefully performed their perennial swan song, and Karen was busying herself with clearing up the garden patch ahead of the cold season so the bushes could stay well maintained during their dormant period. Though the labor was of little importance, especially with the first morning frosts on their way, Karen felt better when she kept herself busy with work nonetheless.

"I see I'm not the only one out enjoying the last stretch of weather!" called a friendly, familiar voice over her shoulder.

"No, Mrs. Gunderman," Karen replied, still kneeling amongst a pair of large rose bushes. "You're not alone."

"And how are you, dear? I haven't chatted with you for a time."

"I'm fine Mrs. Gunderman, thank you for asking," Karen answered sweetly, standing up and turning. She was careful to slouch forward slightly, for while she had developed the habit of wearing loose clothing lately, she was still self-conscious of her growing paunch.

"I hope this isn't the last time I get to see you before you hibernate for the winter."

"Oh, don't be like that, I'm sure you'll see plenty of me."

Her elderly neighbor replied with a *harrumph* and made to lean back over to her side of the fence.

"And I'm not some kind of forest animal, Mrs. Gunderman!" Karen shouted after, sarcastically feigning insult.

"Could have fooled me!" The woman retorted and waved a garden-gloved hand over the fence.

The old woman did have a point, Karen admitted to herself; she would soon retreat to the confines of her home for a period of time. She hated being away from her beloved garden, but it was a necessary stint of reclusiveness. Besides, she reasoned, there would be little to take care of during the late fall and winter months. Nothing to grow, nothing to love and nurture.

Karen gathered her things and headed for her house, taking a long, strained look back at her patch of oasis. *They'll be just as beautiful next year,* she assured herself, *No, even more beautiful.* She turned and walked to her house, one arm folded around a bundle of gardening tools, the other absently cradling her stomach.

~

Another three months and the winter season was in full swing. Her cherished patch of roses was little more than a frozen graveyard of withered skeletons. During the cold months it was her habit to spend her idle moments sipping tea in front of her kitchen window, where she could gaze passively at her lifeless garden and allow her mind to wander. While she mindfully kept herself occupied with her at-home job, Karen's hands still itched to be outside, toiling away in the soil.

It won't be very much longer, she reassured herself to quell the anxiety. As she rolled the comforting words around in her mind, she absent-mindedly rested a hand on her now-bulging belly. *No, not long at all.* She noted her wandering hand and let her mind continue its reflective train of thought as she began a casual pacing through her home. Eventually, she found her way to the closet of the spare bedroom and slid the door open. There was little clutter, and Karen easily located and extracted the small shoe box she had come for. With one hand she wiped away the loose layer of dust that had accumulated in the year since she had last taken it out of the storage closet. Opening it, she gave the contents a cursory inspection, mostly a collection of benign household items and tools, before closing it again.

Taking great care, she stood and left the room with the box cradled under an arm.

~

Karen was positive it could not have been a more beautiful early-summer day. There was not a cloud to be seen, the sun was at its zenith dominating the deep blue sky, and a soft cool breeze danced its way invisibly through her garden. As usual for a summer day, Karen was kneeling amongst her rose bushes weeding, tilling, and clipping the day away. Occasionally, while she busied herself with her plants, Karen would gently cup a billowing rose blossom in her hand and deeply inhale the rich fragrance.

It was true that she was known in her neighborhood for her talents in cultivating stunningly beautiful specimens, and this year was by no means an exception. The bushes were full and healthy, the large, supple blossoms boasting a deep, satin red flourish. Studying her handiwork with a motherly pride, she even entertained herself with the notion that this could be her best year yet. That is not, she quickly corrected herself, to diminish any of her past labors.

"Well, my goodness!" exclaimed the familiar voice of her ever-present neighbor, who evidently was also making use of the picture perfect day. "Maybe one of these years you'll give yourself a rest so that some of us might have a chance to look good."

"Maybe one of these years, Mrs. Gunderman," Karen humored her good-natured neighbor. "Just maybe."

"They're simply gorgeous, just gorgeous." Mrs. Gunderman admired, slowly shaking her head from side to side in admiration. "And the size of them! There isn't a single one of them smaller than my fist."

"Why, thank you," Karen replied, genuinely blushing at the compliments. "I'm quite proud of them."

"Perhaps you would be interested in sharing some secrets then, too?"

"Perhaps you would be interested in sharing your recipe for Mr. Gunderman's favorite stew?" Karen returned slyly.

"You wicked girl. Hardly any way to treat a little old lady."

"Oh, don't be so serious. You know I was kidding."

Mrs. Gunderman issued a patented *harrumph* and sagged her shoulders in a pout. "And not even a scrap for a friendly neighbor."

"Honestly, there's really not much to say," Karen started, turning her head back to face her workmanship again. She felt an overwhelming sense of pride whenever she stood there admiring them. She knew it seemed silly to people, to most they were just roses after all. But these were *her* roses, her little babies. To her they were not something that she even *grew*, rather, something she *raised*.

"Just love and care," she continued with a warm, compassionate smile spreading across her face. "The kind only a mother can give."

About the Authors

Santiago Eximeno is a Spanish genre writer that has published several novellas and short story books, mainly horror literature and flash fiction. His work has been translated to English, Japanese, French and Bulgarian. You can find him at www.eximeno.com or *@SantiagoEximeno* on Twitter.

Christopher Nadeau is the author of 'Dreamers at Infinity's Core' through COM Publishing as well as over two dozen published short stories in such august publications as The Horror Zine, Sci-Fi Short Story Magazine, Ghostlight Magazine and several anthologies. Chris has also served as special editor for Voluted Magazine's 'The Darkness Internal' which he created. His novel 'Kaiju' was recently released through Source Point Press and "Echoes of Infinity's Core" is slated for 2016 release.

A former member of the Great Lakes Association of Horror Writers and a current member of the Dark Fiction Writers Guild, Chris resides in Southeastern Michigan with his wife Lorie and two petulant, long-hair Chihuahuas.

MP Johnson's short stories have appeared in more than 50 publications. His debut book, 'The After-Life Story of Pork Knuckles Malone' was a Wonderland Book Award finalist. His most recent books include 'Dungeons and Drag Queens' and 'Cattle Cult! Kill! Kill!' He is the creator of Freak Tension zine, a B-movie extra, an amateur drag queen, and an obsessive music fan currently based in Minneapolis. Learn more at www.freaktension.com.

Brian Culp is a novelist, screenwriter, and 2014 alum of the Iowa Writers Workshop. He's sold over a million words of nonfiction, along with several short stories. His work includes a 2015 Sundress Publication Best of the Net nomination. He lives in Kansas City.

Find him on Twitter: @hmsbrian

Mark Patrick Lynch lives and writes in the UK. His short fiction, mainstream and genre, has appeared in print anthologies and journals ranging from Alfred Hitchcock's Mystery Magazine to Zahir. His book, *Hour of the Black Wolf*, is published by Robert Hale Ltd in hardcover and FA Thorpe in paperback. A novella, *What I Wouldn't Give*, is available for e-readers. His next book from Robert Hale Ltd is *No Fire Without Smoke*. You can find him online at:

markpatricklynch.blogspot.com.

Louis Rakovich writes sometimes-fantastical literary fiction. His short stories have appeared in Bartleby Snopes, The Fiction Desk, Criminal Element, Goldfish Grimm, Phobos Magazine, and other places. He's inspired by authors such as Truman Capote, Gabriel Garcia Marquez and Edgar Poe, and filmmakers such as David Lynch and Andrei Tarkovsky. He grew up in Jerusalem, Israel, and currently lives in NYC, where he's working on his first novel – a psychological thriller with theological undertones. You can find more stories by him at www.louisrakovich.com, or follow him on Twitter at @LouisRakovich.

Eric J. Guignard writes dark and speculative fiction from the outskirts of Los Angeles. Read his novella, *Baggage of Eternal Night* (a finalist for the 2014 International Thriller Writers Award), and watch for forthcoming books, including Chestnut 'Bo (TBP 2016). As an editor, Eric's also published the anthologies, *Dark Tales of Lost Civilizations* and *After Death…*, the latter of which won the 2013 Bram Stoker Award. Outside the glamorous and jet-setting world of indie fiction, Eric's a technical writer and college professor, and he stumbles home each day to a wife, children, cats, and a terrarium filled with mischievous beetles. Visit Eric at: www.ericjguignard.com, his blog: ericjguignard.blogspot.com, or Twitter: @ericjguignard.

Travis Burnham teaches middle school science and college-level composition, meaning he loves words and blowing things up. He currently lives in Upstate South Carolina with his wife, Chika, but he grew up in Massachusetts, is from Maine at heart, and has lived in Japan, Colombia, and the Northern Mariana Islands. He can by cyberstalked at:

www.travisburnhambooks.com

www.travisburnham.blogspot.com

Tim Jeffreys is the author of five collections of short stories, the most recent being 'From Elsewhere', and a novella, 'The Haunted Grove'. His short fiction has been published in various international anthologies and magazines. Tim is also a talented artist and gained a university honours degree in Graphic Arts and Design in 2000.

Originally from Oldham, UK, Tim now lives in Bristol with

his partner and two young daughters. He remains a northerner at heart, misses the rain, and retains a stubborn refusal to suffer fools gladly.

Visit him online at www.timjeffreyswriter.webs.com.

Robert G. Ferrell was born in Houston, Texas, USA, in 1957. He holds a B.S. in Biology, almost an M.S. in Avian Ecology, and has drifted in and out of graduate programs in Pre-Biotic Chemistry and Medicine. Robert has been published in three humor anthologies: 'My Funny Valentine', 'My Funny Major Medical', and 'Open Doors: Fractured Fairy Tales'. He has been a popular columnist for :login: magazine since 2006. He is the author of three books: *Tangent* (2004), *Ex Mentis Saxonicum* (2012), and *Goblinopolis* (2013).

Robert lives with his wife Adrienne and roughly three cats in rural Wilson County, Texas, outside of San Antonio. When not writing, Robert can be found engaged in Ham radio, playing/recording music, reproducing medieval calligraphy and illumination, or floundering around in his pool.

Find Robert online at http://www.robertgferrell.com and Twitter: @RobertGFerrell

Anna Yeatts is a horror and dark fantasy writer hiding out in Pinehurst, NC. Her short fiction has appeared in Penumbra eMagazine, Daily Science Fiction, Stupefying Stories, and Bad Dream Entertainment among other venues. Anna publishes Flash Fiction Online (www.flashfictiononline.com). Follow her on Twitter @AnnaYeatts or on her website annayeatts.com

Gerri Leen lives in Northern Virginia and originally hails from Seattle. She has stories and poems published in: Daily Science Fiction, Escape Pod, Grimdark, Sword and Sorceress XXIII, She Nailed a Stake Through His Head: Tales of Biblical Terror and others. She is editing an anthology, A Quiet Shelter There, which will benefit homeless animals and is due out in 2015 from Hadley Rille Books.

Find her at http://www.gerrileen.com.

Jay Seate is the winner of Horror Novel Review's 2013 Best Short Fiction Award, and writes everything from humor to the erotic to the macabre, and is especially keen on transcending genre pigeonholing. Over two hundred of his stories have appeared in magazines, anthologies and webzines.

Website: www.troyseateauthor.webs.com.

Birney Reed was a proud member of the Columbus Creative Cooperative (columbuscoop.org) while living in Columbus, Ohio, where his gritty character-driven short fiction was featured in anthology releases such as *Overgrown*, *While You Were Out*, and *Columbus, Past, Present, Future*. His first single-author collection of short fiction, *The Tales of Victor Coachman* was published by Bad Dream Entertainment in 2014. Sadly, Birney passed away shortly after the release in early 2015. He is sorely missed by all.

Brett Reistroffer is a writer and editor living in the Pacific Northwest. He founded Bad Dream Entertainment in 2013 as a home for story-driven dark fiction from new and underground writers.

Webiste: www.BrettReistroffer.com

www.ingramcontent.com/pod-product-compliance
Lightning Source LLC
Chambersburg PA
CBHW020928120726
47905CB00008B/2433